Merry Christmas
Mary
From Esther

FABLES *for* PARENTS

FABLES *for* PARENTS

BY DOROTHY CANFIELD

NEW YORK

HARCOURT, BRACE AND COMPANY

ACKNOWLEDGMENT is here made to the editors of *The Bookman, The Country Gentleman, The Delineator, Story, The Survey Graphic, The Woman's Home Companion,* and *The Woman's Journal* for permission to reprint stories first published in their pages.

Designed by Robert Josephy
PRINTED IN THE UNITED STATES OF AMERICA
BY QUINN & BODEN COMPANY, INC., RAHWAY, N. J.

To dear Mary Westenholz

CONTENTS

vii

SECTION ONE

The Rainy Day, the Good Mother, and the Brown Suit

AND YET she had done exactly what the books on child training assured mothers would ward off trouble on a stormy day. She had copied off the list of raw materials recommended by the author of "The Happy Child Is the Active Child": colored paper, blunt scissors, paste, pencils, crayons, plasticine—she had bought them all, well ahead of time, and had brought them out this morning after breakfast, when the rain settled down with that all-day pour. But, unlike the children in the books, Caroline and Freddy and little Priscilla had not received these treasures open-mouthed with pleasure, nor had they quietly and happily exercised their creative instinct, leaving their mother free to get on with her work. Perhaps her children hadn't as much of that instinct as other people's. At least, after a little listless fingering of colored paper Freddy turned away. "Say, Mother, I want to put on my brown suit," he said. Little did she dream then what the brown suit was to cost her. She answered casually, piling up the breakfast dishes, "I washed that suit yesterday, Freddy, and the rain came. So it's not dry yet."

He trotted back and forth after her as she stepped to and fro with the slightly nervous haste of a competent woman who has planned a busy morning. "But, Mother," he persisted, "I *want* to put it on. I *want* to." He raised his voice, "Mother, I want to put my brown suit on."

From the pantry where she had just discovered that the cream she had planned to use for the dessert was soured, she answered him with some asperity, "I told you it isn't dry yet!" But she reminded herself of the excellent rule, "Always make children understand the reasons for your refusals," and added, "It's hanging on the line on the side porch. Look out there, dear. You can see for yourself how wet it is."

He did as she bade him, and stood staring out, leaning his forehead on the glass.

Yet a little later as she stood before the telephone, grocery list in hand, he tugged at her skirt and as Central asked, "What number, please?" he said with plaintive obstinacy, "Mother, I *do* want to put on my brown suit."

She said with considerable warmth, "Somerset three six one. For heaven's sake, Freddy, that suit is WET. Is this Perkins and Larsen? How *could* you put it on! What price are your grapefruit today? Freddy, let go of my skirt. Grapefruit, I said. No, no— G for glory, r for run—"

But when she turned away from her struggle with the clerk, Freddy plucked at her hand and whimpered in the nasal fretting tone she had sworn (before she had children) no child of hers should ever use, "Mother, I waa-a-nt to pu-u-t my brown—"

"*Don't whine,*" she told him with a ferocity so swift and savage that he recoiled and was silent. She thought remorsefully, "Oh, dear, to scold is just as bad as to whine."

Going back into the pantry she recalled with resentment

4

that the psychologists of family life say the moods of children are but the reflections of moods of the mother. She did not believe a word of it. "Did *I* start this?" she asked herself unanswerably, and, "How can anybody help being irritated when they're so perfectly unreasonable!"

But she was really a very good mother. She remembered that the basis of child-rearing is to understand each child at all times, and went resolutely back into the other room, determined to understand Freddy, if it were her last act. Disconcertingly, it was not Freddy, but Priscilla who ran to take her hand, who said pleadingly, timidly, as if appealing from the cruel decree of a tyrant, "Mummy, Fred *does* so want to have you let him wear his brown suit this morning!" The mother contained herself, collected the children—three-year-old Priscilla, five-year-old Fred, six-and-half-year-old Caroline—led them to the window and said, "Now just look at that suit! How could I let Freddy wear anything that's as wet as sop?"

At least that was what she thought she said. What the children distinctly heard was, "You're in the wrong, wrong, wrong. And I am right, right, right, as I always am. There's no use your trying to get around that!"

They stared gloomily out at this idea rather than at the wet clothes. Their mother went on, "What in the world does Fred *want* to wear his brown suit for, anyhow? What's the matter with the suit he's got on?"

What the children heard was, "No matter what Freddy said his reason was, I'd soon show you it was all foolishness." They attempted no answer, shaken as they were by wave

5

after invisible wave of her impatience to be done with them
and at something else. Indeed she was impatient. Why not,
with her morning work all waiting to be done. She held her
children for a moment with the bullying eye of a drill-
sergeant, and then said, challengingly, *"Well—?"* She meant,
and they knew she meant, "I hope you realize that I have
you beaten."

Something in Fred—it was something rather fine—exploded
with a crash. His round face grew grim and black. He
looked savagely at his mother, thrust out his lower jaw and,
keeping his eyes ragingly on hers, kicked a footstool, vi-
ciously, as if he were kicking her.

"Fred-*dy*," she said in a voice meant to cow him. But he
was not cowed. He kicked again with all his might, looking
at his mother and hating her.

And then—he was only a little boy—he broke. His hard
defiant face crumpled up into despair. He crooked his arm to
hide his suffering from his mother,—from his mother!—and
turned away to lean against the wall in the silent, dry, inexplicable misery which often ended what his mother called
"Fred's tantrums." Little Priscilla began a whimpering. Caroline put her hands up to her face and hung her head.

Their mother thought, her nerves taut with exasperation,
"I'd just like to see one of those child-specialists manage *my*
children on a rainy day! They'd find out a thing or two!" But
she loved her children. She loved them dearly. With her next
breath she was ashamed of being angry with them. The tears
came to her eyes and an aching lump into her throat. Bewildered, dismayed, she asked herself, in the purest surprise,

6

"Why, how did we get into this dreadful state? What can the trouble be?"

She went back into the pantry, took a long breath, took a drink of water, tried to relax her muscles, cast her mind back to the book about what to do on a rainy day. But she could recall nothing else in it but that appeal to the creative instinct. She had tried that, and it had failed.

She heard the front door open. The voice of a young cousin, no special favorite of hers—cried, "Ye gods and little fishes, what weather!" He slammed the door behind him. Although he was nineteen, he still slammed doors as if he were twelve. He had come as he sometimes did when it rained, to wait in the living-room for the bus that took him to college. One of its stopping places was their corner.

Priscilla, the literal, asked, "What does 'gods and little fishes' mean?"

"Mean?" said the freshman, laughing and flinging his books and his rain-coat down on the floor. "What do you mean, mean? You mean too much, Prissy. What does this mean?" As she began to wash the dishes the mother could see that he had flung his heels in the air and was walking on his hands. "He's too old for such foolishness," she thought severely. And sure enough, out of the pockets of his adult suit of clothes, now upside down, little-boy junk rattled down around his hands. The children squealed and made a rush towards the bits of string, dirty handkerchiefs, knives, fish-hooks, nails, pieces of cork, screws and pencils. "No you don't!" said he, returning his feet to the floor with a bang. "Everything there is a part of an important enterprise."

7

"What's a 'portant enter—" began Priscilla.

"Whatever I do," he told her coolly, "were it only to make a mousetrap. If *I* made mousetraps there'd be a four-strip concrete road to my door in a week's time, you bet. No mousetrap of mine would ever have let out Uncle Peter's mouse, believe me."

"What? Who? What's Uncle Peter's mouse?" clamored the children.

"Oh, surely you know that story. No child of our family gets brung up without hearing that one. No? Well, one morning when Uncle Peter and Aunt Molly came down to breakfast—Priscilla, do *not* ask who they were and where they lived, it's no matter—they found a mouse in their trap. It was the kind of trap that catches the mouse alive, so they got the cat, and they all went out on the porch to open the trap and let the cat catch the mouse. Priscilla, do *not* say this was horrid of them, it was, and I can't help it, but that was the way it happened and it was so long ago probably they didn't know any better. So there they all were"—he illustrated how tensely they stood, stooping over an imaginary trap—"the two children and Uncle Peter and Aunt Molly. And the cat. She was scrooched right close in front of the cage"—he quivered and crouched with such vivacity of acting that the children began to laugh—"while Uncle Peter s-l-o-w-l-y, s-l-o-w-l-y lifted the door of the trap till it was open enough for the mouse to get out." He drew a long breath and made a dramatic pause. The children gazed at him, mouths open, eyes unwinking. "And then—!" he sprang into the air, "the cat jumped!" He clutched at Fred. "Uncle Peter hollered!"

8

He ran to Caroline and seized her arm. "The children yelled bloody murder!" He flung the children to right and left. "Aunt Molly shrieked!" He sank back on the floor. "But the mouse was gone!"

He gazed with enormous solemnity at his spell-bound listeners. "The cat was prowling around, sniffing and lashing her tail"—he sniffed the air and getting up on his hands and knees lashed an imaginary tail—"but—there—was—no—mouse."

He sat cross-legged and earnest and went on, "Well, Aunt Molly was terribly afraid of mice, and she always had the idea that all a mouse wanted to do was to run up folks' clothes, so she was sure the mouse had done that to one of them. So she took one child and then the other, shook them till their teeth nearly dropped out"—he shot out a long arm and seized Priscilla, Caroline, and Freddy one after the other, shaking them hard and setting them into giggling fits—"and put first one and then the other inside the house and shut the door, quick! Then she shook herself hard. And went into the house and shut the door. Then Uncle Peter shook *him*self hard. And went in quick and shut the door. And then they all had breakfast, wondering all the while about where that mouse could have gone to. And after they'd finished breakfast, Uncle Peter stood up to go to the office and took hold of the lower edge of his vest to pull it down"—he seized the lower edge of an imaginary vest vigorously and stood appalled, a frantic expression of horror on his face—"*and there was the mouse!*" The children shrieked. "It had been right under the edge of his vest and when he grabbed the vest he put his hand right around it, and when he took his hand away the mouse was in it, squirming." He showed them how it squirmed, and then, speeding up to express-train speed, finished the story all in one breath, "And he was so rattled he flung it right away without looking to see where, and it went spang into Aunt Molly's face and she fainted dead away—and the mouse beat it so quick they never did see it again."

He grinned down at the children, literally rolling on the floor, as pleased with the story as they. "Say, kids, what-d'you-say we act it out? Let's. Who'll be what? I'll be Uncle Peter. Priscilla, you be one of the children. Caroline, you be Aunt Molly—that's a swell part! You must yell your head off when I throw the mouse in your face. Fred, you be—"

"I'll be the cat," said Fred, scrambling to his feet.

So they acted out the little drama, throwing themselves passionately into their roles, Caroline so magnificent with her scream and faint at the end that Priscilla said, "Oh, *I* want to be Aunt Molly."

So they did it over again, Priscilla screeching as though she were being flayed alive, and fainting with fat arms and legs outstretched.

"I'd kind o' like to be Uncle Peter," said Fred.

"Okay by me," said the student. "I'll be the cat."

By the time they had finished it again they were out of breath, what with screaming and running and laughing and acting, and sank down together on the floor. Little by little their laughter subsided to a peaceful silence. Freddy sprawled half over the knobby knees of the tall boy, Priscilla was tucked away under his arm, Caroline leaned against him. From the pantry where, unheeded, the mother washed the dishes, she thought jealously, "What do they see in him? That story is nothing but nonsense." And then—she was really an intelligent person—it came over her, "Why, that is just what they like in it."

Out of the silence, almost as though she were thinking aloud, little Priscilla murmured, "Freddy was bad this morning." There was compassion in her tone.

"What was eating him?" asked the student, not particularly interested.

"He wanted to wear his brown suit. And it was wet, and he couldn't. So he kicked the footstool and was bad."

"What's the point about the brown suit, old man?"

The question was put in a matter-of-fact tone of comradely interest. But even so Fred hesitated, opened his mouth, shut it, said nothing.

It was Caroline who explained, "It's got a holster pocket at the back where he can carry his pretend pistol."

The mother in the pantry, astounded, remorseful, reproachful, cried out to herself, "Oh, why didn't he tell *me* that!" But she knew very well why he had not. She had plenty of brains.

"Oh, I see," said the student. "But why don't you sew a holster pocket on the pants you've got on, boy? On all your pants. It's nothing to sew on pockets. You girls, too. You might as well have holster pockets. When I was your age I had sewed on dozens of pockets." He took a long breath, and began to rattle off nonsense with an intensely serious face and machine-gun speed, "My goodness, by the time I was fourteen I had sewed on five hundred and thirty-four pockets, and one small watch-pocket but I don't count that one. Didn't you ever hear how I put myself through college sewing on pockets? And when I was graduated, the President of Pocket Sewing Union of America sent for me, and—"

"But you've only just got in to college," Priscilla reminded him earnestly.

(In the pantry, her mother thought, with a stab of self-knowledge, "Why, is that *me*? Was I being literal, like that, about rainy-day occupations?")

"Priscilla," said the college student, sternly, "don't you know what happens to children who say 'go-up-bald-head' to their elders—oh, but—" He clutched his tousled hair, and said, imitating Priscilla's serious little voice, "Oh, but I'm not bald yet, am I?"

A horn sounded in the street. He sprang up, tumbling the children roughly from him, snatched his books. "There's my bus." The door slammed.

The children came running to find their mother. "Oh, Mother, Mother, can we have some cloth to make pockets out of?"

She was ready for them. "I've got lots of it that'll be just right," she said, telling herself wryly, "I can get an idea all right if somebody'll push it half way down my throat."

12

But for the rest of the morning, as the children sat happily exercising their creative instinct by sewing on queer pockets in queer places on their clothes, she was thinking with sorrow, "It's not fair. That great lout of a boy without a care in the world takes their fancy with his nonsense, and they turn their backs on me entirely. I represent only food and care— and refusals. I work my head off for them—and the first stranger appeals to them more."

Yet after lunch they put their three heads together and whispered and giggled, and "had a secret." Then, Caroline at their head, they trotted over to the sofa where their mother had dropped down to rest. "Mother," said Caroline in her little-girl bird-voice, "wouldn't *you* like to play Uncle-Peter-and-Aunt-Molly-and-the-mouse? You didn't have a single chance to this morning—not once—you were working so." They looked at her with fond shining eyes of sympathy. "Come on, Mother! You'll love it!" they encouraged her.

A lump came into her throat again—a good lump this time. She swallowed. "Oh, thanks, children. I know I'd like to. What part are you going to have me take?"

The secret came out then. They let Freddy tell her, for it had been his inspiration. He looked proudly at his mother and offered her his best. "Ye gods and little fishes! We're going to let you be the *mouse!*"

She clasped her hands, "Oh, children!" she cried.

From their pride in having pleased her, a gust of love-madness blew across them, setting them to fall upon their mother like soft-pawed kittens wild with play, pushing her back on the pillows, hugging her, worrying her, rumpling

13

her hair, kissing her ears, her nose, whatever they could reach.

But Priscilla was not sure they had been clear. She drew away. "You don't have to get caught, you know," she reassured her mother earnestly. "The mouse wasn't caught—never!"

Good Growing Weather

PEOPLE had often said to Lolly, "Well, well, there aren't many little girls nowadays who have a real live great-grandmother!" But now that Mother and Lolly had gone to visit her, what was she? Just a little bit of an old woman who sat all shucked together in an armchair, hardly ever saying a word, and when she did, getting everything mixed up. Lolly much preferred her daughter, Great-aunt Augusta. She was a postmaster! She had a post office in the wing of her house. People came to get their mail all the way from the village to the house set in the fields. Lolly could step in from the dining-room and stand behind the wall of mail-boxes, watching Aunt Augusta canceling stamps, bang! bang! bang! with her right hand, while her left steadily pushed the envelopes into the right places. Lolly liked the way Aunt Augusta banged with her cancellation do-funny; she liked the way she pushed letters into pigeonholes—like lightning and yet not in a hurry—she liked the way Aunt Augusta talked, not many words at a time, sometimes not a whole sentence, yet settling the matter with a bang, as she canceled stamps. And she admired the way Aunt Augusta took care of her queer old mother. No bang! bang! about that. Such a comfortable, cheerful way of talking to her, with little jokes about what would have been embarrassing if you hadn't made a joke of it—Grannie's weak old hands that trembled so she often couldn't hold her tea-cup to her lips, and her weak old mind that made her forget what time of year it was, and whether she'd had her breakfast or not, and sometimes not know who the people around her were—not even Aunt Augusta. The door to the post office was always open, and no matter how busy Aunt Augusta was with letters, she always kept an eye on Grannie, and was ready, any minute, to step back into the dining-room to do something for her.

She was really only a thin old woman, Aunt Augusta was, with bony hands and white hair that was never tidy, and the plainest country clothes. But Lolly sort of liked her.

It was funny to hear her and Mother talking together. There'd be a long string of words from Mother that went on and on. When she stopped, Aunt Augusta would say, "Well, maybe—" or "Why not?" Lolly, playing with her doll in the dining-room, could see Aunt Augusta through the open door, sorting letters silently while Mother said, "I keep the closest watch on vitamins. It's wearing. There are ever so many of them, and you have to remember which comes in which kind of food. But it is absolutely *essential* for the children to have *all* the kinds, or else—" And so on and so on, till she'd stop to get breath and Aunt Augusta would say, "So I've heard," like dropping a stone into a pond of water. Then she'd glance around to see that Grannie was all right. Lolly didn't mind what Mother said about vitamins and all that, but when she got to talking about protecting children "at all costs" from nervous strain and shocks, as she often did —that made Lolly cross. For ever since they had come to visit

Aunt Augusta and Grannie she'd been under a terrible nervous strain, and Mother didn't even see it, because Lolly had too much pride to make a baby of herself. When Peter the Great came padding into the room, his pointed toe-nails clicking on the floor, his huge mouth—that was on a level with Lolly's shoulder—wide open to show glistening white fangs that could crunch a little girl's hand to bits with one snap, Lolly always stood very still and hoped he wouldn't notice her. If he did, and came to puff his hot breath into her face and loll out his horribly wet red tongue, she said in a low choking voice, "Good doggie, good doggie." But she kept her hands behind her back and froze all over and couldn't breathe till he had gone somewhere else. Once her mother said, smiling, "Children and animals! I pity the child that grows up without a dog friend." But Aunt Augusta knew. She never said anything to Lolly about it, but whenever she saw Peter the Great move over towards the little girl, she told him sharply, "*Get* off, Peter! *Get* away!" with a masterful wave of her hand that sent him walking sadly out of the room, his tail drooping. Lolly had a hopeless, envious admiration for that tone of voice, for that wave of the hand! How ever had Aunt Augusta learned to do it, she wondered?

It was hot on the last Sunday of their visit to Greatgrandmother and Aunt Augusta. After dinner was over and the dishes washed up, Mother read the newspaper for a while and then stepped into the back yard to see if enough raspberries were ripe for supper. Grannie slept soundly in her

17

chair, Aunt Augusta sat reading on the front porch, and Lolly played with her doll. Out of the back window Lolly saw an old-lady friend of Aunt Augusta's stepping slowly along the path on the far side of the garden and heard her call to Mother, "Come along for a walk, why don't you? I'm going into the village to see the Frasers." Mother answered, "All right, I will. I don't need a hat, do I?" Lolly heard the back gate click. There was a quiet pause. Grannie snored lightly. Then a car drove up to the front of the house and a man's voice, all in a hurry, asked Aunt Augusta to— well, Lolly didn't pay enough attention to hear what it was he wanted, except that it was about a sick person—Aunt Augusta was always being asked to go and do something for sick people. The car drove away. "Well," thought Lolly, buttoning up her dolly's nightgown, "Mother thought Aunt Augusta was here, and Aunt Augusta thought Mother was here." It was rather a joke, she and the sleeping Grannie being left for a few minutes to keep house all by themselves. She smoothed the tiny nightgown down, and considered where she would lay Rosie to sleep.

Someone stepped lightly into the room behind her. She turned around with a start. There was Grannie up on her feet, her lips sucking in and out of her toothless mouth, strange sparks burning in her eyes. She smiled secretly and nodded her head at Lolly. "She's gone!" she said. "Mother's gone. There's nobody here. We can play with matches. Come on, Delia, let's have some fun!" She went tottering over to the sofa, where the big sheets of the Sunday newspaper lay tumbled in piles. She had a match in her hand. "I've been

18

saving this!" She showed it proudly to the little girl. Over her shoulder, "Let's light a fire," she said with a chuckle.

Lolly's hands, clutching at her doll had, with her first sight of Grannie, set as hard as rock. She could not unloose them. Her jaws felt like that, too. Set like iron, as though they could never open. She was more frightened by the strange look in Grannie's dreadfully bright eyes than she had ever thought anybody could be. She tried to scream for her mother and could not open her mouth, could not make a sound. And then she remembered that her mother was out of earshot, that even if she screamed, nobody could hear her, the house was too far from neighbors. She was alone with this awful thing that looked like Grannie but was not.

The old woman struck the match, and stooped, laughing slyly, to touch the flame to the piled-up papers.

It was struck out of her hand, fell to the floor, and was stamped out by a small sandal set hastily on it. Another little girl was saying breathlessly, "I *beg* your pardon—I'm sorry—wouldn't we better— Oh, I tell you, let's go into the kitchen and light a fire in the stove and play keep house. That'll be lots more fun. Come on."

Grannie yielded to the hand tugging at hers. Her little playmate was saying, "We can make pretend cookies and bake them in the oven." Yes, Grannie said, that would be fun. "But fire too! There must be fire, Delia, or I won't play." Oh, yes, indeed, said her little playmate, they would make a fire. A real one. A big one.

But in the midst of getting the paper and kindling into the stove, while Lolly was desperately listening for the longed-for step of somebody returning to the house, Grannie pulled away, looked around her wildly, said, "Why, where's my mother gone to? *I want my mother!* I don't like this house. I want to go where my mother is," and was off, out of the front door, scurrying along the main road that led away from town, off towards the woods; where on this holiday afternoon the automobiles were tearing by one after another at top speed; where Lolly, big girl that she was, was never, never allowed to take a step alone, for fear she'd be run over. And Grannie who could hardly see anything with her dim old eyes! Lolly darted after her. An automobile came roaring down the road. Lolly didn't know what she did—snatch at Grannie? Push her to one side? Stand between her and the car? She must have done something, anyhow, for the car swerved sharply and whirled by, the startled driver yelling an angry protest to the heedless two in the road. Lolly's teeth were chattering so that for a minute she could not speak. When she did her voice was very shaky. She said as politely as she could, "Don't you th-think, Grannie, it would be s-s-sort of nice to w-walk over on the side here—on the grass?"

Grannie was delighted. "I'll pick a bokay of flowers to take to my mother," she said, eagerly. "She loves flowers, my mother does. Does yours?" She broke off a burdock and added a stem of long grass to it. "There!" she said proudly.

Lolly's legs were as shaky as her voice—oh, where was *Mother!* Grannie kept walking along fast, and right away from town. They were already far, far from the house—was this sweat running down into Lolly's eyes, or tears? Never mind what it was, she wiped it away with a fierce sweep of

20

her little hand, so that she could keep track of Grannie, wandering to and fro in the dusty weeds, and also watch the turn of the road, around which a car might emerge at any minute. There was one now, rushing towards them like a charging bull. Lolly stiffened to attention, waited till the car was closer and said, *"There's* a pretty flower, Grannie, there!"

"Where? Where?" asked Grannie.

The car had rushed by, the burst of the displaced air all but upsetting the old woman and little girl, clinging together. There were children in the car, snuggled up between their father and mother. They waved their hands as they swept by. Would Lolly ever, ever again sit safely in a car between Father and Mother—? Her lower lip began to tremble, an unswallowable lump came into her throat.

"Oh, where have you been, bonny boy, bonny boy?" sang Grannie, happily, letting the broken green litter in her hand drop, without noticing it.

A car was coming from behind them. Lolly rushed to stand between Grannie and the road. "Look *out* there!" yelled the driver in a panic, wrenching at his wheel.

"Now, Delia, what do you do that for?" asked Grannie crossly. "Don't you suppose I know how to take care of myself?" Tripping over her long skirt and almost falling, she walked out to the middle of the road. A car burst into sight around the turn. Lolly, her heart beating wildly all over her, ran to pull her back. She was just in time! The car missed them by inches! With a scream of brakes it reeled to one side, tipped wildly, settled to all four wheels and was gone, the people in it rising in their seats to look back indignantly.

"There, you see," said Grannie, tossing her head, "I was all right."

Lolly thought hard. Then, "I'm kind of afraid of automobiles, Grannie," she said, the way she'd tease any grown-up to get her own way, "I want to keep off the road—I'm 'fraid of all these cars."

"Why, of course, child," said Grannie kindly, stepping to one side. She forgot about the cars at once. "Oh, there's a daisy!" she cried, stooping to pick a weed. "My mother loves daisies. Did you ever make a lady out of a daisy? I'll show you how." Another car swayed by, flinging the dust around them, the people in it looking out indifferently at the two by the roadside. There was nothing to be hoped from them, Lolly knew that. Nobody would think of stopping, nobody would dream anything was the matter.

But something wonderful had happened to Lolly—she could not have told when—she wasn't afraid any more, there was no lump in her throat, her legs were not shaking. It was all right. What had she been so scared about? She was just taking care of Grannie till somebody could find them. It was easy to take care of Grannie. All you had to do was to keep making her think of something cheerful so that she would forget the road and the automobiles. A car whirled from the turn, quite close to them now. "Grannie, Grannie, what's that bird?" called Lolly. "There, on the telegraph pole?"

"My goodness, Delia, don't you know a meadow-lark when you see it?"

"Oh, of course, a meadow-lark," agreed Lolly, keeping

22

between Grannie and the road. They went around the turn and were in the woods, quite out of sight of any house.

Now it came to Lolly that she hoped it would not be her mother who found them. Mother would make such a fuss. She might even get to crying, and that would give Grannie a scare. She was so quiet and comfortable now, singing to herself and thinking she was picking flowers. Oh, if it could only be Aunt Augusta that found them,—coming up from behind in the old Ford—

Grannie was getting very tired. She stumbled, she was bowed almost double, she tripped on her skirt, she stumbled again. Lolly ran towards her but she fell headlong on the dusty ground. Lolly sat down quickly, saying, "Gracious, Grannie, but I'm tired! What do you say we sit here and rest for a while?" She pulled the white head into her little lap as she spoke. "Let's tell riddles. When is a door not a door?"

"When it's ajar," said Grannie. "I know that one." But she lay quietly enough, her head on Lolly's lap. She was breathing very fast. "I don't seem to walk as well as I used to," she remarked in a surprised voice.

"Well, I'm all out of breath too," said Lolly, making her chest heave up and down.

And then Aunt Augusta came. There was the old Ford, bummeling along towards them, Aunt Augusta behind the steering wheel. She saw them, she waved her hand, she stopped the car and got out. She didn't look scared, she didn't look rattled, she looked just ordinary. "Well, Mother!" she said with a laugh. "Don't you realize we can't afford to keep you in shoe leather if you're going to tramp around this way."

She was simply *swell,* Aunt Augusta was, thought Lolly.

They got Grannie into the car between them, leaning against Aunt Augusta, Lolly sort of propping her up on the other side. Aunt Augusta steered with one hand, and put the other arm around her mother, who went at once to sleep, her head on her daughter's shoulder. Lolly was very tired too. But not at all sleepy. She sat looking at Grannie's hand, limp on her knees. By and by she took it between her hard, dusty little palms. How soft it was, as if it had no bones in it, how soft and withered to nothing—it was ever so much weaker than a baby's hand! Lolly held it between hers. Poor Grannie! Poor old Grannie! So old—and wanting to go to find her *mother!* Holding the strengthless withered hand in hers, Lolly sent up her first prayer. It was of gratitude. "Oh God, I'm so much obliged to you for letting me take care of Grannie!"

When they got home Mother, who had gone the other direction to look for them, wasn't back yet. Lolly was glad. And so, she guessed, was Aunt Augusta. Grannie was safe upstairs in bed, and Lolly was too, a half-hour later when Mother came rushing in and began those tears and exclamations which Lolly had dreaded, but which from a distance, as they were now, hardly reached her.

And the next morning, when Lolly, very late, got up and dressed and went down stairs, Mother was almost quiet about what had happened, just kissed her extra hard. (Lolly wondered if maybe Aunt Augusta had suggested to her to go sort of easy.) She put Lolly's breakfast on the table and went off into the post office. Grannie was tucked up on the sofa where Aunt Augusta could keep an eye on her. She was sound asleep. Lolly sat putting absent-minded spoonfuls of cereal and cream into her mouth, watching a fly buzzing on the window, turning her eyes once in a while to the door into the post office to watch Aunt Augusta sorting mail. Mother was talking. "I'll never forgive myself, never!" she was saying—Lolly dreamily wondered what was the matter now? "But how *could* I have guessed? I don't know *what* Jim will say when I tell him. He'll be *wild!*"

Peter the Great came lumbering in from the porch and went up to the table, sticking his great head close to Lolly's face as she ate. *"Get* off, Peter!" she said, impatient with him. *"Get* away!" She waved her hand imperiously towards the door, watched him walk sadly away, his tail drooping, and turned to see Aunt Augusta's eyes on her. "Hello, Lolly," said Aunt Augusta. Lolly said hello back to her, and lifted another spoonful of cereal to her mouth, her eyes on the fly.

West Wind! West Wind!

INTO the clearing high up on the side of the mountain drove a car, somewhat haggard with fighting water-bars and washed-out places on the long steep back-road. It was, like the family which owned it, a middling car, neither very inexpensive nor very costly. In it were two ladies, both in bright-colored cotton dresses with tight scanty tops and very full skirts, both with bobbed waved hair, both tall and correctly flattish as to figure, both with long bare legs and short socks—looking indeed almost exactly alike, yet even from a distance you could tell that they were mother and daughter. Back of them, in the rumble seat was a round-cheeked rosy little girl of ten or so, her fat legs in khaki shorts, a sort of bandanna handkerchief tied over her front, leaving her plump brown back quite bare. Now you know what kind of a family they were.

They had driven up to picnic on this ancient abandoned farm with another family, friends who had two prep-school boys visiting them. And because they had made a late start from home (you'll see why in a moment) they had hurried as much as it was possible to hurry over that infernal wreck of a road. At least they had hurried as much as the driver thought possible. The one who was not driving had kept saying nervously, "Oh, for heaven's sake, step on the gas, why

26

don't you? You're simply poking!" But as they emerged from the woods and saw that the yard in front of the bleached, eyeless skeleton of the old farmhouse held no other car, the driver said, "There, you see, Carley. In spite of your making us late in starting we're in *plenty* of time. There was no need whatever for you to be in such a hysterical hurry. That blue dress was perfectly all right, anyhow." The little girl fell out of the rumble seat, crying, "Oh, gosh! Look at those blueberries. Ripe a'ready!"

The two she had left continued to sit on the front seat of the car. There was nowhere else to sit. And they were not interested in blueberries. The younger one got out a compact and looking earnestly into its tiny mirror, began to add another gooey layer to the sealing-wax red already thick on her lips. Her mother said nothing. Not a word. Not one single *word*. In a stony silence she looked off at a very fine view of airy spacious valleys, wooded mountains and sapphire-blue distant peaks—none of which she saw. You have probably encountered silences like the one she made (perhaps you have made them yourself) so that it will not surprise you to hear that the girl stuck out her chin considerably farther than was necessary, and smeared the lipstick on with a swish. Also that she shut up her compact with a hard click which, in the sunny silence of the clearing, was as militant as the crack of a pistol. Once more her mother said nothing. Still shaken by the jangling over their late start, she was thinking, "I will *not* let her provoke me into losing my temper again, as I did over that pig-headed changing of her dress at the last minute. This is just the foolish age they all go through. We'll

27

survive it, I suppose—I hope!" All of this which she thought was locked up in her own mind, was of course written in large letters all over her, from compressed lips and stony eyes to taut hands still gripping the motionless steering wheel. The girl began to whistle the air of a popular song, the words of which were none too refined. Her mother's silence deepened to so ominous a degree that she was a little scared. So she whistled all the more shrilly. She felt sore and sorrowful about her mother's intense disapproval. She really did not care a thing about the boy she had been in such a hurry to meet here promptly and for whom she had changed her dress—she only strung him along to show that she could if she wanted to—she felt tragically isolated and increasingly doubtful about whether it was worth while to go on living (she was rather hungry by this time although she did not know it)—so she crossed her bare legs in the sprawling way she knew her mother did not like, took one ankle in her hands and whistled like a steam siren.

Her little sister came bouncing up to the side of the car, her face smeared with blueberry juice, long streaks of it down her handkerchief front. "Gosh! These are good!" she said thickly through a mouthful of fruit. "Here, Carley, take some." She made a generous offer of the bruised bleeding berries cupped in her two hands, from which the crisp young lady in the car shrank in disgust, crying out, "Barbara, don't come *near* me with that nasty mess!"

"Want some, Mommie?" Barbara said good-humoredly, paying no attention to Carley's rebuff.

"No, thank you, dear, I don't think I care for any just

28

now. But it's very nice of you to think of us," said her mother with an underlined politeness aimed at her older daughter.

"I'm terrible," thought Carley, "jumping down my little sister's throat that way, when she's trying to be nice. I'm simply terrible anyhow." So after Barbara had gone back to her berry-bushes she said aloud, coldly, "I suppose you know that you let Barbara do all the things you take the heads right off the rest of us if we *think* of doing them. Anybody would know she's your favorite."

"What do you mean!" cried her mother indignantly, very indignantly indeed, for far within her something was admitting, "It's true. Barbara was the last baby I'll ever have—I do have a special feeling for her." So she said aloud in a more and more astonished voice, "What are you talking about?"

"I know what you'd say to Jim or me if we said, 'gosh!' every other word."

"Oh, *that*—" said her mother, relieved. "Why, children are always getting hold of some expression and running it into the ground. If you don't pay any attention to it they soon drop it. They do it partly to get attention, anyhow."

Carley thought bitterly, "That's the underhand way she manages me, too. She sees right through us. She probably knew just why I wanted to change my dress. I can't keep anything to myself. I look to her the way Barbara looks to me. She's seen me do so many fool things she doesn't believe I *can* ever do anything else. Oh, I wish I could go and live with people I'd never heard of or that had never heard of me. I could draw my breath then. I could *be* somebody. But

29

would they dream of letting me? Not on your life. Everything for Barbara, and the leavings for Jim and me."

There was a long silence, during which Carley got hungrier and hungrier, though she thought she was sadder about life being worth living. During which her mother thought in intensive detail of how she could cut corners with a lessened income, send Carley away to college in the fall, keep up Jimmy's music lessons, have Barbara's tonsils out and still not have her husband think he ought to give up the golf which was about the only pleasure he had. One thing was sure, whatever else had to be given up, Carley *must* get away to college. She was at the age when she needed a new background as much as she had ever needed orange juice and spinach in her childhood.

Presently the mother looked at her wrist watch and remarked, "They're really very late. We've been waiting here more than half an hour. And we were late when we came."

Carley pounced. "I thought you said we were in *plenty* of time," she said savagely, imitating her mother's accent.

"Oh, Carley," said her mother, with the quiet, rather sad adult dignity that always reduced Carley to an inner rage of envy. "How does she *do* it? How does she know just how to make you feel like a naughty kid. And it's not fair. She did say that. And now she shows she never thought it for a minute."

Barbara came heavily back from her berry picking. "Gosh, I'm hot," she said, crawling in on the floor of the car. Her sister hastily moved immaculate white sandals away.

30

"Don't say 'gosh' so much, dear," said her mother. "It's not very nice."

"Why, gosh! What's the matter with it?" asked Barbara in astonishment.

"Aren't you hungry, Babbie? It's an hour past our usual lunch time."

"I never want to eat again," said the gorged child, leaning her head against the door of the car.

"I don't know what to do," said the mother to Carley. "Something must have happened to the Bradfords. But you'd think they'd send word. I can't wait much longer. I left the living-room all torn up and half cleaned. I must settle it before your father gets home. Not to speak of getting dinner."

Her own ear did not catch the overtone of complacent martyrdom in her voice. But Carley's did. "It's all foolishness fussing so much about the housework as you do, Mother. You're the only one that thinks everything must be just so."

Her mother was hurt by the child's ingratitude—at least she thought it was by that, although really she half knew that an unadmitted truth winged the shaft home. "Carley!" she exclaimed. "When you *know* that my whole life is given to make our home what it should be for you children and Father!"

But Carley, too, half knew something—that she had spoken a truth. And she wholly knew that—oh, joy!—for once she saw something her mother did not. She pressed her point zestfully home through the crack in her mother's omniscience. "We wouldn't mind—you know we wouldn't. Why, I've heard you complain that we wouldn't so much as notice if you *never* cleaned house. It's not for us you do all that. It's for yourself."

But she was horrified at her mother's stricken look. "Oh, I'm a beast," she thought. "A beast! What'd I have to go and tell her that for! She does just work her head off for us. Why shouldn't she do something for herself once in a while?"

She was ready to cry. Her mother's eyebrows were drawn into a knot. They sat in silent pain—all the ingredients of happiness heaped high around them—their hearts sore and aching.

From below their knees, Barbara inquired with astonishment, "Well, did you ever know that bees *suck?* I thought it was only lambs and babies."

"What are you talking about?" they both asked her at once.

"It's a book," said Barbara, emerging from their skirts, a book in her hand. "I found it in the door-pocket. It says, 'Where the bee sucks, there suck I.'" She began to laugh. "'There suck I.' Can you beat that?"

Carley snatched the book from her hand. "You little idiot," she said, "that's *poetry*. Here, read it this way." She read liltingly,

" 'In a cowslip's bell I lie;
    There I couch when owls do cry;
    On the bat's back I do fly
    After summer merrily:
    Merrily, merrily, shall I live now
    Under the blossom that hangs on the bough.' "

"Did you ever hear the tune to that?" asked their mother, opening the picnic basket and getting out some sandwiches. (She was as glad as Carley of the change of subject.)

"No, I never knew it *had* a tune," said Carley.

Handing around sandwiches, their mother began to sing, the lifts and falls and turns of her voice echoing sweetly on the summer air.

"Yes, it really is prettier that way," admitted Barbara, through a sandwich. Carley's first had already gone—like a plummet to the bottom of the sea. She had not dreamed she was so hungry. She reached for another, ruffling the pages of the book with the other hand. "Do you know this one?" she asked. "Is there a tune to that too?" She read, her fresh young voice like running water,

" 'Hark, hark! the lark at heaven's gate sings,
And Phoebus 'gins arise.' "

"Oh, yes," said their mother, "a lovely tune that Schubert wrote." She sang it through, her sandwich-gulping daughters' eyes fixed dreamily on her. She was thinking, "Carley is right. I'd much better do more with my music even if the house isn't so clean. I didn't realize they'd have any interest in such songs. You always forget how fast they grow."

"Good gosh, Mother," said Barbara, "I never knew you could sing like that."

She flushed with pleasure. And with remorse. Had it been so long since she sang? Carley said now, "Here, you haven't eaten a thing yet. Take some." She herself was just swallowing the last of her fifth sandwich, and was turning an apple

33

around, considering where to sink her teeth into it. Most of the commercial red had been rubbed from her rosy young lips. She passed the package of sandwiches to her mother. "The shrimp ones are swell."

Her mother said, "Well, I've sung for you. Suppose you read me something while I eat. I'd love to hear you. You read Ariel's song beautifully." She could see, by the tremor of pleasure that passed over Carley's face, how her praise went straight to the girl's hungry self-doubting young heart. "I don't know what you'd like," said Carley.

"Let's take turns picking out things," said Barbara. "You begin, Mommie."

A dark undercurrent in the mother's thoughts, that usually ran deep, flooded up to the surface for an instant, "How about 'O, that 'twere possible'?" she asked. And then, astonished at herself, "No, no, that's too sad for you, of course."

Carley lifted a glowing face. "I simply *adore* sad things!" she cried, and read, her bitten-into apple in one hand,

> " 'O, that 'twere possible
>   After long grief and pain
>   To find the arms of my true love
>   Round me once again—
>   Ah, Christ, that it were possible
>   For one short hour to see
>   The souls we loved, that they might tell us
>   What and where they be.' "

The beautiful, poignant words fell like viola notes into the silence. The mother sat looking off at the distant blue peaks—

she saw them now—thinking of the little first-born son who had died. The corners of her mouth twitched.

Laying down the book, Carley murmured ardently, "That's just too lovely to endure."

"Isn't there anything cheerful in that book?" asked Barbara.

"Let's see," said her mother, taking it. Carley dreamily began to eat a wedge of chocolate cake.

" 'Spring, the sweet spring is the year's pleasant king,' "

read the mother, making her voice brisk and laughing,

" 'Then blooms each thing, then maids dance in a ring,
    Cold doth not sting, the pretty birds do sing
    Cuckoo, jug-jug, pu-we, to-witta-woo!' "

The bird refrain at the end of each stanza sent Barbara into delighted giggles.

Carley, wiping cake crumbs from her mouth, reached for the book. "Do you know this one?

" 'These pools that, though in forests, still reflect
    The total sky almost without defect,
    And like the flowers beside them, chill and shiver,
    Will, like the flowers beside them, soon be gone,
    And yet not out by any brook or river,
    But up by roots to bring dark foliage on.

" 'The trees that have it in their pent-up buds
    To darken nature and be summer woods—
    Let them think twice before they use their powers
    To blot out and drink up and sweep away

35

These flowery waters and these watery flowers
From snow that melted only yesterday.' "

When she finished, *"No,"* cried her mother, "I never heard that. How exquisite!—it takes your breath away with beauty, doesn't it? Read it again." She was thinking, "Why, Carley is a spring pool, soon to be gone!"

Carley, as proud as if she had written the poem, read it again, lingering with love over each musical syllable.

"How about one for *me?*" asked Barbara.

Her mother fluttered the pages, opened the book wide, took a deep breath and began chantingly,

> " 'White founts falling in the courts of the Sun,
>   Don John of Austria is going to the war—' "

"Oh, *swell!*" said Carley, beating time with one hand.

Barbara listened, open-mouthed, to all of the marching, shouting, trumpeting lines. At the end, "That was a beaut!" she exclaimed.

"Your turn, Carley." The mother handed over the book.

"Can you stand a long one?" she asked her mother, and not waiting for the answer began—the familiar, magnificent lines rolling out in glory,

> " 'There was a time when meadow, grove and stream,
>   The earth and every common sight
>   To me did seem
>   Apparel'd in celestial light,
>   The glory and freshness of a dream.' "

36

She read on and on, her young voice round and honey-sweet as a thrush's. Her mother could not take her eyes from the flowerlike face bent over the page. Why, Carley was a lovely young woman! And not only lovely to look at—thrilling to lovely things, to music, to poetry—even to great poetry like this—taking the first steps into deep-hearted womanhood.

"'Thanks to the human heart by which we live,
Thanks to its tenderness, its joys and fears,
To me the meanest flower that blows can give
Thoughts that do lie too deep for tears.'"

Carley drew a long breath of perfect satisfaction, looked up from the book and saw her mother's eyes, deeply bent on hers, full of tears. "Oh, oh," she cried, flinging her arms around her mother's neck, "does it make *you* cry, too, when something's too beautiful?"

The long murmur of the rhythm had sent Barbara to sleep. She woke up now, yawned, and said, "Well, those old Bradfords must be dead or something."

Carley and her mother had forgotten about the Bradfords. They looked at each other and laughed, wiping their eyes. Barbara went on, "But we've had a lots better time than if they'd come."

"I'll *say* we have!" agreed Carley. She had an inspiration. "Mother! What do you say we all go and have a swim in the river? Our bathing suits are in the rumble. It'd be fun. Us three girls together." Her eagerness dimmed. "Oh, I forgot about the living-room."

"Let's go," cried her mother. "I don't care if the living-room *never* gets settled!"

From Barbara, scrambling up and falling over into the rumble seat, there came, "Gosh, Carley, what swell ideas you do have!"

Married Children

The young wife:

"Good-by! *Good*-by!" she turned the golden brown of her tanned face up towards the two pale, indoor, middle-aged faces at the open window. "It's been *won*derful to have you!" The train began slowly to move. Walking along on the platform beside it, she clasped her father's clean wrinkled hand, and said affectionately, "Dear old Dad!" Her mother's, a little knotted with arthritis, but carefully kept, she kissed. The train picked up speed. She let them go. "*Good*-by! Come again!" she shouted, waving her hand. They were gone. A flurry of dust settled down to stillness. She stood a moment looking after the train, the smile still on her face. She was thinking with satisfaction, "Well, the first visit went off all right."

She walked home at a brisk pace, smiling all the way, and let herself into the living-room. It looked empty and deserted. Elated, she stood a moment to expand into the roominess left by departing guests and stepping into the kitchen, *her own kitchen,* began cheerfully to wash the dishes left from lunch.

As she worked her eyes roamed regally around her domain. "I love it all, *all!*" she thought. Every object she touched had been part of a happy hour. She set a washed bowl down on the drain-board and remembered how Christopher's eyes had shone the day he came in with it under his arm. He had been making it himself in odd moments to surprise her. It had come over her all of a sudden how *grand* he was—she thought of some of the girls back home who had married awful poker-playing boys—men who prided themselves on being sports and went right on spending their money on the races the way they had before they were married, grudging every cent for housekeeping, husbands who wanted to live in one room and go out to dance in a road-house every evening.

"Oh, Chris! How did I ever have the good luck to get you!" she had cried, and fell into his arms so hard they both went down on a chair—and it had gone to pieces! And there they had sat on the floor in each other's arms—in the midst of scattered chair-rounds and legs—laughing and laughing. "Like a couple of silly kids!" thought the wife. In the memory of it her face bloomed with gaiety. What good times they had had together! "No matter how rich we ever get, or how many children we have, or *anything*, nothing can ever be lovelier than this first winter." She could have kissed the very door through which Christopher came in from work, always cheerful, not only always loving her, but always *liking* her, no matter what she did. Dad was the salt of the earth, of course. But he always found something sharp and sarcastic to say if anybody unfolded the newspaper before he did, and the way he looked at his plate if the breakfast sausage wasn't cooked to suit him certainly did take away everybody else's appetite. She hadn't known but that all men were like that at home. Christopher, who took everything so easily, who thought it was too wonderful of her to cook his meals at all, anyhow; Chris—always tickled to death all over again every time he came back to the house to find he really was married to her and had a home—well, Christopher simply took her breath away.

She had finished the dishes now and set herself, singing at the top of her voice, *"Mis*ter and *Mis*sis is the name!" to getting the wash ready for old Maria Half-Wolf when she came loping up on her pinto, her black braids flying. If that old red-skin wasn't exciting to have around—like a movie—compared to Hennessey's Steam Laundry delivery wagon! How romantic and picturesque and interesting every bit of the life here was anyway! As she came and went, singing, sorting over and gathering up the laundry, her eyes were often on the magnificent golden spaciousness outside. Those miles of sunlight! That clear strong tireless wind! Compare what she saw now out of her window to the postage-stamp of lawn, the smothering heavy-leaved trees, the crowded commonplace suburban houses that had shut in her life until now. "Honest, it makes a person feel like flying," she thought. "I could fly, I know I could, I feel so wonderful!" and stopped short, startled to realize that the reason she felt like flying was because Father and Mother had gone away. And with them had gone the—the *weight* they put on her. Why was it they always made her feel unsure of herself—like a child again? Was it because they had been grown up so long before she had? She had been dismayed to have that old doubt of herself, the wonder if she was doing things to suit them, come back in her very own home. "My! I'm glad we don't live next door!" she thought, and then, "I'm terrible!

41

I'm simply awful!" she reproached herself, thinking hard about how generous Father always was, how much Mother loved her. "They're sweet. They're swell. I owe them everything," she went on, but rebounded from this dutifulness into, "But, oh, gosh! Does it seem good to do things the way *I* want them, not the way Mother thinks best. I'm going to make milk gravy for dinner, and *thicken it with flour and water!*" Laughing at the thought of how shocked her mother would be at this revolt from Law, she moved gaily to begin her cooking.

But as she worked alone, happily, free from criticism, from supervision, even from observation, in her very own kitchen, she felt little by little as if a cold draught had begun to blow, that, after having had somebody else there, it was queer to be alone by yourself in the place. Once she turned to say something to Mother and was daunted to see how empty the kitchen looked. Why, Mother was gone! Already far away. Her heart sank. Suppose something should happen! Suppose she should get sick! What could she do if she got sick, all alone so far away from Mother!

Well, Mother would come, of course. Stooping to set her biscuits in the oven, it came over her almost as though it were the first time she had ever thought of it, that goodness gracious, she was lucky to have a mother like that, somebody you could count on, abso*lute*ly. Let them be in China or Alaska, or Timbuctoo, Mother would be with them in thought, in love. And if there was trouble—she'd always taken it for granted, but really it was wonderful to know that Mother would be with you as fast as travel could bring her, wanting nothing but what would be best for her children, ready to do anything to get it for them—*Mother!* "Gosh, I wonder will my children feel that way about me!" thought the young wife soberly, and asked herself with concern, "How do you suppose anybody gets that way?"

And then Chris burst in, Chris rushing off to wash and change his clothes before the ceremony of greeting her and coming back in a hurry with open arms to kiss her a great many times all over her hair as well as her lips and cheeks and neck. "I simply adore your hair this way, Judy darling," he said. "You look like Garbo herself."

As they ate dinner they talked about their visitors. Christopher, as an orphan, was quite impressed with parents, quite taken with his wife's parents. She listened, pleased, to his appreciation of her father's geniality, uneasy, to his praise of her mother's skill, steadiness, competence. "Set that woman down anywhere, no matter where, and she'd take right hold and get things straightened out!" he said. His accent, his words, his admiration brought back to his young wife the shadow of her girlhood's dimmed jealous uncertainty of her own powers. She held her head down as she ate, and thought forlornly, "Nobody'd ever say that about *me*." "But," added Christopher thoughtfully, "she's not my kind of woman, of course."

His wife lifted her head quickly. "What do you mean?" she asked.

He thought she was indignant at a criticism of her family, and quailed a little; but held his ground honestly, too. "I don't mean she's not fine. She is. As fine as they make 'em.

But she's just not the kind of woman I'd ever take to. I don't know why. Too darned practical, maybe. I like 'em foolish—and young—and soft—and—" He put his hand over his wife's and looked at her fondly.

Before the young wife there opened a door, the door she had secretly feared would always be closed to her, the door that led to her place in life, her own place. There was a place for her then, a place that nobody of the overpowering older generation could fill. She stepped gladly through to take that place of her own, leaving her mother behind her.

And now she was safe, freed from that pervasive pressure, how she loved her mother! Happily. With all her heart. No silent reservations. "Yes, Mother is certainly *swell!*" she said earnestly, and put up her napkin to wipe her eyes.

The mother to the grandmother:

"Well, all right, Mother, I'll try to tell you about it, but you'll hardly believe it if I do. I never was so shocked as when I got off the train and saw that forlorn town. A dozen cheap ramshackle bungalows set down anyhow on the desert. You'd never *dream* from Judy's letters what it's like. Nor what kind of a place they live in! Only *half* of one of those miserable little wooden packing-cases. Three bare rooms looking out into a desert of dust. That alkali dust! You eat it, you drink it—it took Charles and me three days after we left to get the gritty taste out of our mouths."

"Never mind about the dust, Etta. How is *Judy?*"

"Well, she *says* the climate and the altitude and everything agree with her. But you should see her skin. That rose-petal

44

skin of hers! All dried up and brown! I don't believe she half takes care of it. You never saw such a change in anybody's looks! She's had to have her hair bobbed, to make it easier to take care of. For there's not such a thing as a hairdresser within ten thousand miles of that place, I'm sure. The last of her permanent has grown out and been cut off—her hair's as straight as a string, she looks like a squaw. She just runs the comb through it without so much as a glance at the mirror. Judith! You know how careful she used to be of her hair. But she has no time to think of her looks now. And nobody to notice them, either. Christopher would never know if she didn't even wash her face. He just takes her for granted. And there's nobody in that town—*nobody*—that would know enough to notice looks. Or anything else! I never saw such a place. Everybody looked to me as though they were just roosting for a while before they moved on. But who'd want to settle down in a desert? For it's the real desert, you know, too dreary for words. Simply impossible to keep house in. Absolutely no help to be had, except Mexicans or Indians. Judy has *no*body to do a thing for her except a dirty old half-and-half Mexican-Indian woman who does her washings. And how! But of course the water is so stiff with alkali dust nobody could ever get anything clean."

The grandmother laughed. "Oh, goodness, Etta, don't sputter so. I don't care how they get their washings done. I want to hear about Judy's husband. How'd you like him now you've seen him at home?"

The mother looked off into the distance and said neutrally, "Oh, well enough." She shifted in her chair and admitted,

45

"He's all right." She swallowed, folded her lips and repeated, dryly, "I don't say he's not all *right*—a nice boy. Easy-going around the house, and that sort of thing." She came to life, her eyes snapped, she leaned forward and asked with energy, "But will he ever be the provider Charles has been? That's the question! Do you know I don't believe he ever sells any insurance. As far as I can see, all he makes is out of a filling-station they run. Yes, a regular road-side filling-station, selling gas to automobilists! And when he has to be away, Judy answers the bell and runs out and pumps it up for them and makes change and everything. What do you think of that?"

"Does she mind?"

"Well, I wouldn't say she *minded*. She's still so childish she doesn't take in the meaning of things. And you know what a sweet disposition she has always had. She'd never complain. Christopher is lucky to get her, if he did but know it. There are not many girls who'd be as cheerful as she is, in the life she has to lead. You should see the furniture in that rattle-trap little house. Cheap to begin with, and I suppose the glue all dried out by the heat. It falls apart if you look at it. Charles and I never sat our whole weight on a chair all the while we were there."

"Oh, well, daughter, you and Charles didn't have such a lot of furniture when you started in housekeeping. I remember the first time I visited you, you were serving your meals on the table in the kitchen because there wasn't another in the house big enough to eat off of."

The mother flashed a resentful look at the grandmother and said quickly, "Why, I don't remember that at all." And then, reluctantly, "Well, yes, perhaps—but that was at the very beginning." She looked hard at the older woman and said with heat, "You're just bringing that up to be contrary, Mother. This isn't the same thing at all. Times have changed —the home Judy came from was—" She shook her head, gave that up, appealed to her mother's deeper understanding, "And anyhow, it's not the furniture—it's the—it's the loneliness, the desolation of it all. She's absolutely isolated. Not a soul around that she can say a word to, not a real word. You know how she's always kept up with her music—in church, in the chorus here! I don't suppose there's a soul there who knows what good singing sounds like. Judy practically admitted she hasn't done a bit of practicing since she was married. And no kind of social life either—no club, no speakers— I don't suppose there's a book in the whole county besides the Sears, Roebuck catalogue—no friends, nobody but a lot of— Well, all I can say is that any man who'll take a girl from a good home out to the middle of a desert and expect her to— Where's my handkerchief?"

The older woman said sadly, "Etta, do you know why you're crying? It's not because Judy is having a hard time. It's because she isn't."

The other put down her handkerchief with a sharp gesture of resentful astonishment. "I don't know what you're talking about!"

The grandmother went on, "Oh, yes, you do. Till now you've never *believed,* no matter what you said, that Judy could really be happy away from you. It's because you saw

47

for yourself that she's through with you, that there's no need for you anywhere in her—"

"*Mother!* How can you say such a heartless thing! I'm *not* thinking of myself. I'd give my right hand for Judy's happiness, and you know it."

"Nobody's blaming you, Etta," said the grandmother dreamily, as if thinking of something else. "You're a good mother. Everybody knows that growing-pains hurt."

"But, Mother, you've got this all wrong! Listen to me! I'm not jealous of Judy. I don't want to keep her for myself. *I love my daughter.*"

The grandmother sighed and said with profound sympathy, "My poor Etta, you've just got to learn to love her another way." She put her wrinkled hand on her daughter's.

There was a silence—then the younger woman said in a low faltering tone of pain, "Mother, at the station, when we were going away, Judy ran along beside the train, saying good-by—" she stopped to wipe her eyes and blow her nose, and, her lower lip trembling, murmured piteously—"and she looked so—so *cheerful!*"

An involuntary rueful laugh broke from her mother. "Well, darling, so did you twenty years ago."

They laughed. They clung to each other. They reached for their handkerchiefs.

The father to the grandfather:

"—a pretty tough time of it, as far as money goes. I don't suppose there ever was a harder time for a young fellow to get a start. His insurance business don't amount to a whoop,

48

I take it. He's had to hustle right out and find *some*thing—got himself a filling station to run. No, not much money in that. Pretty slim pickings for them all around, I take it. Not that it takes much to live on as they do, in half of one of those little shacks, with three sticks of furniture."

"Oh, well, they're not the only ones to have a hard time getting started. It all depends on how they take it. How *do* they? Are they good sports? Do they make out to stand it?"

The father unhooked his spectacles from his ears and polished them thoughtfully on his handkerchief, looking down at them with a smile. "How do they stand it?" He repeated the question, and putting his glasses back on, answered it in a tender voice, "They don't 'stand' it at all," he said. "The nice kids, they don't even notice it!"

The First Grandchild

"IF YOU think I ought to stay in, I will, of course," Jocelyn told her parents in the voice which meant she had no intention of doing anything of the kind.

Her father and mother understood her. With an air of giving her up altogether, her father silently raised before his face the newspaper he had laid down when the telephone rang.

"Of course, Joy, I can understand it would be a little difficult to explain." Her mother hastily presented the girl with a talking-point. Jocelyn pushed it away.

"Heavens, no! what would be difficult? I'd just as soon as not tell the crowd my married sister has gone to the hospital to have her first baby, and my early-American parents think it wouldn't be decent for me to go off and dance till we get the great question settled of whether it's a girl or a boy."

Jocelyn's father folded back the newspaper to the editorial page with rather a loud crackling of paper. She answered this protest crisply, "Those are the facts, Dad. What is so indelicate about mentioning them out loud?"

"Your father means," Jocelyn's mother murmuringly interpreted, "that if you yourself don't *feel* as if it would—"

"Well, I don't," said the girl. "Why should I? It's not as if there were anything I could do for Felicia. You and Father live back in the pre-hospital, pre-trained-nurse days, when all the family felt it a duty to stand by to keep the tea-kettle boiling and scrape lint."

Her mother broke into an unwilling laugh. She knew it irritated Andrew to have her frivolously see something funny in a situation which annoyed him. But the glimpse of Jocelyn's notion of the past was too much for her.

The girl's complacent young jauntiness was somewhat shaken by the sparkle in her mother's eye. She looked at her with an uneasy inquiry.

"It was our grandmothers who scraped lint. You're only two generations out," explained her mother. Andrew rebukingly turned his paper inside out to get at the financial page. Well, he was right, she told herself, there was nothing funny in that, now she thought of it from his point of view. She recognized in herself Aunt Jennie's silliness which in her childhood had so often irritated her. She knew just how Andrew felt.

The front door-bell rang. "There's Hank now," said Jocelyn. "What shall I tell him?" As if she had not decided what to tell him!

"Oh, go *along!*" said her father with a sudden angry explosiveness, from behind the paper.

Jocelyn's eye met her mother's and saw, kindling behind the veil of conscientious seriousness, another of those sparks of amusement. For an instant mother and daughter looked at each other as if both were mischievous girls.

Then Jocelyn leaped at her mother for a good-by kiss,

51

called to her father, "Well, since you insist, I will," and was
gone.

"I oughtn't to do that!" thought her mother, remorsefully.
"It's not fair to Andrew. He'd never do such a thing behind
my back!" She sighed, the sparks quenched. "That's Uncle
Elmer's underhanded ways coming out in me. I don't seem
to get over those faults of mine at all— You'd think by this
time—with a grandchild just about to appear!"

Noticing that the Corot "Morning Mist" hung crookedly,
she walked across the room, pulled at one corner and stepped
back as if to make sure it was now straight. But she did not
see it. She saw the Christmas morning when Andrew had
given the photograph to her—little Andrew prancing round
in his tiny pajamas, his stocking hung before the fireplace
in the "old house," the small cheap house that had been
their first home, when Andrew had been only an instruc-
tor, where young Andrew was born, where their first child
had had his first Christmas.

She reached for the ball of yarn and her needles, and sitting
down began to knit and to remember.

Behind his newspaper her husband was saying to himself
suitable regretful words, saying them but not thinking them,
"I oughtn't to snap at the children that way! Joy hadn't done
anything to have me take her head off, so—but good God!
what a mess girls of her age are!" He ruminated wrathfully
on girls! Half they were shallow children, and half, self-
willed egotistic young women. Wanting the pleasures of
both ages with none of their obligations. Jocelyn's demand on

life was to be allowed to do just as she liked and yet have the older generation go through the motions of approving everything she did. Hard-boiled little idiot, priding herself on her vulgar English and lack of natural feeling!

Well, that was too strong perhaps. About Jocelyn anyhow. As his irritation cooled down, he admitted he had gone too far. A misgiving pricked him. His temper was certainly not improving with age; would he, later on, develop into one of those undignified choleric old gentlemen at whose rages everybody laughed behind his back? He put the idea aside, told himself, "Anyhow I deserve some credit for not having let Phebe see how that silly laugh of hers rubbed me the wrong way." He went back to thinking about his younger daughter. She was no worse, he supposed, than any of her gang, her half-naked loud-voiced sorority sisters who, when he came in of a late afternoon, seemed to fill the living-room with miles of silk-stockinged legs as they lay back in low arm chairs and crossed their knees, dropping cigarette ashes all over the books on his reading-table, and laughing like hyenas over each other's wisecracks. He couldn't see that all this modern education had changed girls. What could anybody see in them! When he thought that some men of his age were crazy about them—

His arms felt that the usual time had passed since turning over a page and folded the newspaper into a new shape. Not supervised by the brain they brought only the advertisement of a department store under his eyes. His gaze fixed itself docilely on electric toasters and overstuffed chairs while his brain, shunted by the interruption to another track, found there a very disagreeable thought; was it only because he was an old man that he was not stirred as other men seemed to be by liquid eyes and gleaming hair and provocative tricks with full soft lips? He recalled a little Cleopatra among Joy's friends, who, marooned with him for half an hour one evening as she waited for Joy, had automatically turned on him the batteries of her eyebrows and lips and Clytie-like shoulders. How drearily he had seen through her, not even amused, bored. A dried-up juiceless old college professor, he was, about to be publicly thrust into the prison of old age with the key turned behind him by the birth of a grandchild. And without ever having had his share of life—a well-worn path seeming to open before his thoughts at this point, his mind slid along it as water flows downhill—without ever having lived for an hour in the grand style careless of consequences, going fullspeed ahead with the current—as one could at the side of some reckless, full-blooded, deep-bosomed woman.

There was not a sound in the room except the clicking needles of his wife. But he drew back quickly as though he had been laughed at. Long years with Phebe had taught him just when she would be likely to see something funny in what impressed other people. The unheard tinkle of her laugh now made him remember that if she knew he had been thinking himself defrauded because she had never driven him mad with passion, she would remember with involuntary hilarity what he had always felt about what are called seductive women. It was not because he had grown old that he had been bored not kindled by the blandishments of that pretty girl. He had always detested the complacency of girls who had found out they were physically seductive to men. They were, he had often thought, like ill-bred new-rich vulgarians, flaunting their unearned power over life with every accent and gesture. From his youngest days on, a woman who had turned on him what she thought was sex-allure had roused to frenzy all his capacities for exasperation. He could no more resist being rude to her than he could keep back the "damn!" when somebody stepped on his bad corn.

Yes, as the minutes slid between him and the idea about his never having lived in the grand style, it was more and more apparent that it was a papery idea out of a book. His mind had slid into it only because the literary grooves to it were worn smooth. As a man of intelligence, he found it a revolting feature of human life that you could not even count on thinking your own thoughts, having your own emotions; that you were likely to find embedded in your brain some muddy cheap conception that bore the same relation to reality as the yearnings of shop-girls over a movie-hero.

He pushed the whole subject away with distaste and tried to remember what he had been thinking about when he had been shunted off on this side-track. He had been thinking—and this was real reality—that tonight found him on the threshold of old age, and without ever having done what he'd like to have done.

And he knew why! Because he had had children to provide for. Because it had taken all that he could earn in his profession to bring up two girls and a boy. Everything else had been put aside till they should be grown. And now they had— Looking blindly at the advertisement of an egg-beater, he thought, "The children—!" And remembered how in babyhood and childhood they had seemed mystic priceless unique treasures, such as had been entrusted to no other human beings in the world's history. He and Phebe had groveled before their three small idols, had beaten loudly on the tom-tom of the tribal religion, had poured out their hearts' blood on the altar before the three celestial treasures. And with the years the celestial treasures had grown into— just three more human beings, strongly resembling several not-very-much-loved aunts and uncles and grandparents.

The clock struck eleven. "I do wonder how Felicia is getting on," murmured his wife over her knitting.

He made some appropriate noise to show he had heard her. His arms, very tired of holding up that unseen newspaper, laid it down and reached for his pipe.

Phebe took advantage of this appearance of not being occupied to ask, "Do you remember the night little Andrew was born?"

He nodded and said, "It was awful."

"Oh, I don't know," she murmured in a low tone as if her thoughts were sinking back into her mind.

He did not hear her. He was living again through that ordeal. The purity of its suffering had been gone a long time. It was lurid now with anger. At the time he had been in too agonizing a fire of terror and pain to do more than suffer like a brute. But when he remembered that night, it was with a Promethean hatred of its suffering, so resentful that it made him hate life. Why should unoffending human

56

beings be sent through such hell as that in which his harmless wife had struggled and screamed. He had been trying
to forget what was happening tonight, but here it came—
his daughter was in that hell this instant, his harmless sensitive little girl who always cried so when she cut her finger.
An echo of her screaming in his inner ear came out in cold
dew on his forehead, took him back to the hideous hospital
corridor where he had leaned against the wall, rigid, stiffly
silent, assuming the only rag of human dignity left to him,
the "manly" pose of Apache insensibility. The Hindus were
right! Life is nothing but an endless chain of miseries. To
escape is the only—

He caught a glimpse of his wife's steady eyes bent on her
work and took back hastily this confession of unfaith. Not
that Phebe would have laughed. She would just have laid
down her knitting and reminded him that as a matter of
plain fact, "endless chain of miseries" was laying it on rather
thick, wasn't it? Phebe was so natural. The excesses of melodrama were rebuked by her mere presence. Strange, having
as little ability as Phebe for what anybody would call con-
secutive thinking, how she kept—but of course it wasn't by
the intellect at all that she kept that unshakeable sense of
proportion.

The telephone rang. Phebe flung her knitting from her
and went hastily to answer with her little trotting step. He
said to himself, "She's mistaken. It's too early for any news
from the hospital. I won't even listen." So he listened, every
pulse halted, every muscle taut, his eyes fixed on Phebe's
back, as in a silence that seemed eternal she held the receiver

at her ear. A boy? A girl? Perhaps—across his heart flickered a flame from the night when his own first child was born—"perhaps Felicia is dead."

Phebe spoke at last. She said, "I think three dozen will be enough, don't you? We can't expect many people out at this time of year."

Damn! *Damn!* Some of her Ladies' Aid stuff! He drew loudly on his pipe and took a book off the nearest shelf at random, so that when she turned back, she would not know he had been so frightened. He would make her think—he held the book up looking at it intently—that he had forgotten what they were waiting for.

As she crossed the room to go back to her chair and her knitting, she gave one glance at his eyes fixed intently on the page, and thought in shocked anxious sympathy, "Oh, poor Andrew! He'll worry himself sick before this is over! How he feels things! How terribly hard he takes everything! There's not a callous spot on his heart anywhere. It wears him out." She sat down, took up her work, and began to remember how he had suffered when their babies were born. "I'm sure it was harder for him than for me. I used to be so sorry for him, grinding his teeth to keep himself from flying to pieces. And nothing I could do to make it easier for him. There never is. I'm so—*ordinary* compared to him." She turned her knitting, "He always takes it out in thinking that everything is worse than it is. Well, I suppose that's like grinding his teeth, sort of a nervous relief. But it tires him out nowadays, to get really worried, as he is tonight. He can't stand it as he used to." She asked herself suddenly,

"Why doesn't he retire? Even with half a pension we'd have enough money—living the way we like to. With Mother's bequest, we'd have enough to travel once in a while. Andrew always wanted to travel. We could go to England, and he could look things up in some old library. He'd love that."

As if he had read the words on the page before him, he found in his mind the idea of retiring from active teaching. With it, always the other half of that idea, was the old question of whether he could stand life without the steadying grind of daily work. Wouldn't leisure shove him over the edge of the danger-thought he tried to ignore? He began to imagine what it would be not to go to college every morning. Never to go to college again. Never to throw the pearls of scholarly interpretation at the feet of the swine of—he glanced uneasily at his wife and took back that figure of speech—well, to make it a colorless literally factual statement such as Phebe insisted on, never again to try to force the significance of human history down the throats of young barbarians who cared about nothing but football and girls. Even Phebe would admit they were barbarians, although she now wordlessly reminded him of gray-haired men who once in a while looked up at him at their sons' Commencements to thank him for some deepening of understanding which they traced back to a lecture of his.

Suppose he should retire—how would it seem to wake up every morning not with a full schedule of work before him, but free to choose whatever seemed really worth while to do —he was slipping, he was lost, that chance phrase had plunged him over the edge into the danger-thought he had set himself not to have. He had it. What he feared was that if he ever had time to look around freely for something worth doing, he would see that there is nothing really worth doing. Nothing.

Clawing hard at the words in the book before him, "Abundant examples can be found alike in Hellenic and in foreign history—" he clambered back to ordinary ideas, and although he was breathing rather fast, went on reading resolutely.

His wife had thought herself around to the opinion that it would be a mistake for Andrew to retire now. "He really adores teaching, for all his talk about football morons. What he lives for really are the two or three students a year who see what he's driving at. They are what makes living seem worth while to him. Without them, he'd be lost. No, it would be a great mistake for him to retire."

She held up a small half-made garment, wondering if she had made the tiny sleeves small enough. A baby in the family again! What fun! How she talked—as though the little thing were already there! Well, that was the way she felt, as sure as though she had the new scrap of life in her arms, this minute. She supposed she ought to be horribly anxious and tense, like Andrew over there, half-frantic as he was tonight. But she wasn't. She was sorry, of course, for Felicia's suffering. No, she wasn't either. She was glad for her, she was trembling with gladness for this other woman! Was there anything like that certainty that came with the pain of child-birth—that you were strong enough to stand anything! The worse it had been—at least for her—the more strength had come rolling up like great mid-ocean waves, miles deep, to carry her forward. Those were among the few hours in her life when she had felt strong enough for anything. She leaned back on the memory of them when something happened to make her feel she really didn't amount to enough to take up house-room.

Strange, where that strength came from! Into such an insignificant snip as she. It seemed to have nothing to do with her, at all. The immense endurance she had felt when Andrew was so sick with pneumonia—that had been another time when she had known she was strong enough for anything. She hadn't been afraid, at all. She had stood up to Andrew's danger as strong as it, or anything! And in the first year of young Andrew's marriage when he had been so horribly troubled about the quarrel with his wife—where had the power come from that had flooded her with the certainty that the quarrel would pass, was nothing. In spite of her son's white face and scared angry eyes, she had known so certainly that she had made him know it too that this explosion was only a part of their getting down to share life with each other. Andrew had said long afterwards, "Mother, you saved our marriage." But he was wrong. That was absurd. She as a person would be incapable of saving anything. It was the strength pouring out through her from that unseen reservoir that had saved it. And could save anything.

"In consequence of the peace, the Athenians sent to recall Iphocrates with his fleet; besides which—"

No, it was no use. Xenophon could not protect him from the fact that he would soon be responsible for the existence of another human being in the world. He saw endless circles of responsibility, widening to infinity around the meeting, years ago of the life-ignorant boy and girl he and Phebe had been. Because they had fallen in love—whatever that meant—more than a quarter of a century later another human soul—call it "soul"—was summoned out from safe non-existence to suffering.

"I never knew Andrew to have a worse one of his blue fits than tonight," thought his wife, sadly; "of course I might have known he would take it hard, crazy as he's been about the children. It's always scared me, the way he's loved them. He's tried not to, too—he's always thinking up intellectual things to say about how it's no more than animal instinct. But mercy! let one of them be sick, or in trouble, and poor Andrew is beside himself. If I were any good, I'd know what to say to help him get through this." She thought wonderingly, "Why don't *I* feel worried? I am, a little, on top. But underneath—I never felt happier. A baby in the family! Perhaps it will be a little girl. That would be *nice!* I'd love a little girl. You can make such darling clothes for them. Perhaps they'll wear bonnets again. Jocelyn always looked adorable in her bonnet. What fun they are when they're little! And big, too. More fun all the time. Joy's never been lovelier and funnier than now—rushing ahead into being grown up—and so deliciously silly, with those newfangled trimmings of modern manners hung around her!

62

Yes, daughters were great! To have two women in the world so close to you as Felicia and Joy—for Joy was a woman now, too, a warmhearted, loving, dutiful, responsible woman—gracious! what swear-words the child would emit if she heard such adjectives applied to her!" At the imagined expression on Joy's face, a gust of amusement all but swept her mother into another untimely laugh. She repressed it, glancing apprehensively at her husband. "I'm a trifling, light-minded woman. Aunt Jennie's nothing to me. It's no wonder I get on Andrew's nerves."

It must be, she thought, because she had had such a happy life, that high spirits were always so irrepressibly near her. She'd never known any of the traditional miseries of life—the best husband in the world, far too good for her, commonplace as she was, a man so fine, so scrupulous, so sensitive, honored by all who knew him, looked up to by his children. This very intensity of feeling that was making him suffer so tonight, it had made life memorable for them all. They'd have been the dullest, flattest family in the world without Andrew's quivering perceptions. They were the lamp, the oil, the wick. Andrew was the flame. They saw by his light. No wonder that every Commencement, some middle-aged man or other, long out of college, came to thank Andrew for—they always said the same thing, even the dumb inarticulate ones—for the inspiration he had been. And such children as she had had, so good to her, never holding off as they grew up and being distant and hateful and hostile, the way modern children do in books. Such funny darlings, with their fits and starts of being grown up, and their lapses

63

into being twelve-year-olds. Only think, if the new baby were a girl, what fun ahead of her! "Perhaps some day she'll sit, about to become a grandmother, and look back over her life and thank God for it."

At this, her foolish wandering thoughts stood still in a panic, as if she feared that Andrew might read her thoughts. That was one thing she couldn't bear to talk to Andrew about. He always seemed to think when you said "God," you couldn't mean anything but the old policeman with a white beard who spies on you through a hole in the clouds. And she was so dumb about explaining, she always got shy and clumsy when she was moved, she never could even make a beginning of telling him that when *she* thought of God— well, they none of them could live a minute without God. What else was their love for each other a piece of, if not of God? What *she* meant by "God." She had asked herself a moment ago where that strength came from when you needed it most. She knew. Where *could* such a flooding of power come from, save from the unimaginable power of that unimaginable goodness that was God. You knew that, be- cause it never came when you wanted something for your- self. Only when you'd left yourself behind and needed strength for someone else. Then it never failed you. Even a poor absurdity like Phebe, Andrew's wife, was swept along by it to wherever she needed to go.

Andrew was looking through the unseen Xenophon at the thought of his descendants, "Tonight completes the circle. With the birth of a child to one of my children, the door of escape from the treadmill is closed. Around and around it the great tribe of my descendants will plod towards nothing. Treading on each other's heels, never a step nearer the goal they all set out to reach." He stood in darkness, watching these doomed great-great-grandchildren of his, plodding around and around to nowhere. And then even this stir of life dwindled, began to die down. He watched it anxiously, as a man in the dark would watch the single spark of light left to him. Like a dying spark it grew dimmer. Went out.

The clock struck midnight.

"I do wonder how Felicia is getting along," murmured Phebe in a low tone. But she was not thinking of Felicia. Or of the new baby. Of Andrew. Across the room, he sat quiet enough, his face bent over a book, his pipe in one hand. But his jaws were clenched and working. With all the invisible antennae of the spirit she knew him to be in danger, terrible danger, the only danger that ever threatened him, from his dreadful power to torture himself. This was not just anxiety about Felicia. This was the Enemy that had come only two or three other times. Looking across at the dear gray head, and aching in the reflection from his misery, she began to pray passionately, calling on God for help, in the only prayer life had taught her, "Dear Andrew! Dear Andrew! *Dear* Andrew!" she prayed with all her might.

Across the black nothingness in which he stood, his heart dying to ashes, a faint light appeared. It grew brighter—came

65

nearer—priceless beyond thought in that dark void. It was close. Phebe was bringing it to him. Phebe came trotting towards him, with her unquenchable light, putting the nothingness to naught by not knowing it was there.

His relief was a shock, a sort of physical shock, like the relief of a man in a bad dream, falling endlessly who, with a great start, wakes and finds himself safe, with morning light bright across his bed.

It had been like a bad dream. It *had* been a bad dream. Were there not waking nightmares?

He filled his lungs with a heave of his chest, and found that he had been half-asphyxiated by forgetting to breathe. Carbon dioxide poisoning. That was what was the matter. That always gave people strange notions. The moment he remembered to draw oxygen into his lungs, he was all right. He had had a moment of dizziness, that was all.

He turned his head and saw that his wife was looking at him. Had he given an actual bodily start, like the man who wakes from a nightmare?

She saw from his face that the Enemy had gone. He laid down his book, looked at his pipe, felt in his pocket for a match. Easily, naturally. Oh, it was *really* all right. "It's hard to wait, isn't it," she murmured.

"Yes, it's given me the jim-jams," he told her, trying to belittle by a trivial word the waking nightmare which had made him forget to breathe. He got up and went to a wastepaper basket to knock out the ashes from his pipe. How enormous the relief was to come to himself out of that

66

smothering helplessness. To come to himself and find Phebe there. For an instant he must have forgotten that Phebe would be there. Why—the new grandchild would find Phebe there, too! He had not thought of that. Still stooping, and tapping his pipe against the basket he said over his shoulder to his middle-aged wife, "I was just thinking that the new baby will get along all right. He's got nothing to complain of. He'll have you for his grandmother."

Phebe heard the words but got no meaning from them. "What is Andrew talking about?" she asked herself, "what does he mean?" Then she knew what he meant. He meant he loved her.

Instantly—it was always the same, as if she were a girl again and he a boy telling her for the first time—she burst into a rosy inner flowering of joy.

But she was shy and clumsy as she always was when she needed specially not to be, and could not think of anything to say except to murmur as she bent her head over her knitting, "Oh, he'll be all right."

"*I* was the one who said he'd be all right," Andrew told her. He sat down beside her. "Let go of that knitting," he said, laid it on the table and took one of her hands in his.

Ah, this was one of their good hours, she thought, one of the hours she'd remember when her time came to die.

After a while the door opened. Jocelyn came in. "A boy," she said, "a seven and a half pound boy with the requisite number of eyes and noses and fingernails." But her eyes were very soft.

67

They had been too much astonished by her appearance to stir. "Felicia is all right, she's getting along like—" She stopped, looked at them, and said, "You look kind of nice, Darby and—" but her lips began to tremble and she could not go on.

She turned away abruptly to hide her face, and cast off her cloak with an exaggeration of her boyish willful lack of grace.

Her father had turned very white when he saw her come in. As she spoke, the color had come back into his face, more with every word. He put his hand up now over his eyes as though the light were too strong for them, and leaned back limply.

But her mother had sprung up and run to her, crying, "But how in the world—?"

"Oh, in the middle of the party, I got sort of sick of the crowd and told Hank to go play by himself. And I took the trolley out to the hospital." She reached for a cigarette, "I thought it would be a lark."

She lighted the cigarette and sat down in a low armchair. "I wouldn't let them telephone you. I was bound I'd be the one to throw the bomb."

"Joy, you naughty girl, how you act!" cried her mother. "You make me want to shake you. *Tell us about it*. Did you see Fred? Did you see Felicia? Did you hear whether—"

"No, gosh, no! I thought Fred had enough on his mind without a sister-in-law butting in. I didn't even go up to the floor where Felicia's room is. I just stuck around downstairs till they came and told me the baby was there all right, and Felicia was O. K."

She crossed her knees and dangled an endless length of silk-stockinged leg. "Emmy Ward's aunt is a nurse in that hospital. She showed me around some while I was waiting. Took me in to the baby-ward."

She opened her mouth wide and let out a cloud of smoke. "They're kind of cute," she admitted, her eyes following the upward swirl of smoke.

SECTION TWO

The Forgotten Mother

IT WAS one of Dr. Burrage's sayings that neither he nor his son—his adopted son, that is—knew anything about mothers. "Dr. Wright's died at his birth. And I lost mine when I was between four and five. Can't remember her at all. Well, yes, I do have a dim picture of someone with brown hair, rather soft and light, with a lock that often fell over her forehead. I can remember how she used to brush it back with her hand. Queer, how a meaningless gesture like that should stick in a child's memory. Then there's something connected with her in a recollection I have of walking along a beam laid on the ground. You know how kids love to do that. She was there at the time, I presume."

Once, four or five years after his beloved adopted son had gone into practice with him, another faint memory of her emerged into visibility from nowhere, as things from the past do come back to people approaching old age. The two doctors had been sitting late before the fire in a sociable silence. They often ended their days by such a quiet time together. The bond between them was so close that they scarcely needed words to share each other's thoughts. The clock striking midnight aroused them from this silent communion of comradeship. "Well, son, we must get to bed," said Dr. Burrage, heaving himself up from his armchair. He

73

added, "Odd! Just now, I seemed to go back to some time when I sat quiet like this with my mother."

"I thought you couldn't remember her," remarked Dr. Wright, winding his watch.

"Well, of course I can't. Not really," admitted the older man. "I was too young when she died to remember her."

He was repeating what people always say about children whose mothers die young; what had been said in his hearing a great many times when he was a little boy of five. "No, he won't remember her. He's too young." Especially had this been said by the handsome, energetic young woman who, when he was six, became his stepmother, and who from that time on ran the family life so competently that his father, from earning very little, made constantly a bigger and bigger income and blew his brains out in a fit of jealousy and drunken melancholia when he was forty-two. His handsome stepmother soon married again and went away to live in the Philippines. From that time on Henry Burrage—but he was twenty then—had to manage by himself without any parents at all. For the few recollections of his mother, vivid at the time of her death, had long ago been blurred to nothingness by time and by his stepmother.

He must have been eight or nine, a smartly dressed pert little boy, badly spoiled by his stepmother's indulgence of his whims, when the episode of the hawk finally faded from his mind. There was nothing much to it anyhow. His mother (his own) had when he was quite small, taken him to spend the day on a farm—he never knew whose, nor why. Probably it belonged to a cousin or uncle of hers. There were other children there, older than he, good-natured country children used to playing with all ages, who carried him out to a game of tag in the back-yard.

He had not liked that back-yard from the moment he set eyes on it. Even before, he had not liked being taken away from his mother by strangers, although the strangers were only boys and girls bigger than he. A back-yard that did not have his mother in it, might have—he didn't know what. The first thing he saw as he looked suspiciously around was an apple tree between the house and the barn, and he didn't like that, either. A dead limb on it pointed stiffly off towards a grove of old oaks set so thickly that he could not see what was in the darkness under them. Only a strip of plowed field lay between the yard and the darkness under the trees. It was too narrow to suit Henry. He wished his mother had come along. Without her, everything in this new world held a menace. The kind, masterful older children sent him to and fro in the game. His feet trotted docilely wherever he was told to go; but in his heart a dark pool of uneasiness brimmed slowly up towards fear. The dead branch kept pointing so.

After a time the big little girl who was directing proceedings sent him to hide behind the lilac bush, next the house. It was close to an open window. As he squeezed himself down into his hiding place he heard through the window two grown-up voices speaking in dark secret tones. The game was blindman's buff. It was the first time he had ever played

75

it, and he found it terribly exciting. His heart rose sickeningly into his throat every time the hooded "it" came near, groping dreadfully with those blind clutching hands. Once they grasped and shook the thin branches of the bush that were his only poor shelter. His throat drew together convulsively into a knot. When the game's center shifted to the other side of the yard, he sank down on his heels, worn out with tension, trying to get his breath through that knot. But now behind him, a man's bass voice, rumbling ominously, said, "Hand me my gun, will you, Ella? There's a hawk in the woods. I want to be on the safe side."

A hawk. A hawk! What was a hawk, the little city boy asked himself feverishly, that a man—big he must be to have a deep voice like that—should be so afraid of it that he must take his gun with him. He stood up to peer fearfully through the twigs of the bush over at the dark trees, hiding something so dreadful that great grown-up men were frightened of it, and covered his face in his arms. If a *man* was frightened of it—Henry's legs gave way under him. A hawk! what is a hawk? He whispered the evil-sounding word over to himself, crouching behind the lilac bush. Fear oozed out of the woods, as out of a cracked bottle, and, thick, clammy, black, flowed sluggishly across the field towards Henry. The other children had stopped playing, and were talking. He had forgotten them. The vague menace that had darkened the air ever since he had left his mother, grew blacker. He could not stop whispering to himself, "A hawk. A hawk—" although he could feel how every repetition of the evil word drew towards him the unknown danger out from the darkness under the oak trees. Cold sweat burst from his pores, trickling down his back like ice water. Never again in all his life from that moment on to his dying hour, did Henry Burrage feel such strangling terror.

And now the older children turned and ran back to the little guest, putting out their hands, dragging him out, saying kindly, cheerfully, "Come on! We're going over to the woods to play. Come on!"

This saved the little boy's reason. For the shock pierced through the numb nightmare helplessness in which he had been crouching, frozen, silent, crazed, and awoke his instinct for self-preservation. Here was no dangerous unknown that muffled a little boy in blackness without showing anything against which he could fling himself in self-defense. Here were real arms and legs and bodies he could fight. Here was good flesh and blood which he could bite and kick and scratch. They would never take him to the woods where the hawk would get him. Never. Never. He would kill them every one before he would go to the woods.

He was seized and held high in the air. The grown-ups had run out of the house, rushing to the struggling screaming children. The farmer, his rifle still in one hand, had seized the little boy with the other and torn him bodily from his murderous attack. Through his own frantic sobbing the little boy could hear that everyone was loudly talking, the bewildered frightened children protesting, "No, we were *not* teasing him. We weren't even anywhere *near* him. We had

77

only—" the elders saying, threateningly, "If he were *my* child, I know what I'd do!"

He heard a man's voice say, gloatingly, "You've *got* to punish him, Mary, this time. You've *just got* to *whip* him. If *you* don't, I will."

A woman cried out, "Look what he's done to poor little Ella's dress. He ought to be spanked till he can't—"

Then his mother's voice—*his mother's voice!* He had forgotten that he had a mother. "Give him to me, Ed. Don't you touch him, Aunt Ella, he's *my* little boy. You leave him to me. Leave him alone, I say!"

He was in her arms now, in his mother's arms, he was clutching at her with all his might, she was carrying him around to the other side of the house, away from the forked tongues of anger licking hotly around them.

She sat down on the ground in the shade of a big currant bush and took him on her lap, in her arms. She put her cheek against his and let him cry and cry and cry, holding him close till—could it be true, could it be true!—he felt that if he could keep on crying only a little longer, he would have wept away the dreadfulness that had seemed the end of life. With his every sob, he could feel it going away. The muscles of his clenched hands began to loosen. The relief made him cry harder than ever.

When the last wild burst of sobs was over, he was himself, not a fear-crazed maniac, just Henry, sitting on his mother's lap and feeling something smooth and soft in his hand. It was the ribbon at her throat on which his hand had been clenched so tautly that he could not when he first

78

tried, open his fingers. That ribbon was blue, wasn't it? Seems as though it had been blue when he saw his mother tying it before the mirror, this morning, ages ago, before they had come to this place. He opened his hand and lifted his head to look at the ribbon. His eyes were still swimming, he was still drawing long convulsive breaths that sounded like sobs. They did not feel like sobs. They felt like coming up into the air where you could breathe, after having been held a long time under water. His breathing slowed down. He began to finger the crumpled blue ribbon with grimy little hands.

At this his mother smiled at him and set him down on the ground beside her. "What do you say we lay out a pretend farm?" she proposed. She cleared a space on the earth with a sweep of her hand and began to make a wall of pebbles around it. "Where do you think the road ought to go?" she asked him.

He showed her where he thought the road should be. She leaned forward to draw the line of it as he pointed, and a lock of her soft brown hair fell down over her eyes. She put it back with her hand. Henry reached for a bit of old shingle that would make a bridge. "Let's have a brook," he said. He had meant to go on to say, "I like brooks, don't you?" but his voice was so shaky he didn't try. "Yes, brooks are sort of nice," his mother answered.

They worked together, making fields and the barn-yard, looking for stones small enough and flat enough to be stepping-stones. The little boy's breathing and pulse gradually slowed down till they were nearly all right. His mother did not ask him—she never asked him—what had made him act so naughty. But presently he asked her something. In a trembling whisper, and keeping his head bent very low, he asked, "Mother, what is a hawk?" She told him, and added a story from her own country childhood about a brave mother hen who had fought off a hawk from her baby chicks.

He sank his head still lower. "It's not a—a—a dragon?" he breathed.

"No, oh, no," she told him quietly, "only a bird, not as big as that rooster over there." As she told him this, she sat up, and put back her hair from her forehead with her hand.

He lifted his head then and looked into her eyes, deeply into his mother's honest eyes.

They went on making the play-farm, the little boy moving pebbles here and there, his mother making a rail fence out of twigs. They scooped out a place for a pond, and put moss around the sides. He said, "I'm going to make the road go a long, long way, clear off to town."

All the while there was flowing into him the knowledge that he was safe, that there was nothing to fear, that a hawk is only a bird no bigger than a rooster. He had been filled to the last smallest cell of his body with terror. Now that was gone, and into the empty little Henry that was left poured confidence and courage. Flooding rich and warm, this tide of faith in life began to circulate in his every vein and artery. It did not come from his mother. It came from his having learned what the things you are afraid of, really are. Those old oak trees—they were nothing but trees. The stiff evil pointing branch—it was only a piece of dead wood. A hawk is only a bird.

The knot that had been strangling him loosened, loosened, fell away.

Presently his young mother saw that her little boy had fallen asleep, so soundly asleep that he did not wake up till they were at home again.

He never spoke of that day. Nor did his mother. During the next year he learned so many new things—trains and telephones and how to go to the grocery store alone, and how to tie his own shoe-laces—that when he remembered his mistake about the hawk he was quite ashamed that he had ever been such an ignorant baby. So he forgot it.

There was no such reason for his forgetting the time he walked the beam, and all his life he kept a few shreds of memory about that. Not long before his mother died, a long squared timber—perhaps left behind by the builder who had just finished a new cottage next door—lay for a day or two across the front yard of the little one-story brown house that was Henry's home. One morning when Henry's young father came out on the front porch after breakfast and saw this, a gust of the boyishness such a short time behind him blew him up on it to run lightly from one end to the other, setting his feet down on the narrow beam with nimble precision, and leaping off at the other end with a pirouette of triumph. So of course little Henry must do this. He stepped happily up on the end, as his father had. But when he lifted one foot to put it in front of the other, he fell off. The grass was soft. He was not hurt at all, but very much surprised. He rose at once and tried it again more cautiously. Again, before he could set down his advancing foot he lost his balance and tumbled off on the grass. His father laughed good-naturedly at the clumsy child, looked at his watch, kissed his wife good-by, pulled down his vest, and went off to the factory office to work. But half-way down the street he turned and came leaping back to kiss his wife good-by again. "You look like sunshine," he told her. This was because she wore a yellow dress with ruffles, she said. He shook his head, put his hand gently on her head and went away again. She stood on the porch, looking after him and smiling.

Henry had been thinking hard about walking that beam. He felt that his two falls were due to his not having really put his mind on it, and with great care stepped up once more. He fell off at once. At this he lost his temper, scrambled up to his feet and kicked the beam with all his might. It was very hard, and Henry's foot was soft. He hurt his toes dreadfully and gave a yell of rage.

"What's the matter?" asked his mother, turning her head towards him. She was still smiling although by this time Henry's father had turned the corner and was out of sight.

"I want to walk this thing the way Father did," he told her, frowning and sticking his lower lip very far out.

"Well, why don't you?"

"I ca-a-an't!" he complained in a nasal whine.

"Yes, you can if you want to." She stopped smiling, gave her attention seriously to her son's problem, and stepped down from the porch to where he stood. "You can do any-thing—if you want to enough to learn how," she told him.

"How do you learn things?" he asked dubiously.

"You keep trying to."

So he began to try and she to keep him trying. He was soon ready to give up, but she reminded him a good many times what fun it would be to know how to run along as his father had, so after resting and eating another piece of bread and butter, he tried some more. It went better. He took two steps without falling. His mother clapped her hands and looked proud. He learned that it helped to wave his arms around as he stepped cautiously forward. His mother brought out a basket of mending and sat on the edge of the porch, watching him as he took those two steps over and over—and fell. Presently he took three before he fell. "Goody!" said his mother. "Try again."

But he was hot and tired, and sorry that he had ever be-gun this stupid business. What did he care about it! He turned around to his sand pile and went on with a mountain he had started there yesterday. His mother said nothing. A little anxiously, he called her attention to the bigness of the mountain he was making. She nodded and smiled pleasantly. But she did not clap her hands or look proud. "Oh, dear!" said little Henry crossly. He went on patting and poking at his mountain, but he did not see it. "Oh, *dear!*" he said. Presently he went back to the beam.

"That's fine," said his mother.

But it wasn't fine at all. It wasn't a bit of fun any more.

It was just work. Yet somehow, it didn't seem quite so hard to do. By and by, he had taken six tottering steps before falling. And then seven, and then eight. He and his mother looked at each other proudly.

After lunch and his nap, when he went out on the front porch the tiresome thing was still lying across their front yard, as he felt it lying across his mother's mind. Yielding to this pressure, he went back languidly and practiced some more. His mother came out beside the beam to watch. "You're getting along *well*," she said. He tried harder.

"Why," said his mother, holding out her hands to show, "you've only so much more to go, to do it all."

Then it came to Henry. Before he had even once shakily teetered his way from one end to the other of the beam, he was not shaky any more. Something in his head that had been holding out against his wanting to do it, gave way. Something in his legs that had been wavering and uncertain, straightened and steadied. Henry knew how. Straight and true he trotted to the far end of the beam and jumped off. He was tired, quite tired, but happy. "Watch me!" he told his mother, and stepping up, trotted all the way back. Whatever had made him think it was hard to do?

"Well, *Henry!*" said his mother.

Henry knew by the way she said this that she was just as proud of him as she could be. It was not the first time his mother had been proud of him, but it was the first time he had known she was. It was glorious! His heart shone. He ran to her to hug her knees with all his might. She was a Friend, Henry's mother was, so she had quiet Quaker ways and did not squeal and call him darling and honey-bunch and such things. But Henry knew what she meant.

There were no other Friends in the town where Henry's father had taken his young bride, so she had no Meetings to go to. But sometimes she and little Henry had Meeting by themselves. Once in a while of a winter afternoon, before the stove (his parents were poor as well as young and had only a stove, not a furnace), once in a while in summer, out in the side yard under the very old oak-tree that overhung the tiny cottage, Henry's mother would say, "What do you say we have Meeting?"

Henry liked Meeting pretty well, although there wasn't much to it. All you did was just to sit quiet. Sometimes when he was still very small, he sat on his mother's lap. Sometimes he sat beside her and held her hand. She let him do whatever he felt like doing, so long as he was quiet. Sometimes, when they had Meeting out-of-doors, he slid down and lay on his back on the ground, looking up into the strong, crooked, rough branches of the old oak-tree, and through them at the blue, blue sky. Once or twice he dozed off into a nap. Once or twice his mother prayed. Always the same prayer, "God please make my little boy strong and good." The first time, "What is 'God'?" he asked her curiously, but shyly, for a string inside him had been softly plucked by the sound of her voice when she said the word. She answered him, "When a little boy wants to do what's right, that's God in his heart."

But mostly there was no talk at all. Just a stillness, and

Mother's face so quiet and calm that it made Henry feel quiet and calm to look at it.

Then she died and he began to forget her. It did not take long. He was so young, four and a half years old. And his stepmother was so devoted to him. She was the daughter and only child of the rich man who owned the factory where Father went to work in the office, so of course after she married Father he got a better job, and after that a better one yet. There was soon plenty of money, instead of too little. They moved to a new home. It was so large and so different from the little brown cottage, that his stepmother told his father there was really no use to try to use any of the old furnishings. So they didn't try. Everything was new. There was nothing, not a chair, not a picture, nor a scarf, nor so much as a handkerchief that could remind little Henry of his mother who had died.

"You're *my* little boy now, honey-bunch!" his pretty stepmother often told him, hugging him hard. "And *I'm* going to give you *a . . . good . . . time!*" She never said anything to him about his mother, but he heard her, talking to other people, pity him because his mother had deprived him of the toys and candy and clothes every child needs to be happy. "Think of it! He had *never* been to the circus! And he had never had a toy with wheels—not so much as a little express wagon! Nor any fun either. His mother was a Quaker. She didn't know *how* to have a good time!"

Henry's stepmother, whom he was taught to call by her pet name of Tulip—knew all about having a good time. She saw to it that Henry's father did, too. They were always dressing to go out in the evening, to dinner, to a country-club dance, to a restaurant in a city forty miles away, to the theater—or perhaps for a week-end in New York. Henry learned to dodge them for a few days after a New York week-end because they had headaches and were cross. "I can't ever make up to my poor husband," Henry heard her say to other people, "for those poky moldy years of his first marriage."

Once a visitor asked her, idly, "Did you ever know his first wife?"

Tulip's face darkened. "Yes, I did! That is, I met her once or twice. I remember her very well." Her voice was sharp.

"What was she like?"

"I always hated her!" cried Tulip. "She was one of those horrid women who are satisfied no matter what they have! She was always smiling. I hated her."

Another time, some years later, one evening when she had had a good many cocktails, and was talking to someone who excited her, she said she didn't care *who* knew that she fell dead in love with Henry the first time she saw him, a young employee in her father's office; and had nearly died of jealousy of the plain, dowdy Quakeress he was married to. "It runs in our family," she said proudly, "to have strong feelings. No Quaker blood in *us!*" And sure enough, by and by, her feeling for the man who excited her grew so strong that Henry's father shot himself.

But that was later, after Henry had grown up, or almost, and was in college.

Nobody had ever thought of such a thing as his going to college:—Tulip because she thought it a hideous waste of time for anybody to bother with books; Henry because he was lazy, spoiled, and ignorant; Henry's father because he always thought just what Tulip did. As to the rest of the people who knew Henry and his father and Tulip, half were sure the kid would be in the reform school by the time he was old enough for college, and the other half couldn't see any more sense in book-learning than Tulip did.

After a while, eight or nine years after her marriage, Tulip began to get tired of Henry. It was just about the time when she had finally succeeded in killing and completely burying his mother. Perhaps she knew this. Perhaps it was because he had all of a sudden stopped being a cute kid with cute ways and had grown into a gangling, clumsy, long-legged boor with the worst manners in this world. So Tulip told his father that though it simply broke her heart to be separated from the dear boy, she felt he ought to be in a good military school where he would be handled by *men*. Of course his father felt so too, as soon as Tulip told him to.

From that time on, Henry had no home and no mother and no father. In June he went from his prep school into a summer camp, and in September back to prep school, staying in Tulip's house only a few days in between times. The first year he was at school was one long horror to him. Badly trained, badly taught, badly spoiled as he was, nobody liked him, and he hated everybody. The school was what is called "well run," that is, run so that on the surface nothing could be seen of what was really going on in any boy's life. Setting-up exercises, cold showers, meals, drill, classes, studyhall, drill, hikes, cold showers, chapel, games, drill, meals —every minute of the day was spent in doing something active—*left!* right! *left!* right!—under the eye of a supervising officer, and plenty of them, one to every six boys. All that was Henry (and a good deal of him had accumulated by this time) lay festering in the dark, far beneath the school's flawless varnish.

His first summer camp began in the same way—why not, the camp being run to make extra money by three of the officer-teachers on the school faculty. But it was worse, because by this time adolescence—whatever we mean by that— had come to him. In the well-run school it meant that when those strong qualities which were to make Henry a man of power, for good or evil, came violently into life in his personality they found him shut up in solitary confinement in a lightless cave. Like waves from an ocean immeasurably greater than Henry, they thundered along under the low rocky roof of the cavern which was now the only place the real Henry had to live in—flooding over him, lifting him off his feet, half drowning him, battering him against the sides of his prison till he was all one bruise. At the meeting where the officer-teacher-counselors of camp put their heads together about how to keep the boys in order, "Keep your eye on that Henry," they said. "He's got bad blood in him." So the guard set on Henry redoubled. To the right and to the left of him, wherever he was, stretched ranks of other boys, under the same discipline as he—they called it discipline—a watchful teacher-officer at each end of the row. It was a very well-run camp. His mother, quite forgotten, lay in her grave far away.

But one of the teachers liked to go fishing. One morning in July, he felt like having a day on the lake and needed a boy to help him with the other oar of the heavy lake-boat. Henry, because he was big for his age and because nobody else wanted him around, was told off for this duty. After they were well out on the lake, the teacher, guided by those unseen weather signs legible to fishermen, decided that he would have better luck if he fished from an island at the other end of the lake.

By the time they had landed there, the teacher had thought of a way to get rid of the disagreeable hulking fellow who would certainly make a noise if he stayed near. He said in a tone of imitation geniality, "Wouldn't you like to try your hand too? Take this rod, and go around to the cove at the other end of the island, and see how you make out with casting." He added indulgently, longing for a whole day of quiet for his own fishing, "Take your lunch along so if you have good luck you won't need to stop."

Henry, fishing rod in hand, clumped heavily on his big feet through the woods to the other end of the island. It was not more than a mile away from the fisherman-teacher. But every step of that distance took Henry into a realm where since his little boyhood he had not in a waking moment set foot, not once—into quiet, solitude, and silence. A huge weather-beaten granite rock, shaded by an age-scarred oak tree, lay like a fallen giant, half in the water of the cove, half on the beach. Henry climbed up on it and hung his feet over the edge, his huge clumsy feet that made him awkward and showed he was to be great in stature among men. He fastened the imitation fly on his line as he had seen his teacher do, and made a few casts, not very successfully. It was not very interesting. Presently his arm tired. Having no watchful supervising teacher near him to keep him active, he laid his rod down to rest.

It was great, he thought, not to have anybody around to spoil his sitting and doing nothing, if he wanted to. He looked down idly at his feet. Funny how light it made a person feel not to be slogging along, *left,* right, *left,* right, hammering down hard and heavy on the earth. It must make your feet surprised to be floating, nothing but air under them. He swung them idly to and fro to feel their lightness. Then, forgetting this, he let them hang down and stared at the sunlit water, brim-brim-brimming up on the beach of the little cove where he sat, quiet and still for the first time since—he could not remember when he had ever sat so still as this. Back of him a bird dropped a sleepy summer note into the woods. After a while he slid down on the warm rock, stretched himself out and put his arms under his head. Strange, as he looked up into the strong, crooked, rough old oak-branches, strange how light he began to feel, all of him, not just his feet. The rock was so strong. It bore him up as though his hulking overgrown body that was too big for him, weighed no more than that of a little tiny boy on his mother's lap.

He lay thus a long time. An hour? Two hours? Once he thought, looking up at the arch of the sky, bent over the lake, that it was as blue as a piece of blue ribbon.

He had lain thus, motionless and relaxed, for most of the morning, when he shut his eyes, pinched them shut, with a shudder. He had felt surging towards him one of those frightful waves of feeling that left him battered and bruised to the bone. But this was not shut up and driven with savage force along a tortuous narrow channel deep in blackness. It had the whole universe to spread out in. It flooded over him from everywhere, from the sky, from the earth, the kind sun, the lake's calm stillness. He had been relaxed too long to stiffen himself against it, and when it reached him—soft, warm, mighty, gentle—it floated him off as light as air, up and up like a thistle-down into the vast spaciousness above him where there was room for everything! Those terrific wants were only a part, a small part, of him, of living, of what was before him. There was room for them, for everything—sunny, limitless room in which life's different parts fitted together in their true proportions, made one shapely whole which a lonely big boy almost a man need not dread, need not fight, need not be ashamed of.

The knot that had been strangling him, loosened, loosened, fell away.

When he was dropped again, light as thistle-down, on the strong sustaining rock, Henry, big overgrown boy though he was, rolled over on his face and began to cry. There was

92

no one to hear him. He could cry as much as he wanted to.

When he had cried as much as he wanted to, and sat up again, he felt better—why, he could hardly believe it, he felt so much better. And, good gosh! was he hungry! He ate his lunch to the last crumb, strolling up and down the little beach. Then he tried seriously to fish and did catch two rock bass, little fellows. After that he went in swimming, and after that he just lazed around, playing with pebbles. Some, the flat ones, he skipped across the water. The pretty rounded ones he arranged vaguely in designs, stars and diamonds and things, thinking to himself how much better everything looked when it was arranged in a design.

When he heard the teacher coming, crashing through the woods, he was a little ashamed of being such a kid and brushed his hand back and forth to smooth out the designs he had made.

"Well—?" asked the fisherman-teacher. He looked at the two bass, small ones. It was four o'clock. They had been fishing for eight hours. He himself had nine pounds and a half of fish. His face told Henry what he thought of Henry as a fisherman. But he had studied the rules of pedagogy, remembered that a teacher must give his students plenty of encouragement and always think of something positive not negative to say, so he smiled and said in a cracked, imitation-cheery voice, "Pretty good, Henry. Pre-t-t-tty good, for the first time."

But Henry didn't hate his falseness and pretense, nor want to strangle him for it, as he would yesterday. He thought

93

to himself with sympathy, "Gosh, it must be fierce to have a job like that."

After that most of Henry's leisure time was spent in fishing. He never became very expert at it, that is, he never brought back from his long solitary days of angling any very big catches. But he continued to go. And fishing is such a right masculine sport that nobody at school, or camp, or even in Tulip's house, interfered with it. They interfered with him less anyhow after that first summer. There was less need to. "He was," they said proudly at faculty meetings, "coming out all right after all." As with so many other troublesome boys, the right school turned the trick, gave him just what he needed. He turned the corner of adolescence without disaster and became another person, a credit to their teaching. They were actually sorry to have him graduate.

When he did, he told his father and Tulip that he was going to study to be a doctor. They tried their best to dissuade him from this absurd idea. And so did everybody else who knew him. Tulip told him a thousand times, earnestly, "Now, Henry, don't be foolish! You *know* you'll never be able to stick it through! Don't you realize that it would take *eight years!* You'd simply die of boredom! You'd *never* have yourself a good time! Not once. Eight of the very best years of your life, when you might be having the best times, you'd be leaning over sick people and catching their diseases. Wherever in this world did you *get* such a crazy idea, anyhow?"

She repeated this with variations a good many times.

Every time, when her breath gave out and she had to stop, Henry told her sheepishly that he guessed he could stick it out all right. But he never told her wherever in this world he got such an idea, because he did not know.

Stick it out he did for those endless eight years, during five of which he had to support himself, his father dying and leaving no money and Tulip, of course, having no call to spend her substance on another woman's son. One year was spent in business, making enough money to go on with.

He was a big, grave, rather graceless man of twenty-seven, when he finally had M.D. to put after his name, and began the practice that was to bring him such rich rewards, was to bring his patients help, protection, consolation. Old Dr. Hepplewaite took him in at once as assistant—"I don't say Henry's brilliant. But there's something—perhaps something about his character—that'll be useful to him in the practice of medicine."

There certainly turned out to be, although people differed as to what its name was. Some of his patients called it dogged persistence. "Dr. Burrage just *won't* let go of a patient," they said, comforted when he came lumbering into the sickroom. But others insisted it was his fearlessness. "You can feel it all over old Dr. Burrage—he simply doesn't know what fear is," they said. And indeed when someone once asked him about this, he said he didn't know but that that was so, he really couldn't ever remember being seriously afraid.

He was a very fortunate man, one of those to whom the

95

right things happen. Good luck seemed to be with him in all his personal relations, as well as in his professional work. He did not marry one of the stylish, lively, professionally coiffed society girls who fluttered around the young doctor, any one of whom would have brought him money, social prestige, and influence. To their annoyance he married a quiet, brown-eyed little thing ("not even neat! You should see her hair. It's always falling down!" they said scornfully) who brought him nothing but a heart so pure and loving that when she died young, it went on beating faithfully in the doctor's memory, making him happier than any flesh-and-blood woman he might have married to take her place.

Of course the greatest piece of good luck for him, all alone in life as he was, was his adoption of the orphan who turned out such an ideal son. The quiet, undemonstrative love between the older and the younger man was so serene and steady that all who knew them saw their own paths more clearly in its light. Yet who else would have picked out that child, of all others! He had been a regular little demon, the doctor's older patients said when they told the story, as they often did. Left an orphan at four, he had been taken in by a family who did not want him—they had plenty of nice children of their own, older, and were dismayed by this passionate bad little boy. But they were distant relations of his parents, and there seemed to be nobody else willing to give him a home. Dr. Burrage must have seen him, many's the time, as he came and went in that house, taking care of the old grandmother who was paralyzed and bedridden. And he knew of course, the way doctors know everything, that the little boy was not a welcome addition to the family. But he had never seemed to pay any attention to him till one day, stepping into the house, he found the children—the grown-ups too—in the midst of a frantic storm. The little fellow—the one who grew up to be Dr. Wright—was in a frightful tantrum, acting like a mad dog, screaming and kicking and scratching and biting the other children. The father rushed in just as Dr. Burrage arrived, and pulled the child away. The mother was crying and saying, "Just look what he's done to poor little Betty's face. *This* time he's got to be punished! If I have to do it myself he's going to be whipped till he—"

But the doctor had taken one long step forward and snatched the child into his own arms. "Leave him alone!" he said. "Don't you touch him. Leave him to me!"

No, he never claimed to have had any sort of prophetic divination about what the little boy's qualities really were. In later years, when people asked him, he always said honestly, "Why, I couldn't tell you what made me do it. I really haven't any idea. I just did."

A Family Alliance

SHE HAD never read Thomas à Kempis's axiom that temptation can do no more than show what stuff you are made of. For that matter she had never heard of Thomas à Kempis or any other literary classic not included in the required reading-list of the Blue Falls High School. So far but not a step further up the educational ladder; her country had coaxed the reluctant Jigger. (Her name was really Gladys, but that along with many other things about her was not known to the young crowd she ran around with in New York. The first evening, before Dora Warren had a chance to introduce her, one of the boys several inches shorter than she, had asked ironically, "Who's the cute little jigger with the cock-eyed bob?" And Jigger she remained thenceforward.) But if she ever had heard that axiom she would have called the worthy Thomas a darned old liar. For she was convinced that her troubles were to be laid to temptation alone, and that the stuff she was made of had nothing to do with the matter.

Temptation's name was Dora Warren. Like every insidious danger Dora seemed harmless. She wanted nothing for herself but to think that everything Jigger did was cute. They had met only a few months after Jigger had clawed her way to the New York job she had set her heart on from the time

98

she could read *Vogue*. She had only just had time enough to find out that her clothes were impossible and where to get others, where to have her hair done and where to buy shoes, and in general to get her New York legs under her, when Dora who had broken into the big town all of a year before, dropped in one night to see if the food in that boarding house was any better than in the others she had sampled. It was not; but she thought Jigger marvelous. They had about the same kind of job and made about the same salary. They both came from small places and were crazy about New York. Dora proposed that they join forces, rent a studio apartment—they called it that—and have some decent eats. Not to speak of latch-keys.

They were different enough to get on well together. Dora's typewriter stood in a publisher's office, and Jigger's in that of a silk importer. Dora was rather plain—that is, she was pretty in a dowdy old-fashioned way, plump and little and smiling, with curly hair, amiable blue eyes, rosy cheeks, and regular features. The kind our forefathers thought "looked good enough to eat." With that 1880 outfit, the poor girl had learned early, of course, to expect little in the way of admiration and to take thankfully what she got. Jigger was plain in the way that is pretty now—long-legged, flat-hipped, sleek-haired, with thin dark face and high cheek-bones. Along with her clothes she had picked up the weary, slightly sinister expression that went with them, and successfully gave the desired effect of being something that would poison you in no time if you ate it.

They settled down very soon into the roles to which in 1937 they were destined by their looks, Dora the one who did the kissing, Jigger extending the cheek. Jigger, introduced by Dora to her crowd, instantly took precedence over her, in virtue of slinky hips, irregular features and a snugly fitting aura of bad medicine. Dora, humble through long practice, took up the second fiddle without resentment, and fell into the role of satellite, doubled with that of press agent. For, used to getting her limelight by reflection and being really very warm-hearted, she enjoyed nothing more than telling people nice things about Jigger and her family.

How could anybody expect Jigger, inexperienced in life as she was, to foresee the danger lurking in Dora's pleasant little puffs? She had hardly noticed them at first. She certainly never encouraged Dora's propaganda, although she had not rushed to contradict her with priggish accuracy every time she heard a Dora-ized version of the facts floating around. For that matter she couldn't have contradicted her. When Dora let fall the statement that the Pratts, Jigger's people, "were one of the old land-owning families in the upper Hudson Valley," she was telling the truth. And so she was when she told the crowd that "Jigger is running up to spend the week-end at her people's country place." You couldn't object to that. Jigger didn't, anyhow. Nor to "Jigger's mother is a professional woman too. A musician— pianist." You couldn't object, not what you'd call *object*, when she said, "Her father was an Army officer before he returned to civilian life to take over her grandfather's affairs."

Every word of it was so. What could Jigger have done about it?

As far as that goes (just as a person who constantly hears a foreign language comes to think in it) she slid into using Dora's lingo herself. She not only said but thought that "I'm just running up for the week-end to my people's country place." She was, wasn't she? And on the first evening she met Spike Hunter it was she herself, not Dora at all, who let fall that her people were one of the old land-owning families in the upper Hudson Valley, and that her mother was a professional pianist.

But she was so flustered that night she would have said anything. If she had thought it might make a better impression on Spike, she would have said she was an orphan, or a Hungarian countess. She mentioned her folks only because someone had just told her young Hunter was a Yale graduate, son of a fine old Ohio family, and she hoped a hint that she too had A Family might attract his attention. For she wanted him to like her from the minute she saw his queer dark face with its fuzzy funny eyebrows and its black eyes and its bulging forehead. "Don't tell me that I look like a Russian!" he stopped her first exclamation. "You would be the three thousand and sixty-fifth to say that and I want to keep you in the one and only class where you belong."

She liked his line. She liked his eyebrows. She liked his voice. She was also a little afraid of him, which did no harm. It was not because she was getting awfully tired (though she was) of living in one room and pretending it wasn't the bedroom; and of delicatessen food; and cooking over a gas ring; and dressing as though she earned more than she did; and talking about things she didn't know anything about; and making the same old rackety noise whether she felt like it or not; and in general living according to a pattern that fitted her looks better than it did her. She was twenty-four years old now, Jigger was, had lived with Dora in one or another "studio apartment" for longer than she ever admitted, and there were moments when she panted like a hart after a kitchen with a coal-range. She seldom allowed herself to think of that coal-range, because when she did her mind was almost instantly out of control. Before she could open the copy of the *New Yorker* on her knee, she was swept from the airy kitchen in which the dream-range stood, out to a breeze-swept, vine-shaded, back porch on which sat a non-poisonous Jigger shelling peas out of her own garden, and from there to a real dining-room not an alcove, and upstairs to a bedroom with a real bed in it. A double bed.

But this was not why she was crazy about Spike Hunter, any more than spring is why seeds sprout. They wouldn't sprout if it weren't springtime of course. But there have to be seeds before springtime can do anything with them.

Whether it was the mention of her family or something else, Spike liked her all right. She hardly dared believe he did as much as he seemed to. Before long they stopped going around with the crowd and went around together. A striking couple they were, who might have stepped right out of the advertisements of a transatlantic steamship line—you know, the spiffy quietly upper-class couple who play shuffleboard and lean over the rail; and on the dock are not cringingly ashamed but in a well-bred way proud of their baggage. Jigger knew they looked like that, but it didn't seem so important to her as it would have five years ago. In fact it seemed less important to her with every minute. Sometimes, when she and Spike were with astonished awe discovering yet one more idea or feeling they had in common that nobody else had ever shared, she forgot all about how she looked for half an hour at a time. This was a great rest to her.

Spike had made no secret of the fact that he had taken to Jigger on sight and getting off to a fast start he kept on burning up the track. Before long, a paltry two months, he was adoring her, and telling her so and Jigger was so happy that she ached, and might have lost the discontented sullen expression that made her look so distinguished, if a secret uneasiness gnawing at her heart had not fastened it still more firmly on her face. But then, defying convention in the courageous way that made her love him so, Spike asked her to marry him, not companionately, permanently, even though he wasn't making very much money yet, just as her father had asked her mother; and Jigger cried heartily for joy just as her mother had, and said, yes, sure she couldn't think of anything she'd like better and she didn't give a damn about the money. (This sentiment if not the turn of the phrase was also like her mother.)

And then—they went to tell Dora, and she said, "Oh, how marvelous! You'll have the wedding at your people's country place, of course." And Spike, who had had to listen a good deal to Dora's line while waiting for Jigger to get dressed to go out with him, said, "Sure, where else?"

But it was not then she heard the breakers crashing. She was still in too shining a cloud of glory to look ahead. She said, "Oh, *yes!*" and sank into a dream at the very idea of her wedding day.

It was the letter from Spike's father and mother that gave Jigger her first intimation of the trouble Dora had made for her. She and Spike had written the news of their engagement to their families the same day. But the answer from Jigger's parents, living much nearer, came first. Naturally they wrote to Jigger as they always did only more so, and Jigger being in an emotional state, shed some more happy tears over their motherly and fatherly love and anxiety and hopes for her happiness. They each had written a note to Spike too, enclosing them in the same envelope with her letter. "Sweet!" Jigger thought these notes. But Spike was out in Ohio on business and was taking advantage of the trip to visit his parents so she couldn't hand her own parents' greetings over to him at once. They too, of course, looked forward to her being married from her own old home. "Mamma says wait till June when the peonies will be out," wrote her father, "and if you do, I'll get the barn and chicken-houses painted." It was one of the family jokes—getting the barn and chicken-houses painted.

Two days later came the letter from Spike's family, the Hunters of Ohio. Jigger opened the big square envelope, and read the well-turned phrases (there was a marked family likeness to Spike's style in them) written in very black ink on thick creamy linen paper, and although they gracefully expressed welcome to her as their son's fiancée, her face was very grave. She took out her parents' letters. They had been written on sheets torn off the family pad, and she guessed by the looks the ink had partly dried down in the bottle and her mother had added a little water to make it run better.

That afternoon after office hours, a tall, dark, sophisticated-looking Park Avenue girl with a worried expression went into a chic shop to buy a box of the most expensive cream linen paper in stock and a bottle of the blackest ink. And that evening Jigger sat down to write her father and mother. She said she was sending them some New York letter paper, and would they mind using this when they wrote Spike. And perhaps—she consulted Spike's parents' letter—she'd just write out a few phrases that they might care to use. She tore that beginning up and started again. This time she wrote that she had told them so far, only about Spike himself, but of course parents'd be interested in his family too. The Hunters were an old Ohio family, more or less in politics like all Ohio people. Spike's mother's family were Southerners. "I'll probably have to endure a good deal of old-black-Mammy and Big House and Southern charm stuff from them," she wrote, putting it in New Yorkese so that it wouldn't sound like boasting. "His father is owner and editor of the largest daily newspaper in the place where they live—it was his father's before him. He is Trustee of one of the Ohio universities. Spike's sister is married and she and her husband are now living in Paris." She hesitated, wrote, "France, you know," was ashamed and tore up that letter. The next time she began boldly by asking them right out if they would mind not referring to each other as Mamma and Papa when they wrote Spike because he . . . She started again, saying she knew they would take it just as a joke as she meant it if she . . . She started again.

To make a long story short, Jigger wrote letters to her parents all night long and in the morning tore them all up and burst into tears. Not of joy, either! If she'd been there at home *with* them, she might perhaps have made them understand. But you couldn't write that kind of a letter to your father and mother. At least Jigger couldn't. Not to *her* father and mother. I haven't spoken about it before—it was something she would have blushed to have the gang suspect —but Jigger was rather a nice girl.

She decided the simplest thing was not to show their letters to Spike when he came back but to tell him they had sent all kinds of good wishes to him and their commiseration of his hard luck and so forth and so on. When he actually saw her again, Spike was so astounded to find that Jigger was still there, still engaged to him, that he hadn't dreamed her, that nobody else had run away with her yet, that he never noticed about her parents' letter one way or the other.

He had a raise in salary that spring (the up-turn in business coming just at the right time for him) and so much encouragement from his boss (he was on the selling end for a big firm of wholesale druggists) that they fell to calculating minutely the cost of life in the suburbs. One of the surprising things these two young New Yorkers had in common was a curious notion that it might be sort of amusing to live in a house with a yard around it. Then Jigger went to her boss (the silk importer), and told him cheerfully that she was going to get married and that she would be leaving next week to go home and get her things ready.

You must know by this time what kind of folks Jigger's father and mother were, and can imagine just how they looked as they got out of their Ford at the station at Blue Falls, well ahead of time because Mr. Pratt wanted to ask the station agent about a new sprayer which should have arrived before this, and Mrs. Pratt wanted to speak to him seriously about his small daughter's practicing. "If Laura can't get in at least her hour a day, Mr. Elmore, it's a waste of time for her to take, at all. I'd feel I was getting your dollar a lesson under false pretenses," said Mrs. Pratt. She spoke firmly. She did not like false pretenses of any kind.

The train came chugging around the curve, and they hurried out on the platform. The tears were in Mrs. Pratt's eyes, a lump in Mr. Pratt's throat. Their little girl was coming back home for the last time—at least the last time she would still be theirs.

Some of the New York make-up and a good deal of the New York expression had evaporated from Jigger's face during the trip from Manhattan to Blue Falls, and when she saw her father and mother waiting there, with their muddy country rubbers on their feet and that steady loving look in their eyes, she ran to them on her high heels and flung her arms around their necks and shed a few more tears.

But all the same, all the same . . . ! When she got into that battered middle-aged Ford, smelling slightly of sulphur spray, and drove over muddy roads to her "people's country place" and saw the square clapboarded dark-brown house with the mansard roof and the jig-saw work under the eaves; the bay window filled with geraniums and wandering Jew; the golden oak dining-room set; the front parlor with its long lace curtains draped back from the windows and its comfortable furniture upholstered in brown rep; and her mother's battered black upright piano and round piano stool screwed high for the children who "took" of Mrs. Pratt,—there was something queer about her smile. They had a surprise for her, they told her, something done in honor of the wedding. Proudly watching her face they drew her into the front hall.

A brand new maple floor had been laid there, and new paper was on the walls. "Well, Sister, what do you say to that?" asked Mr. Pratt. (For at home Jigger was not even Gladys, but Sister.) Sister-Jigger, feeling their eyes on her, looked at the shiny varnish on the light yellow floor and at the pretty little sprigs of flowers on the new wall paper and cried out with enthusiasm that it was *perfectly mar*-velous! Knowing her every inflection from babyhood up and having the advantage of twenty-five years more of life's battering than she, they perceived at once that something was very wrong. And they were very much afraid they knew what it was.

They had tried to put out of their minds the uneasiness they had felt when they read their daughter's letter about the University Trustee, newspaper owner, living-in-Paris family she was marrying into. But it came coldly back now, filling the newly done-over front hall with dismay. So they all began to talk in loud cheerful voices and moved on to take Jigger to her own room. They left her there to unpack and went downstairs together, heavy-hearted.

Looking around the fresh new hall, "Gosh, I wish it was over!" said Mr. Pratt, plucking at the loose skin on his brown weather-beaten neck.

"Now, Papa, don't get nervous. The father of the bride is always fit to be tied, they say. It'll be all right." This was what Mrs. Pratt said. They both agreed that one look at Sister's face showed her young man was what she wanted, and what else mattered. But after her husband had put on his overalls and had gone out to boss the spraying of the far orchard, Mrs. Pratt stood a long time by her old piano looking fixedly at the cover of "The Mulhausen Album for Beginners," although she must have known every word and letter in it by heart. She was thinking so deeply that she did not notice the arrival of a little boy till he was there behind her. Coming to herself she caught sight of her face in a mirror opposite and was startled to see how somber and foreboding she looked. "I'll have to do better than that," she thought, and said with an artificial cheerfulness that alarmed the little boy, "Oh, how are you, sonny? Let's start our five-finger exercises today with *both* hands. Don't you think that will be *nice?*"

Jigger had taken off her city shoes and put on a pair of sneakers, had changed her dress for an old skirt and sweater she always left hanging in her closet, and was now in the side yard under the grape arbor. A wild idea had occurred to her that perhaps they could have an outdoor garden-party wedding, with a striped tent for refreshments and a banked-flower altar, and not have to go inside the house at all. But one look was enough. The side yard was just the side yard, no more. There were, it is true, lilac bushes, clumps of tulips in bloom, a big bush of snowball, and a hydrangea; but there were also big rhubarb plants in the corner, and a line of currant bushes at one side; and from it you saw the *out*side of the house! Also the barns and chicken-houses, which had not been painted. Jigger stood still to look at the outside of her father's old house standing sturdily high and square on its green grass, the new leaves on its locust trees throwing a pattern of shadow on its shingled roof. From the open windows came the sound of five-finger exercises, stumblingly played. A hen with some chickens wandered around the corner of the side porch. Some clean dish towels fluttered from a line by the back door. Jigger clenched her fists and said stormily, "I'll be darned if any stuck-up Ohio people are going to make me ashamed of my own home!"

This did not prevent her from having, during the three weeks before her wedding, a great many crazy ideas about how not to go through with what she (and Dora) had started. Every day she said fiercely to herself, "Let them think what they will. It's nothing to me!" And every day she knew that what they thought would be a good deal to her, might easily be a handicap to her all her married life. Every day she reminded herself that it would unendurably hurt her father and mother if now she just ran away with

Spike around the corner in New York somewhere and got married by a justice of the peace or the County Clerk or whoever married people; and every day she thought they might easily be even more hurt if she was married at home under the eyes of those hateful Ohio snobs. It seemed too awful to expose her parents and her home to such eyes, when, if that one contact between the two families could be avoided, the Ohio people need never, never see the old Pratt place and its owners. You can imagine how crazy were some of her plans for escape when I tell you that one of them was to pretend that she had a yen, a positive yen, to be married in an orange grove, and to insist on carrying both families off to Florida. Another was to have a church wedding and the wedding breakfast in the hotel and never go near the house at all. If you had only seen the Blue Falls church and the Blue Falls hotel you'd know that this idea was the last superlative of craziness.

After each of those wild fluttering beatings of her wings against the bars, she managed to come back to her senses and went on discussing with her mother how many chickens would be needed for the salad, and whether the ice cream freezers they had already arranged to borrow would be enough or whether one more wouldn't be safer. The unspoken accompaniment in her mind to all these preparations was an outraged, "How I loathe Dora!"

She put on a grimacing cheerfulness to hide the existence of this undercurrent and she was, naturally, about as successful in hiding it, as in her childhood when she had tried by a would-be-natural manner to hide a misdeed from her mother. Mrs. Pratt grimaced cheerfully back, her heart as heavy as lead. When Mr. Pratt called her to come see how high the peas were sprouting, or to tell him where she wanted the clothesline hung and getting her there all to himself, asked in a low anxious voice, "Don't you think maybe Sister kinda hates to have those folks from Ohio come here for—" or, "Wouldn't it better if we could somehow—" Mrs. Pratt always cut him short, "Mercy, *no!* Fred! What an idea! She's just a little nervous about getting married. All girls are." She wasn't going to have *any*body, no matter if he was Trustee of a University, make her Fred feel apologetic about not having made more money. He'd made enough! Then the two parents would look at the peas or the clothesline and go back to make more cheerful answers to their daughter's cheerful remarks, and say how nice it was they were going to meet her family-in-law.

Then the fateful day came. Not the wedding day. The day the Hunters from Ohio were to arrive. They had decided not to drive, Spike wrote. His mother's back wasn't strong and long drives tired her. They were due on the late afternoon the day before the wedding and Spike with them. The cheerful grimaces had worn pretty thin by that time, and none of the three Pratts even tried to keep them up as they made the last preparations at the house and donned their new street clothes to go to the station. There was little talk of any kind, and what there was, on a note of nervous uncertainty. "Sister, would you rather have me wear my overcoat?" "Which tie would you like to have me put on?" "Oh, Mother, *do* you think I look all right in this jersey? Or had I better put on my voile?" "Will this hat do, Sister? Or shall I go without any?"

In the Ford, Mrs. Pratt and her daughter on the back seat plucked at each other's neck arrangements, smoothed down each other's hair, put on their gloves and took them off and put them on again. On the front seat Mr. Pratt was thinking sadly, "I ought to have got on better. Other men do." On the platform, hearing the train whistle, they arrayed themselves in a row, thought that looked silly, stood back of each other, thought that looked worse, and held their ground despairingly just where they chanced to be. The train stopped. The brakeman came running down the steps, set a stool and turned to give a hand to an undeniably Fifth Avenue traveling costume, surmounted by a severe perfectly fitting little dark hat which proclaimed negligently that it had been made in Paris. Back of this came a custom-made tan camel's hair overcoat accompanied by tan gloves, and topped by a marvelously fine and supple tan felt hat, the brim turned dashingly down in front. Yes, there were people inside those clothes, but Jigger did not see them. Behind the Fifth Avenue costume with the Paris hat and the camel's hair overcoat was a tall young man with soft black eyebrows and bumps on his forehead. He was just as well dressed as the others but Jigger was so amazed to see who it was, she did not notice his clothes at all. It was Spike! Why, there was *Spike!* She gave a shriek of pure astonishment, echoed by one like it from the young man who ran rapidly towards her. Forgetting all

113

her plans for well-bred mannerly self-control she sped as fast as she could into his arms.

When they came back to this life, which took them rather longer than they realized, the Fifth Avenue costume and the custom-tailored tan overcoat had stiffly shaken hands and exchanged formal greetings with Mr. and Mrs. Pratt. Spike and Jigger were presented now and nervously shook hands with all. Spike's father and mother did nothing whatever to put their son's fiancée at her ease. They merely murmured a few guarded cool words which she could hardly hear.

"I hate them!" thought Jigger. "They don't like me! I'll hate them always! I'll take Spike away from them if it's my last act."

Then Mr. Pratt said what had been agreed on beforehand (after the livery-car idea had been abandoned in a tacit resolution to get it over once and for all) as the best thing to say. He didn't do very well with it, did not use the jaunty accent his daughter had tried (trying not to seem to try) to suggest to him as the best way to carry it off. But he said it,— "Well, our good old friend, the family Ford awaits us at the back. It won't hold all six of us. Suppose we let the young people walk."

Jigger, aware at once of suppressed surprise from the Paris hat and the expensive overcoat, ground her teeth and thought, "If I can only live through it!" which is not a desirable way to look forward to your wedding day. Nobody thought of anything to say so they went around to where the Ford was parked. Jigger and Spike helped get the luggage in. It was sophisticated, expensive, going-to-Europe suitcases and a pig-skin kit-bag that made the Ford hang its head. The four elders took their places. Spike shut the doors—yes, the one that sometimes stuck took that moment to do its worst of course. "All right. We'll expect you when we see you," said Mr. Pratt, being over-jaunty now to make up for having boggled his speech about the Ford. They drove away, leaving Jigger and Spike to manage somehow to use up two hours walking the two miles to the old Pratt place.

The first thing that happened inside the Ford was that Spike's father pulled off his gloves. "I see you don't wear 'em," he remarked to Mr. Pratt at the wheel. When he had taken them off, he stretched his hands and wriggled his fingers and murmured, "Gosh! That feels good!" He then hunched himself out of his overcoat, hung it over the back of the seat, ran his fingers around his collar, and took a long breath.

His wife might have had something to say to this if her attention had not been fully engaged by Mrs. Pratt's answer to her first question. She had asked, in a guarded voice, "Have you been away on tours a good deal this winter, Mrs. Pratt?" Jigger's mother had not the faintest idea what this meant, but having a life-long habit of counting on plain truth-telling in all situations, answered, "Oh, no, I never go away from home. I couldn't leave Mr. Pratt. And he can't ever get away for more than a day or so. You know how it is with a farm and orchards. There's always something that has to . . ." She did not finish her sentence. Her eye had fallen on the elegant camel's hair overcoat which hung down from the front seat. It was folded so that the inside was out. Inside the collar was a forgotten price tag, very new and clean.

Mrs. Pratt looked from this to the expensive suitcases. She now saw that they were new, brand new. And so was the pig-skin kit-bag. She looked around full into the face of the woman next her, and saw under the perfectly fitting French hat a face like her own, frankly middle-aged, rather worn, with honest somewhat anxious eyes.

From the front seat came the voice of Jigger's father, making conversation if it killed him, "I understand you are much interested in education, Mr. Hunter." Spike's father looked around at his wife, got no help from her and answered uncertainly, "Not so specially. Newspaper work's my line. I run the little daily my father started—that keeps me pretty busy. I do it all myself—just with one old compositor. I haven't time for much else. Of course I believe in education, but . . ."

"Why, I understood from Sister—our daughter, I mean— that you are a Trustee of one of the Ohio Universities."

"Oh, *that!*" said Mr. Hunter, laughing. "They call it a University. They call anything a University in Ohio, you know. There are seventeen of them, somebody told me once, or was it twenty-seven? It's just a local school, a Methodist institution—only forty-seven students. They were having a hard time to get anybody to take a vacant place on the Board and Mother wanted me—m'wife, I mean . . ."

He went no farther. Mrs. Pratt leaned forward over the new price mark on the overcoat to ask intensely, "Do you mean to say you are *Methodists?*"

116

"Yes," they said. "Why?"

"Why, so are we!" cried Mrs. Pratt.

They were as struck by this as she. "You don't say so!" said Spike's father, turning his head to look at Mrs. Pratt as if he saw her for the first time. "Kenneth never told us that!" said Mrs. Hunter.

"Kenneth!"

"Perhaps Gladys hadn't happened to tell him about it."

"Gladys!"

"Well, anyhow," said Mrs. Pratt, "I've played the organ in our church for twenty-five years."

Over his shoulder Mr. Hunter said, "Mother was Epworth League leader when I first knew her. That's where we got acquainted."

"Well . . . !" said the mother of the bride.

"Well . . . !" said the mother of the bridegroom.

A thoughtful silence followed. Presently Mrs. Hunter asked, "How did your daughter ever happen to *go* to New York?"

"Well, she *wanted* to," explained Mrs. Pratt apologetically.

"Yes, I know." The other mother understood perfectly.

"It's better to let them," wisely commented the Ohio father from the front seat. "They have to get it out of their systems."

There was another reflective silence. This was broken by Mrs. Hunter's putting her hands up to her head, "Would you mind if I took this hat off? It's so tight it gives me a headache. Kenneth would have me buy it."

117

"It's very stylish," said Mrs. Pratt, looking at it on the other woman's knee.

"Oh, stylish!" said Mrs. Hunter impatiently. "I never had such a thing on my head before. *I* think it makes me look perfectly ridiculous."

Mrs. Pratt now asked her acutely, "Did you come by way of New York or straight here?"

"We've been in New York with Kenneth three whole days," said the other.

"You must be tired."

From the front seat Mr. Hunter cried out, "Tired? *Dead!* Once is enough for me. I wouldn't live there if you gave me a million dollars."

"That's what I always say!" agreed Mr. Pratt.

They were now arrived. The Ford stopped. "Here we are," said Mr. Pratt. He had stopped at the side porch and when they got out they faced the row of currant bushes. "My, aren't they far along!" said the lady with the Paris hat in her hand. "They'll be ready to do up before long, won't they?"

"I hope they'll last till some of our early raspberries are ripe," said Mrs. Pratt.

"Yes, I put up mine with raspberries too," said the Fifth Avenue traveling costume.

"Well, well, come on *in,* folks," said Mr. Pratt heartily. "We're awfully glad to have you here."

They all went in and shut the door. And it was not opened again till two hours later when Spike and Jigger appeared, and Jigger, bracing herself and looking discontented and repellent, pushed it open and led her fiancé inside her home.

This is what she saw. In the living-room sitting with her father—who was in his shirt-sleeves—sat a fatherly looking bald-headed man, also in his shirt-sleeves. Both men were smoking pipes, and both were laughing. "Hello there, Sister!" said her father, putting out a hand to her. "What do you think! Your young man's father and I were in the same regiment down in Cuba when we were boys. Can you beat that?"

"Your father had a little the edge on me before it was over," said the good-natured looking man with him—could that be Spike's *father?* "We were both corporals but he got to be a sergeant."

"Only just made it before we were mustered out," said Mr. Pratt. He leaned forward and clapped the other man on the knee. "Say, do you remember the time Lieutenant At-water Dillingham Jones knocked his campaign hat off saluting the Colonel?"

A delighted yell of recollection from the other man drowned him out. "By George, I haven't thought of that from that day to this!" he said brokenly through his spasms, alternately wiping his eyes and holding himself together with his hands. "Ah-hah! hah!" he shouted. "Oh-ho! ho!" He waved his hands, gasped and asked, "Do you remember that slab-sided Kentucky mountaineer who got caught on sentry-go in his bare feet with his shoes hanging around his neck?"

Jigger and Spike turned, looking deeply into each other's eyes, and unnoticed by the laughing fathers, stepped out into the front hall, shutting the door behind them. They were not alone there. Voices sounded from the top of the stairs. Someone was starting down. Looking up, Jigger saw a pleasant-faced, gray-haired, comfortable-looking woman in one of her mother's wrap-around blue aprons. She was saying over her shoulder to Mrs. Pratt on the landing above, "But she's never liked it at all over there. Nor he either. They're crazy to get back to Akron." Seeing her son's fiancée staring up at her, she explained, "I was just telling your mother about Kenneth's married sister, Carrie. He's probably told you her husband works for a company that makes vacuum cleaners and when they thought they'd try to sell some in France, they wanted somebody over there that understood all about the way it works. He's a very good hand with machinery, Carrie's husband is."

Having now come to the bottom step, she looked around her and said, "My, I wish my front hall was as fresh as this. We haven't had it done over since Kenneth was in the seventh grade. But I simply can't get Mr. Hunter to admit how terrible it looks." She looked shyly and kindly at the girl before her and said, smiling, "You must make Kenneth mind you better than I ever have his father." She had a very sweet smile.

"Oh, I love her!" thought Jigger emotionally. "I must be sure not to take Spike away from her."

A roar of laughter came from the living-room. "What a good time those boys are having," said Mrs. Hunter, indulgently.

The two mothers passed on to the kitchen, Mrs. Pratt saying, "We thought it would be nice to have baking-powder biscuits with the salad—little tiny ones, you know."

120

"Yes, I cut mine out with a napkin ring," said Mrs. Hunter.

Alone in the front hall, gazing into each other's eyes, were a couple of distinguished young cosmopolites, just stepped out of their expensive stateroom on an ocean greyhound. Dreamily, almost absently, as if they did not know what they were doing, they put their arms around each other and laid their cheeks close together. "Kenneth," breathed the girl in his ear, "do you know we never can live up to our parents, not if we live to be a hundred!"

He moved his cheek slowly up and down against hers in a nod of assent. "You said it, Sister."

Babushka Farnham

THE WOMEN peering from the near-by houses to see their new neighbor hadn't thought Mrs. Farnham so old as she turned out to be. Her hair was white and her thin back somewhat bowed, to be sure, but there was something springy and forward-looking about the way she climbed down from the little Ford truck that brought her furniture, and stepped up the path to the cottage. She let herself in the front door but almost at once reappeared on the porch to boss the job of unloading the furniture. She had taken her hat off and put on an apron. In the tiny house next door old Mrs. Warner watching from behind the curtains said to her husband, "She looks real nice, don't she?" Mr. Warner said wonderingly, "What do you suppose makes her look so cheerful? Don't seem's though moving into that old shack would set a person up much."

The furniture was light, a white enamel bed not new, a couple of plain tables, a few yellow-varnished chairs, a stationary rocker, upholstered in blue plush, a large trunk and a small one, and a ship-shape bundle of bedding wrapped neatly in a well-washed patch-work quilt. The driver managed alone easily until he came to a battered wooden box something like a seaman's chest. He dragged this as far as the edge of the truck, tried to lift it, let the end fall, shook his head, and said something to the old lady who stood watching him. Mrs. Warner said over her shoulder, "Better get your coat on, Poppa." When Grandmother Farnham came knocking at their door to ask apologetically if they would tell her where she could find a man to help carry something too heavy for one person, Mr. Warner was all ready to show her that the folks on that street expected to be neighborly.

When he came back, "I wonder what's in that box," he said, rubbing his arm, " 'twas as heavy as lead."

What was in it was the only thing they did not learn about the new arrival in the next few days. She showed at once that she was mistress of the art of moving into a new town. Inside a week everybody knew all about her. The name she gave the postman was Mrs. George Farnham, but she said it was usually written Mrs. Rose Farnham, because she had been a widow for many years. She told her neighbors that as a matter of fact she was usually called Grandma Farnham, because she had such a lot of grandchildren. Eleven, to be exact, and one little great-granddaughter in New York City, whom she had never seen. There were photographs of these grandchildren all over the two rooms, living-room and kitchen, which were those seen by her visitors. Her bedroom (not having any family or intimates in town) she never took anybody into. Pictures of her children too were hung on every wall. Middle-aged men and women, nice-appearing people, they were. One of her sons was a wholesale plumber, one a school-teacher, one a hardware merchant. Her two daughters had both married real-estate agents. Like her clean pieced quilt, her *Christian Herald,* her braided rag rugs, her membership in the Epworth League, her stationary rocker and herself, they were guarantees to her neighbors that she was what she seemed—one of them.

Her reasons for coming to live in their town and on their street were as open and understandable as everything else. Until recently she had been needed to take care of a bedridden invalid daughter in Des Moines. After her death Mrs. Farnham had thought it would be better, as long as she was able to do for herself, not to live around from the home of one married child to another, but to find a quiet place and keep house for herself. A relation by marriage of her daughter's husband had inherited this little cottage, quite big enough for a single woman, and let her have it for very little rent. "And that is something I have to think about, for I have only the interest on my husband's life insurance. Ten thousand dollars in the savings-bank, at four and a half per cent. Not but what that's plenty for anybody who's used to managing." Yes, there was no doubt about it, she understood what people naturally like to know about a newcomer.

She was neighborly too. She ran over to Mrs. Cole's familiarly to borrow a needleful of blue silk; passed on the baseball page of her daily newspaper to old Mr. Warner as soon as the mailman brought it, and having a pretty good radio, often called across the street to Mrs. Moore of an afternoon (she was never around in the morning), "That woman who talks about cooking is coming in splendidly. Not a speck of static. Wouldn't you like to bring your sewing over and listen to her?" She was soon accepted and dropped into the class of people to whom nobody pays any special attention because everything they are likely to do is known beforehand.

She had of course, like every grandmother in a dutiful family, a good deal of mail; picture-post-cards with funny kittens or puppies and "Love to Grandma" from the youngest grandchild still in the grades; art post-cards with very pink cherry trees from an older one in the high school; letters from her married daughter with items of home news—the sill under the back kitchen had rotted and they'd set the new one in concrete. Elizabeth thinks now she will stop high school and go to business college, etc., etc.; letters from her sons with so much printed business-heading on the paper that there was little room left for more than "We're all fine and dandy and hope you are too." Sometimes, once in a while, a letter from New York came, from a married grandson, the oldest, George.

He was the only child of the invalid daughter in Des Moines Grandmother Farnham had taken care of for many years, so she had brought up this boy and knew him better than her other grandchildren—in fact knew him very well indeed, so that sometimes she let his letter wait for several days after it came before opening it.

"Dear Grandma:

"Thanks for your nice letter to Natacha. She thought it was as good as a story book. Justine had to read it over and over to her, at bedtime, for four or five nights. And now she's teasing for a squirrel to come up on *her* windowsill.

Poor kid, with a windowsill five stories up. I tried again to make Justine see that we ought to move to the suburbs. Not to speak of Natacha, it's simply impossible for me to get any golf where we are. I tell you what, Grandma, the old-fashioned woman isn't so bad. This modern notion of a woman having a 'career' of her own—it's all very well in books, but when a man comes in late, dog-tired after a day that hasn't had any good breaks in it, and finds the cook's left and—"

Sometimes Grandmother Farnham not only waited several days before opening letters from this grandson, but did not read them all through before lifting a lid from the kitchen stove.

She read almost all, however, of the occasional duty-letters from Justine, her grandson's Russian wife.

"Dear my husband's grandmother:

"How are you now, so far away, never-seen-great-grand-mother of my darling Natacha-baby? I hope you are very happy and quiet in your little own-home. I show your photograph every day to your sweet great-grandchild. I tell her to say 'Babushka Farnham.' Babushka sounds to me more loving than 'grandmother.' We have had a bad cook again. They are all bad; but when there are none, I am worse. What do people in America do for sore throats? I was asked to exhibit again last month, a great honor it was, an invitation from the notable society where only fine artists show work, but could not finish my group because Natacha-dear had two sore throats in three weeks. So sick she was, I became like a wild woman with fear for her. In my studio that whole month I had but pieces of hours, and then always with anxious fright for Natacha. George was so displeased when—"

Grandmother Farnham always tried to skip the parts about George and looked hastily down the page, stopping short in phrase after phrase whenever she encountered his name.

"—to live in a suburb now would mean *I give up my* modeling, never could I leave Natacha with those bad cooks long enough to come in to a studio in the city. George says—"

"—if only I could have, clear free, for my work three years —two years—*one* year! I could show, but George—"

"—like a nightmare so I know not if I ever wake up from when I try and try, always hurrying, and always must stop to run back to see Natacha, at the very instant when I arrive to come, *all of me,* to success with something I sculpture, after long tries when I succeed not."

The English grew more and more excitable and the writing more temperamental. Grandmother Farnham could not understand it very well, and also saw a good many Georges on the last page. So she made a long flight to the end where there were some large circles and "Natacha sends these kisses to her Babushka, and so do I send love to the only mother-father-grandmother I have." Justine's own parents had died before she had left Russia.

When Mrs. Farnham had been living in Des Moines, and such letters from New York came in, the comments of George's Iowa cousins had usually run, "For mercy's sake,

what ever possessed a foreigner to marry George! It wouldn't
be any too easy for a smart Iowa girl to manage him so's to
have any life of her own."

Grandma Farnham had sometimes looked so sick after reading the news from George and his Russian sculptor wife that
her grown-up granddaughters felt obliged to bring out one
or another of the family formulae we all use for making sympathy look like officiousness: "Don't take things so *hard,*
Grandma! You can't carry everybody's burdens." Or, "Now,
Grandma, you've had your full share of George. You've done
your full duty by him, goodness knows. You just think about
something else!" Or, "Oh, for heaven's sakes, let them stew
in their own juice. She married him, didn't she? Let her
make out the best she can, the way the rest of us have to."
They knew George almost as well as his grandmother did.

But now she was alone in her small own-home. There was
nobody at hand to force rough doses of common-sense down
her throat when she began to look sick over a letter from
New York. Sometimes Grandmother Farnham went on looking sick all day, long after the letter she had thrust into the
fire had been burned to nothing.

They came very seldom, however, and in the long intervals between them her neighbors commented on what a lively
old lady Mrs. Farnham was, always moving around with a
bounce like a younger woman, always smiling, always ready
to see the funny side of things. Yet with no professional reason for cheerfulness, being a Congregationalist and not a
Christian Scientist or a New Thoughter. That idea of her
doctor's about having her lie down to rest every morning

must be a good one, for she looked in better and better health all the time, which doesn't often happen to people of sixty-eight.

"Why, Mrs. Farnham, you're getting posi-*tive*-ly fat!"

"I know it. I had to let out a petticoat waistband this morning before I could get it round me. The air of this place seems to agree with me. I have the best appetite for my meals I've had in years. I tell you what, I'm here for life!"

People liked to have her lay her good spirits to the climate of their town, liked to have her enjoy living on their street. They often said, "Wasn't it a stroke of good luck to have such a nice old lady move into the Allen shack!" (It had been a shack before becoming a cottage, and people sometimes forgot.)

The neighbors kept a kindly watch over the elderly woman living all alone. Since she was, by doctor's orders, to be perfectly quiet in the mornings and sleep if she could, nobody ever went over there before noon. But somebody would have run in at once to see what the matter was if she had not come out between half-past twelve and one to take in the mail. One day as Mrs. Warner set the dish of hash on her table and called her husband to eat his lunch, she noticed that Grandma Farnham was just going down the steps from her door. How lightly she trotted along the path, for a woman of her age, thought Mrs. Warner. She seemed to get up from those quiet mornings in bed as spry as a girl.

The hash was all eaten and the pie too before Mrs. Warner got up from the table to clear off. She glanced casually out of the window. Why, there was Mrs. Farnham still standing in front of her mail box reading something. What letter could it be to keep her there so long?

She took the letter presently back into the house, walking very slowly. On the porch she stood still, re-reading a page she had already read many times.

"—that day I had success. Sometimes it comes not, sometimes yes. This was a yes time—the greatest I ever yet feel. I was so happy, no one can be so happy. When they come to tell me Natacha had broken her leg, I could not—just for a breath-long—know who Natacha was,—nor who I. Then— oh, dreadful I think myself a bad, bad mother, not right I should have my lovely Natacha-daughter if I forget her for my work. I forget her, you see, Babushka dear, for just one time to take breath, I forget she live, my own little girl. When I remember, my heart almost break, and I rush, no hat, no coat, to hospital where Natacha. Then I forget my dear clay children, as dear as Natacha, I forget them, all three long days. Not once of my dear clay children did I think till the fourth when, Natacha better, I telephone to the janitor to be sure to keep the cloths wet. But he forgot. He *forgot!*— when I go back to studio, half was crack and spoil. I work— three week now I have work to mend what was spoiled then —but—it is not only time that is lost—the me who lived then cannot live to work so good now. I send you, so you can see— I have drawn in the lines to show where the water would fall, when my fountain would be in place."

Grandmother Farnham opened the door slowly. She had turned the radio on before she went out, but had not stopped to regulate the volume. As she entered she was greeted by a woman's voice like a soured needle, saying, "Keep the rouge up and out towards the temple, never towards the nose."

Mrs. Farnham sat down, looking at a small unmounted snap-shot that had been enclosed in Justine's letter. It was a design for a fountain. Three naked children, with lean, beautiful, unformed bodies, started back in exquisitely angular poses of dismay and delight, as their flimsy dam of sticks broke and let through on them, in a curving gush, the water of a little brook.

Half an hour later, she was still looking at it when a man's raucous voice shouted, "Stand by, folks, to hear the Marsdon quartet sing 'Nellie Was a Lady' like your father used to do." The small room cringed before the onslaught of magnified tenors and basses, but Grandmother Farnham did not lift her eyes from the photograph. She had looked at it long enough now to guess at the poetic meaning of the design—to see how the downward rush of the living water seemed to pour out the three lovely children as the embodiment of its own vital beauty. Was there perhaps a deeper meaning back of that? Did the little playing dam-makers stand for humanity, childishly trying with flimsy barriers of sticks and stones to master the flow of life which at the appointed time bursts through, overwhelming youth with its gush of joyful power?

The loud-speaker was bawling, "Manure that you keep piled up in your barn-yard will *never* grow grain for you!" when she reached for the magnifying glass she used to read small print, and began to examine the photograph more closely. She looked at it, inch by inch, dwelling on every

131

detail—the ruined figure with its craze of cracks spoiling the texture of the surface, the delicacy of modeling of the two that had been repaired. How honest, how faithful to children's enchanting weakness were those angular young joints, those fine tendons, the touching slimness of those little necks, the arch of the small spines. She had thought only the eye of a woman many times a mother and grandmother could see all that. It was after all the artist's eye that saw and divined. She smiled lovingly at the sculptured children—and drew long sighing breaths as she smiled, shaking her head, her chin trembling.

Presently, as though she could not bear to look at it any more, she laid the photograph down and put both hands over her eyes.

A woman's voice, vociferously dripping honey, asked, "How are all the little brides today? Each in your own little love-nest, wondering about—"

By the time the advice to young wives had turned into the stock-market report, Mrs. Farnham had taken her hands down from her face and let them fall on her knees, knotted old hands on thin old knees. She sat thus a long time, empty hands lying on her gingham lap, her eyes, rather sunken now, fixed on the blank wall before her. Her chin was not trembling. It was steady and still and so was her mouth, her sad old-woman's mouth, the corners drooping as though Grandmother Farnham had had about all the living she could stand.

The bed-time story had begun when someone knocked at the door. Grandmother Farnham heard it and stirred. The knock was repeated. She looked about her blankly as though to make out where she was, as if she could not see her own old furniture standing faithfully about her in the twilight. Twilight? The afternoon was gone.

The knob was turned, the door opened. Old Mrs. Warner stood on the threshold, a plate in her hand, something on it covered with a clean piece of white cloth. She was surprised to see Mrs. Farnham sitting doing nothing, facing a blank wall, and looking—well, rather queer. "Oh, I beg your pardon, Mrs. Farnham, for coming in without your saying to. I thought maybe you couldn't hear me knock through the radio. I've brought over a piece of cake I made for our supper. It's made by the recipe you told me about."

She added with concern, "Aren't you feeling well, Mrs. Farnham? Seems as though you didn't look just—"

"Well, I have a sort of a headache," admitted Mrs. Farnham, taking the cake.

The wind from the open door blew the photograph across the room to Mrs. Warner's feet. She picked it up, glanced at it, and looked again, her wrinkled old face breaking into brightness. "Oh, how cute!" she cried. "Why, who ever saw children in a statuary that look the way they really do! Takes me right back to when our girls were little."

"Yes, don't it?" said Mrs. Farnham. "It's lovely work. Lovely work."

She stood looking down intently at the triangle of cake on the plate in her hands.

"Who did it?" asked the visitor.

"It's something my grandson's wife, Justine, has just done. She's a Russian. I've told you about them, don't you remember? She married George, my oldest grandson. I've never seen her or the little girl."

After a pause she added, in a lower tone, "I never saw any of her work before. She never happened to think to send any. I guess she thought I wouldn't be interested."

Mrs. Warner took her eye-glasses off their hook on her bosom and looked more closely at the photograph. "Isn't there something the matter with the little fellow that's squatting down in front? Is that his back? What makes it look so humpy and queer?"

"The clay got too dry," explained Mrs. Farnham. "You know you have to keep wet cloths on clay or it all cracks to pieces. Just when Justine had it where it was the way she wanted it, before she could finish, she was called home to take care of her little girl through a sick spell. The janitor of the studio was to keep the cloths wet. But he forgot. She's spent a lot of time getting it back where it was, she says, but she hasn't quite got it all mended. It's harder after you've been interrupted, to get back to where you were."

"—and right in front of Tommy was a great brown *Bear!*" shrieked the radio.

It made Mrs. Warner jump, "My! haven't you got your radio on pretty loud?"

"I don't know but I have. I hadn't noticed," said Grandmother Farnham.

Even when the Warners knew what was in the chest, that was all the good it did them. "Nothing but dirt," reported Mr. Warner to his wife, the evening of the day he had

134

helped Mrs. Farnham get ready to leave town. "Lumpy grayish dirt, kind of wet and greasy looking. I said—I declare I didn't know what *to* say, when the lid came open—I said, 'Some kind of earth for your geraniums, Mrs. Farnham?' And she said, 'No, nothing alive will ever grow in that.' Then she just stood looking at it. I thought she looked kind of funny. After a while she fetched a long breath and told me, 'Better throw it out, I guess. Maybe your wife would like the box for kindlings. The lid is hinged. It might be handy.' "

"*Well—!*" commented Mrs. Warner.

"I thought she spoke kind of funny," said the old man musingly.

"She's been kind of funny ever since she decided to go," said the old woman.

She asked, "Did you throw it out?"

"Yes, I dumped it around back of the chicken-house."

"What did you do with the box?"

He hesitated, "When I got through cleaning up the yard, the way she told me to, I made a fire to get rid of the trash. And I put the box on and burned it up."

The two old people looked at each other. "That was a good idea," said Mrs. Warner. "I don't believe I'd have felt just right to use her box."

"I thought maybe you wouldn't," said the old man.

Neither then, nor as the years went by after Mrs. Farnham's departure, did they ever again speak of the box full of clay. They let it drop down into the realm of unexplained mysteries of human life, which became steadily larger in their minds as they grew older and wiser.

II

George and Justine were to take the speaker of the evening home for the night. George felt a warm rich satisfaction at snatching a distinguished person away from the Monroes. For six years, ever since he and Justine had moved to Long Hills, he had been waiting for a good chance to land one on the Monroes, who brought their millionaire cousins, their expensive house and their butler into the conversation too often to suit George's taste. His heart sang, as he observed Mrs. Monroe's face change to ruefulness from its usual complacency. "But you aren't *ready* to take in a man like Mr. Lorenzo for an overnight guest, are you?" Her shrillness betrayed her dismay.

"Oh, he'll just have to take what he gets," said George. He looked hard at Mrs. Monroe and remarked, with a relishing smile, "He's no middle-class Philistine, you know. He's not looking for the right kind of doiley! What he wants is a chance to talk to Justine about her work. She's the only person of his kind out here."

They had tried—not very hard—to telephone Grandma about the unexpected guest, but when Central said, "That line is *biz*-zay," George hung up the receiver, saying to Justine, "Oh, let it go. Frieda never objects to company. The house will be all right, just as it is."

Sure enough, when at half-past eleven they led their

136

celebrity in, the lights silently blossoming out as George clicked on the switches showed rooms exquisitely dustless and orderly. There were some good things in the ice-box, too, as there always were, for the midnight lunch George enjoyed setting out for unexpected guests: a bowl of savory potato-salad, ginger-ale bottles frostily nestled against the ice, a bowl of golden apple-sauce, home-made raisin-bread and flavorsome spice-cake, a bottle of George's favorite whiskey standing ready on the sideboard.

Over this food the art critic exclaimed, "What a wonderful cook you must have! I haven't tasted gingerbread like this since I was a boy in Indiana."

"Yes, Frieda is very capable," said Justine.

"You must have a very special gift for managing the Friedas of the world," said Mr. Lorenzo, "to combine such perfect home-making with so very personal a gift as yours. It's plain from the look of your sculpture that you don't try to work in any odds and ends of time as most women who keep house have to."

"I've been very lucky of late years about having good help," said Justine.

"Well, *my* attitude may have something to do with it," said George, with the honest accent of one overcoming reticence to make a contribution to a discussion. "I'm not one of the men who want to be the whole show, and make their wives miserable if they try to do anything but keep house. Let the housekeeping *go* a little, say I," said George, unfolding a perfectly ironed damask napkin, "there are other more important things. I'm *proud* of my wife's success, not jealous of it," he ended magnanimously.

When they went upstairs, George threw open the door to the spare room, turned on the lights and gave a satisfied look around. The furniture was all old-American. "We like to have *one* corner of the house where we keep our family past with us," explained George. He took up a corner of the clean, washed quilt which covered the bed. "That was pieced by my great-great-grandmother."

"Indeed?" said the guest, politely. "That's very interesting. And who made the sampler? And which ancestor did this fine four-poster come from?"

"Shall I open a window for you?" asked George. "Let me just bring you another piece of bedding. There! Good-night. Sleep well."

"What time shall I come down to breakfast?" asked the guest.

"Whenever you like. We don't hold with the provincial, pie-for-breakfast and everybody-down-at-once business. It's a movable feast, as suits our needs. My old grandmother has made her home with us for six or seven years now, since she got so feeble she couldn't look out for herself. Like all old people she gets up early, long before anyone else. Natacha, our ten-year-old daughter, and her little brother usually have their breakfast by themselves in the kitchen alcove. My grandmother claims them then. She says that's really the only chance she has to see them. I take the eight-forty in, and usually sit down to the table about eight. Justine is a regular European, always has breakfast in bed before taking the nine-three in to town to her studio. You know how artists are, can't do a decent day's work if they've had to see people and talk to them first—though of course tomorrow will be a red-letter day when she will have the great privilege of break-fasting with you. How would a quarter of nine suit you? I'll take a later train and we can have an hour comfortably to-gether."

The breakfast was as delicious as the ice-box supper. Over the perfect coffee and the piping hot muffins there was good talk ("that finest flower of civilized life" old Mr. Lorenzo often called it in his lectures), a discussion about America's share in art past and future, mellow speculations about human nature, keen searching technical talk between Justine and her guest about her own work. Mr. Lorenzo had a good deal to say about its development in the last six or seven years.

"I didn't think you had it in you, honestly," said the old critic, looking at her admiringly. "Charm, yes, and delicacy—but a kind of nervous uncertain uneven charm, not this quiet calm power of your later work. It didn't show—I'll stake my honor as a seeing eye, it did *not* show in your earlier things."

"I always felt it," said Justine in a deep thrilling voice. She lifted her chin and laid a beautiful muscular hand upon her breast, "I always felt it—*here*."

"I can't find my rubbers, Grandma!" came in a shrill aggrieved whoop from the hall. "*Gram!* I can't find my *rubbers*. What did you do with my rubbers, Gram?"

"Don't shout like that, Harry, when you want to speak to Grandma," said George reprovingly over his shoulder. "Go where she is." Slow steps came down the stairs, a low voice murmured in the hall, broken by demands in a child's voice, constantly rising louder. Finally, "Oh, hello, Grandma, how are you this morning?" said George. "Mr. Lorenzo, this is my grandmother, Mrs. Farnham."

The tall old guest half-rose from his chair, bowed, clutched at his napkin before it slid to the floor, sat down and reached for the toast. Justine rose, regal in her flame-colored house-gown, and went to greet the newcomer affectionately, stooping to kiss her on both withered cheeks. "Dear Babushka!" she said tenderly. "Dear, dear Babushka Farnham." She pulled out a chair and set it for the other, with a graceful gesture of welcome.

With a jerk of his head George called the attention of the visitor to the picture made by the two women, the parchment-skinned old grandmother like a Rembrandt in her black woolen dress and white collar and apron, Justine all vivid brightness like a Venetian portrait. In an aside he said, "There are mighty few women, let me tell you, Mr. Lorenzo, that'd be so nice to their husband's grandmother as Justine is to mine. Lots of women would feel put upon if they had to take an old person into the family—just an ordinary little small-town old woman, at that."

Justine sat down and poured herself another cup of coffee. The old woman did not at once take the chair offered her. She came up to the table and leaned over Justine, one thin big-knuckled hand on the flame-colored shoulder. "Harry's teasing to have one of the muffins to eat on the way to school," she explained, apologizing by her tone for interrupting talk about the future of America's art.

"Well, why not?" said Justine, indulgently. "Take him two." She pushed the plate towards Grandmother Farnham, dismissed her with an affectionate look, and turned to Mr. Lorenzo, "I haven't the base of that third group in the Iowa war-memorial *simplified* enough yet. It takes so long to learn how to leave out things, and of course it's what you leave out that makes a work of art."

The front door opened and shut with a slam. Through the dining-room windows they saw a small boy trudging forward, a large bulge in one cheek. "Why, where's Natacha?" asked Justine, interrupting herself in her remarks on the elimination of detail. Grandmother Farnham came back into the dining-room from the hall and sat down heavily. "Natacha's a little under the weather this morning," she said. "I thought she'd better stay in bed a day or so." As she spoke she smoothed out her white apron over her black woolen dress.

George laughed and shook his finger at her, "We know your tricks and your manners, Grandma! That's so you can be nurse!" He explained to the guest, "My grandmother is one of the old-fashioned women who're never so happy as when they can get somebody down in bed where they can stand over him and make him take his medicine. Justine and I are positively not allowed even to look at the children when they get some of the little ailments children are always having."

The old woman looked at him steadily and said nothing.

141

Justine turned to the guest, "I'm so-r-r-r-y you're not going to see Natacha. As a fellow sculptor you'd be interested in the modeling of her cheek. You never saw such low relief! And so significant, every faintest change of plane. I've tr-ried to do her many times, but I can never get it subtle enough."

Mr. Lorenzo saw an opportunity to do the polite thing by the old country woman and bring her into the conversation on a level suitable to her mentality. "Which parent does this little girl resemble, Mrs. Farnham?"

George's grandmother answered with an almost disconcerting promptness, "Natacha looks some like her mother, but in disposition she's exactly like George." She spoke a little dryly.

"That means," said George, not sorry to show the existence of tradition in his family, "that she's very much like her great-grandfather. Didn't you always tell me I was like my grandfather, Grandma?"

Mrs. Farnham looked at him. "You're your grandfather all over again," she stated. She added, for the benefit of the visitor, "George's grandfather was my husband."

"Oh," said Mr. Lorenzo, "oh, yes, of course." He wondered if he could look at his watch without getting caught at it.

Justine noticed his wandering eye, understood and sympathized with his lack of interest in the tiresome digression they had wandered into, and tactfully brought the conversation back to a topic where his role would be the leading one, "I thought all of your talk last night was beautiful. But nothing touched me more than the story from your young days

142

you were telling us about the poor country woman, all un-
taught, who had been trying to be a sculptor, and who
brought her little children to the tent-school where you were
teaching."

"What was that?" asked George. "I guess I must have
missed that. Probably when I stepped out to see what the
matter was with those pounding steam-pipes."

Justine explained, "Why, it seems that Mr. Lorenzo in his
youth gave lessons in 'art,'" she exchanged a smile with the
lecturer, "that meant painting, drawing, decalcomania, sculpture, making wax-flowers—anything. In those days they had,
he was telling us, a sort of summer camp in some places
where people came to live in tents, to listen to lectures and—"

George threw back his head to laugh. "Are you trying to
explain Chautauquas to *me?*" he asked, "to an Iowa boy?
Why, we had 'em every summer in our town. Grandma,
didn't you use to go to 'em?"

"Sometimes. Years ago. Before you were born," answered
the old lady, smoothing down her apron.

"Well, this was years ago before you were born, too," said
the white-haired critic, "for I wasn't twenty yet!"

He turned from George to Justine. "But there's really more
to that story than I told last night." He explained to George,
"I wanted to get over to the audience the idea that even ages
ago in crude pioneer America, there were sporadic cases of
artistic talent, and I gave as an example a woman I saw in
my first Chautauqua. Like most of my students, she was a
good deal older than I. In fact, married with three children.
She had brought them along with her to the Chautauqua

encampment because she hadn't anybody to leave them with. They were holy terrors too. Their father thought his wife's notions of being an artist were all foolishness, and I suppose the children got the idea from him that the more trouble they made her, the better pleased he'd be. Well, they made her plenty. I couldn't see how she ever got time to do as much work as she did. Mostly at night, after the children were asleep, I imagine. I used to see her tent lighted up till all hours."

"Did she r-r-really have talent?" asked Justine curiously.

"I thought so then. She was utterly untrained of course, probably had never even seen a decently sensitive piece of relief in all her life. You simply can't imagine what a howling wilderness, artistically speaking, middle-western America was fifty and more years ago. What she did had strange crudities, and of course was absurdly uneven. But a kind of personal quality—you know what I mean,—there are artists with technique at their finger-tips who haven't it."

"I can't imagine what work could be like that was done in entire ignorance of tr-r-radition," mused Justine.

"Well, it had a certain sprightly animation that was really quite charming. I thought of it again when I first went to St. Quentin and saw the Latour pastels."

George lifted the lid from a box of cigars, gazed consideringly into it, chose one, rolled it between his fingers, lighted it and looked surreptitiously at his watch.

The old artist went on, dreamily reconstructing the long-ago scene. "She had only a very small quantity of clay to work with. Very little cash at her disposal. I imagine her husband took care to make it as hard as possible for her. So she worked in miniature. She made a series of small portrait heads—people in her class—and I assure you they had an almost eighteenth-century lightness of poise. I can see them now, those little heads. She made quite an impression on my imagination, as you can see. The first person with real talent I'd found in those tent-schools. Well, I've talked about and taught sculpture for more than fifty years since then, and I've never seen anybody more crazy about modeling. It was really rather thrilling to a youngster as I was, to teach her. She'd never had the slightest instruction, and the few simple technical tips I could give her freed her by leaps and bounds from difficulties she'd been struggling with alone."

"What was the rest of the story that you didn't tell last night?" asked Justine.

"Oh, yes, that was what I started to tell. One day the Chautauqua grounds were swept with a sort of cloudburst—one of those characteristic mid-summer Iowa winds that slammed most of the tents flat. The rain kept on, but the wind was all over in a minute, and then people began running around, making sure their friends were all right and trying to find their things. I'd been in the Assembly Hall which was a permanent building, and not damaged at all, but I'd left some rather valuable books in my tent and dashed out to see if I could get them. I found the tent twisted together in a knot, and was just stooping to see if I could pull the canvas away when along came this woman I've been telling you about. She was running frantically, the way women never ran in those days, her long skirts clutched high, her hair all down, streaming behind her in the rain. She looked as though she were out of her mind. I thought of course she was looking for her children, and I'd just seen them in the Assembly Hall, playing with some other kids, hardly even noticing that it was raining. So I called after her, 'It's all right. They're safe. I saw them just a minute ago in the Assembly Hall.'

"She didn't hear me—she'd gone by like the wind. So I put out after her. Sure enough she was streaking it for her tent. When she got where she could see that it was down, with the wooden supports at each end broken off short, she shrieked, and simply flew. I couldn't catch up with her. As soon as she reached the tent, she flung herself down in the mud, and plunged right under the twisted wet canvas. When I got to it, I could see how she was crawling under it, pushing her way towards where the beds made a sort of hump. I snatched the canvas off, in record time, of course. There she was, smeared with mud to her eyes. She was reaching her arm under one of the beds. I called to her, shouting something about their being safe, but she didn't seem to know that anybody was there, just kept on reaching and then sat back, something on her lap. She was leaning her shoulders far over it to keep the rain off. But I could see that it was the board she kept her little portrait heads on.

"They were in soft clay still, of course, but the bed had kept the tent from crushing them. They were quite all right. Not hurt at all. I understood then. I was as glad as she to see them safe, and said, 'God! what luck you happened to put them under the bed!'

146

"She didn't straighten up—she crouched there in the mud, the rain beating down on her back and shoulders, not a drop falling on those exquisite little creations; but she turned her stooped face towards me, her mud-smeared face all ablaze with relief—and smiled. Well, really you know—I'm an old man, I've lived a long time since then, but I swear I've never seen anything like that smile.

"I thought she might wonder how I happened to have followed her and explained, 'I thought you were looking for your children. I wanted to let you know they were safe in Assembly Hall. But I guess you saw them there, too.'

"She froze then, just as she was, all stooped and twisted, her head turned towards me, her eyes very wide, her mouth a little open, her face as blank as though I'd started talking Greek or Choctaw. And I saw of course that she'd forgotten her children—forgotten she had any."

"How dr-r-ramatic," breathed Justine, gazing unwinkingly at the narrator. "How very dr-r-ramatic." Her fine chest heaved in a long breath. "And then—?"

"Well, all she had to do was to keep still about it. I'd never have said anything. There wouldn't have been anything to say, as far as that goes. She hadn't *said* she'd forgotten about her children. She could have contradicted me. But no—she turned as gray as ashes. I've never seen such a strange color. She sat up straight, she ground her jaws together and said something through her teeth, but in such a strangled voice I couldn't understand any words except "George," and before I could stir she had swept all her lovely little heads from the board into one shapeless lump and was battering on it with her fists."

Justine looked down at her beautiful muscular hands and drew them back into the flowing sleeves of her house-coat.

"At that I let out a yell," went on the old sculptor, "and made a grab to hold her arms. But she wrenched away from me, stood up, threw the lump down, and ground her foot into it. 'I'll never touch a finger to clay again,' she told me, only I didn't think she knew I was there, 'till every child I'm responsible for is grown up.'

"Her children came screeching down the road then, squabbling and whining, to pull at her skirts and complain that it was raining and they were hungry. It would have given me the greatest joy to wring their necks, one by one."

He paused.

"And then—" asked Justine, somberly.

"That's all. As far as I ever knew that was the end. I never saw her after that. She didn't even come to say good-by."

"Why, you haven't had a cigar, yet," said George hospitably, offering him the box.

"You make it too much alive, your story—" murmured Justine. "It brings back—br-r-r-r! our first years! Do you remember, George, how r-r-r-eally hard they were?"

"Have a cigarette?" her husband asked her, handing her one and striking a match.

She took two thoughtful puffs, shook her head and said, "The worst of your story is that it needed not to be—the tragedy. That poor woman was a victim of being born too soon, not of the nature of things. Of course, no one would claim that it can ever be made simple and easy—the being an artist and a woman too. But in modern times, it is so very possible to develop the technique for managing those two sides of a life. It took me some years to master it—I was young, I did not know, at first I did not know. But then I said to myself, "It is a technique; like the technique of any art, it can be learned by anyone intelligent enough to—' "

From behind the swinging doors came a crash of breaking chinaware. Justine looked vaguely and absently in that direction. Grandmother Farnham got up from her chair, stepped through the swinging doors, and beyond the pantry into the kitchen. Behind her, she heard the murmur of pleasant voices, intermingled. Before her stood a brawny woman with a glowering blonde face and a cold Swedish eye, a dirty dishcloth clenched in one fist. At her feet lay the fragments of a china dish.

"Ven do dey tank I get my vork done!" she asked indignantly, tossing her head towards the dining-room where the finest flower of civilized life was blooming. To underline what she meant, she seized a half-loaf of bread and flung it into the garbage pail.

"Frieda, how would you like to take the day off?" asked old Mrs. Farnham peaceably. "Nobody is coming home for lunch except little Harry and I can take care of him all right. I've got to stay in anyhow with Natacha. She has one of her sore throats. It'd be no trouble to me to answer the door and let in the iceman and all that."

"Dey bane yoost so much more vork ven I get back," said Frieda, unappeased.

"Oh, I'll putter around and get things fixed up," said her employer's grandmother. "I haven't anything else to do. I'll make some fresh gingerbread too. I can get your dinner started for you."

"Vell—I might—" admitted Frieda. She laid down the dishcloth and went back towards her bedroom. In the door she hesitated, ruminating gloomily on her grievances.

Grandmother Farnham pulled up her skirt, reached into her petticoat pocket and took out a small old-fashioned purse, rather flat. "Let me stand you treat, Frieda," she said, with a pleasant smile. "Here are a couple of dollars. Take a friend to the movies, why don't you?"

Harvest in the Ripened Years

SHE WAS cleaning the shelves in the attic, the ones that ran back under the eaves. Not that they needed it. Nothing had been touched up there since she had last set them straight. Not a thing. And there was but the thinnest film of dust to be wiped off, the same gray film which was steadily sifting down over everything in the house, and over her. If only one stroke of her cleaning-cloth could reach her heart, to clear it from that slowly settling ash-like dust.

At this she felt a familiar danger near, and stood up to issue her ultimatum, although that was now worn rather thin, "None of that!" she said sharply to herself. "None —of—that!" She would draw nine long breaths. That always loosened nervous tensions. How many explosions of excitable little Caroline's had they headed off that way—"Breathe deeply now, Carrie darling—nine times. I'll do it with you. All ready? *One—two—three*—right down to your toes— *four*—" Alone in the attic Caroline's mother counted and breathed resolutely, remembering to relax her muscles, not to grip the dustcloth as though it were the only thing between her and despair. But it was.

At "nine" she stopped and went on with her work. *Work?* Useless pottering. She had the memory of Caroline vividly in her mind now, hung on a hair-trigger as the nervous little tyke had been. Wonderful to see the disciplined woman Carrie had grown into, all her chain-lightning intensity pouring itself smoothly along the right wires to drive at noiseless speed the shining efficient dynamo of her work. People sometimes said, "How *does* your daughter accomplish so much?" Mrs. Barney knew how. And one of the many glorious happinesses (in the past) of which she continually reminded herself, was Carrie's saying once, "You did it, Mother. Now I have children of my own, I can see just how patiently and ingeniously you kept me from being one of those fly-to-pieces women. You'd better believe I often think of it with my fly-to-pieces little Deborah." What more could any woman want out of life, Mrs. Barney asked herself, her useless dustcloth hanging limp in her wrinkled hand, than such memories as she had. All her memories. She had been fortunate beyond belief. Even the long-ago sorrow of her widowhood was golden with remembered love. And the children—how miraculously they had, all four, from being cranky, or lumpish, or self-willed, or nervously timorous, bloomed out into sturdy men and women, facing the world with their heads up, rooted deep in life. Two of them married well, too. As well as anybody could expect, that is. At the motherishly grudging tone of this she achieved an inward smile of self-mockery. She knew very well that just so grudgingly had her mother-in-law thought about her.

Well, she felt better. Really better. Nothing was so good for a person as to make a little fun of herself. She went back to dusting, and pushed her dustcloth along a shelf far under the eaves. There was something there, a small object. It felt about as big as an apple. But not withered. Hard. She brought it out to the light. It was a frog, molded in green soap. Oh, yes! It was one of those she had bought for Bobby to help him learn to like to wash his darling dirty little hands. He must have grown out of that need before they were all used up. This one—how long had it waited there under the eaves? Fifteen—no, heavens! twenty-five years! All the while Bobby had been passing into and through and out of the suffocating anguish of shyness of his little boyhood, through the hearty roughneck barbarisms of the graded school, through cave-digging and his first dog and those awful Westerns—stories and movies—and the newspaper route and measles and mumps and scarlet fever and learning to swim and whooping-cough and hide-and-seek—and then his four years of high school, and Tarzan and basketball and his new deep voice and the first girls and vacation work in the drug store and beginning to shave. And his four years of college—they fled through her mind in one flickering lightning-flash, football and Latin and Socialism and Edna Henderson and Florence Winser and the Glee Club and Bernard Shaw and planning finances with her—that was when she began to spend her little capital, reckless so long as the children had their education. Bobby was Robert C. by that time, working as dashingly as he played, stoking professors' furnaces and cutting their lawns, pressing other boys' suits, doing without things, developing that power, that endurance, that confident life-loving vitality that carried him with a rush through the working and studying years of law-school into success. "You must be very proud of your son, Mrs. Barney. Everybody says he will be a judge before he is forty."

"Yes, I am very proud of my son," thought Mrs. Barney in the attic, clutching the soap frog in her hand as though it were all that stood between her and despair. "I am very proud of both my sons. Of all my children."

But it was no use. She could not hold the soap frog tightly enough. "Only—" alone there in the attic she said it aloud to herself, plain and clear, the truth at last, "only I haven't any children. They are all dead. They have died, every one of them, and left me alone."

It was at her lips now, the cup which had been slowly filling up, drop by drop, in spite of all she could do, during these months since Allie's wedding, it was full to the brim and now she must drink. It was full to the brim with loneliness and silence and uselessness and desolation. She had turned her head away a thousand times. A thousand times she had pretended it was not there. Ten thousand times she had been sensible and reasonable and had made herself quickly think of something else. But now she was honest. She drank deep of the bitter draught that filled her cup— she was useless, that was the plain fact, she was not needed any more anywhere, she might as well not be at all. She was like a flimsy paper bag that had been round and full and important with the duties and responsibilities crowded into it. But one by one they had all been taken out. She was empty. She was nothing—a poor little crumpled paper bag with nothing in it, blown aimlessly around the universe by a cold black wind. Now she was honest at last. *She had no children*. Those fine grown men and women who called her "Mother" were not her children. She would betray them if she thought of them as her—as anybody's—children. And if there was anything in her past to make her proud, it was that she had never yet betrayed them by wanting something from them for herself.

What did she want from them now? She wanted them to need her. To be a mother was to be needed by your children. But they did not now need anything she could do for them, except to stop trying to be useful to them. Padding tiger-like beside her during these last solitary months, had been a savage memory of how drearily her grandmother's useless attempts to be useful had weighed on her mother's dutiful-ness—how her mother's had weighed on her, God forgive her! No, those four young adults who had been her children were now kind and affectionate friends of an older woman who had done her best for them and to whom they were very grateful. That's what they were, all they were, all they could be. There was nothing they would not do for her—the exqui-sitely renovated little old home around her bore witness to that—they would do anything in the world for her except be children who needed her. "And I wouldn't *want* them to be!" she cried, even as she drank the black bitterness she had so long pretended was not there. She shuddered as she drank, but it could not force her to stoop, even in thought, to be less than her children's mother, who wanted only what was best for them though it would kill her. She hated herself, she fled away down the steep stairs, from the fatal spot where she had been honest, had given up the pretense that she was not desolate.

She was shocked at what had happened there. She was ashamed. She pushed the cup away (but now there could be no more pretense that it did not exist), she remembered to go down the stairs more carefully, guarding herself from accidents, lest she be a bother to the children. She went on into her kitchen, her horrible, tidy, clean, empty old-woman's kitchen, thinking to herself, "I'll start my luncheon. I promised the children I would always get myself a warm meal in the middle of the day."

But she had forgotten the soap frog. It was still clutched rigidly in her hand. She sighed, opened her stiff fingers, and set it on the tin box in which—how foolishly—she still put soft pieces of old napkins, just right to bandage small cut fingers and skinned knees. Beside it stood the battered silver cup that Bobby had learned to drink from. "There are too many reminders of the children around," she thought, like any other mother whose children have died and left her alone. "It would be better if I put them all away. Every one."

But what good would that do? She did not need reminders. Wherever she turned, ghosts of her dead children floated around her, little girls hungry for the cookies which now dried and crumbled unwanted in the cookie jar, bored children who wanted her to stop work and sing them something funny, restless little boys whose awkward arms pushed things off the table to the floor—she would give a year of her present life for the blessed noise of breakage. Of her present *life?*

"This is selfish and morbid!" She flogged herself to self-reproach. "There is no woman of my age alive who has as much to be thankful for as I. What more could I possibly have to make me happy? I have everything any woman could ask for to be happy. I have everything any woman could ask for to be happy. I have everything any—" The tears came like a flood to silence her.

And then she *was* ashamed. And frightened. Suppose one of the children had come in and seen her. She went quickly into the bathroom (Charlie had insisted she should have a second one on the ground floor to save stair-climbing), washed her face in hot water (there was always hot water now with that electric thing Allie's husband had had installed), smoothed her hair, put a little powder on her reddened nose, and said, "I'll go get my potatoes on."

Sitting to pare the potatoes—two poor little potatoes—she thought conscientiously, "I know a thing or two I'd say to any other woman with no more sense than I'm showing." So she said them, the reasonable, logical, unanswerable, futile things—"Yes, of course your case is rather special because your husband died and that let you in for an extra dose of concentrating on the children, but there have been other widows in the world's history who brought up a family alone. Why act as though you were any more of a victim than they? And why all these surprise-hysterics? You knew your children would grow up, didn't you?"

A faint voice, far below this crisp sensible sermonizing, murmured, "We all know about death, don't we? But isn't it sorrow, sorrow, sorrow we feel as we stand beside a grave? And sorrow hurts."

The moralizer, somewhat shaken, granted the point hastily, "Well, leave that, then—and consider how ridiculous it is for you to feel yourself *lonely!* On a globe with millions of other human beings? It's sickeningly sentimental to limit your interests to your children. How about international affairs? And the tariff? And the Supreme Court's decisions?"

The plain elderly home-maker paring two potatoes for herself only laughed a little at this, very sadly. As well ask an old plow-horse to run races.

The moralizer gave this up, too, but pointed out, "If such things are too far away for you to grasp, how about things right around you that you *can* understand—the Sewing Society, the Reading Club, the radio, the public library, the Village Improvement Society—"

She laid down her small pared potatoes to think. Perhaps she could get somewhere with thinking, now that she was honest at last, now that she had given up the grinning falseness of the pretense that—because she should not—she did not suffer. *Why* did she suffer? Let her be honest for herself as well as for the children. Was it only, as this smug censor would have her think, because she was mean, selfish and small-souled, and felt aggrieved because she was no longer the center of her stage? "But—isn't it a shock, usually a fatal shock, to transplant an old, deep-rooted tree? And was I not deep-rooted in usefulness and now wrenched away from it, all those living fibers that brought life to me torn loose, withering and drying up? Can the few small roots that have not been cut—those dry little Reading Club and Improvement Society roots—can they keep *me* alive who drew life abundant from a thousand others? And is not dying painful? Those roots that are left to me, they should be stronger, do you say? I should have given more of myself to them when I was younger, should I? But, see here—I don't complain of this, or glory in it, I state the fact—if I had not given all of myself to learn the art I had to practice, I would have failed. All of myself was not too much to learn how to give my children what they needed. Everybody knows that he who practices an art must give it all he has, or fail.

"Suppose you said to a painter of sixty—my age—who had given all his life to his lovely, living, rewarding art, 'Lay down your brushes now. You've finished your pictures. You'll only spoil them if you go on fussing with them. And don't be so unreasonable and self-centered as to feel sad about this. If you still want to do something, can't you learn how to put on wall-paper instead? Or to make patch-work quilts? That's good, useful, needed work.' "

She put her two potatoes into the little saucepan of water, wiped her hands and looked at the solemn clock, slowly ticking away long minutes that had so raced and tripped and danced and played.

"I'd better go and do some Spanish," she thought. Remembering how depressing she had found her mother's empty sixties, she had invented for the children a great desire on her part to study Spanish. She had always wanted to know that language, she told them (as well Spanish as anything), and it was going to be fun to have plenty of time for it. Plenty of time! What a relief her device had given them—poor dear children, as transparent as glass to her eyes, which had so long watched them close to see what they meant and wanted under what they said. They had straightway bought her one of these phonograph language systems, setting it up as a screen to hide their mother's loneliness. So every day she put on a record and, because she must have something convincing to show them when they dropped in to see if she was *really* all right, she grimly learned lists of words she cared nothing about—*cuchara, ferrocarril*—listening to a man's voice mouthing out the vowels in an affected foreign way she could never bring herself to imitate.

She got out her lesson-book now, found the page, put on the record that went with it, dropped the needle on the whirling disk. A deep, unctuous, Latin voice asked loudly, slowly, PORQUE—DESEAN—USTEDES—something or other. She did not hear him. She had wrestled with herself up and down the world till she was worn out. Her book fell shut. The unheard record ground its way to the end and clicked itself silent. She did not hear it. She had her children with her at last.

Not just those four who had relentlessly grown up and left her—all of her children, the scores and hundreds who had filled her past with glory. Since she could have only their ghosts, she would at least have all of those. In the wide spaciousness of her memories there was room for them as they had looked at all ages, in all moods and humors—as fat babies kicking chubby feet before the fire, as tall adolescents troubled about their algebra marks, as blossoming girls in party dresses, as sick little boys hollow-eyed and feverish with colds, as rough, hard, vital little boys with dirt behind their ears no matter how she washed, as sweet safe little girls playing with dolls, as beautiful sixteen-year-olds, haggard and luminous with the first intimations of love, as naughty passionate little torments who quarreled with each other, as golden-good Sunday-morning children with bright brushed hair and improbably clean hands.

How they romped and played around her now, the ghosts of her little girls and boys who had been so living and were now dead. An immaterial game of blind-man's buff pounced and shrank back and giggled behind her, noisy tag was being played up and down the front porch—listening, she could even hear the echo of past laughter and shouts—and Bobby, darling little Bobby at six, leaned against her knee, watching a funny finger-play he loved. She ended it in the consecrated way—"And so I've got to give—you—a *hug*—" and Bobby drew back, startled, enchanted, his blue eyes shining, his rosy laughing mouth wide open over the adorable two-toothed gap in his front teeth. "Do it again!" he begged her.

But what was that? All the fibers in her body trained to incessant watchful listening, quivered at the sound of a child's weeping. That was Charlie—it must be Charlie—he was not here in the room with her. It was outside he had been playing, and he had hurt himself. She sprang up and—confused, only half awake—walked quickly, a little unsteady on her feet, out to the front walk, looking around her for Charlie.

There he lay, at the front gate, flat on the ground, crying. He had tripped and fallen again. He was always stumbling over his feet, Charlie was. As she hurried towards him, she began the mother-planning for strengthening weak points— she must see that he had more practice in balancing himself —a scooter—little stilts—dancing-lessons. His crying grew louder. He must really have hurt himself. *Suppose this time, he had broken a bone.* She began to run towards the gate.

But of course before she had taken three steps she was quite awake, and knew that the little boy who lay there, crying, could not be her Charlie, Charlie at the moment probably leaning over a microscope in a laboratory. She came to a halt. In an involuntary reflex of reaction she even took a step backward. It was nothing. Just a child who'd skinned his knee. All her flooding anxiety about the possibly broken bone ebbed away to flatness.

But somewhere in that flatness it met a small little shame, very weak and of no importance, but still with strength enough to lift its head and suggest in a thin voice, "Well, really—! Just because it's not *your* child who's hurt—!"

So she walked on to the front gate, a spare, gray-haired, old lady with spectacles. There were two children. Very unattractive, inferior children. She knew them by sight and reputation, though not by name. The worthless bum's family, who'd moved into the old shack at the end of Landon Road, a mile or more away. People said the father was an ex-jailbird. People said the mother was a lazy slattern. People said the children were probably light-fingered. People said that doors would have to be locked from now on.

"Well, did you hurt yourself?" she asked the little boy, sprawling in the dust. It was just the stupid phrase and dry,

162

loveless intonation she had always despised childless people
for using. But was she not a childless woman now?

She stooped over to pick him up. But at the sound of her
voice, he had stopped crying, scrambled up, and, sheering
away from her offered hand, ran behind his sister's skimpy
ragged skirts, clutching them hard in grimy fingers. There
was some blood on the stones where he had fallen. Mrs.
Barney's lips tightened. Children did not run away from her
when she held out her hand. The other child, patting the
little boy's head, said in hasty excuse, "He's turrible scared
of strangers." Through her glasses, Mrs. Barney looked at
the little girl. About nine, probably. Thin. Unkempt. Dirty.
Eczema. Good eyes.

"Well, he must have skinned his knee anyhow," said Mrs.
Barney, pointing to the blood. With another involuntary
reflex, this time to skinned knees, she said, "You'd better
bring him in and let me fix it up. You're too far from home
for him to go on without having it taken care of." In her
matter-of-fact voice—she heard it there as fresh as though it
had not lain unused for years—was the not-to-be-mistaken,
not-to-be-questioned intonation of mother-authority. The
dirty, uncombed little girl heard it too. She looked disturbed
and hung down her head, but pulling the younger child after
her, she followed along the neat walk, up on the nicely
painted little front porch, through the snug living-room with
its fresh cretonnes, through the small sunny dining-room
with the well-polished old cherry table and chairs, on into
the kitchen. Absently scratching an eczema scab, she looked
around her with dazzled eyes. Could this be a *kitchen!*

The old lady who had made them come in was stepping around, getting together a lot of clean pans and cloths and bottles and cotton and scissors—for a skinned knee!

"Now come here—what's your name?" she said now, holding out a hand to him again.

But the little boy clung tightly to his sister, hiding his face in her faded cotton skirt.

"His name is Eddie," said the older child. She undid his fingers, telling him—the not-to-be-questioned mother-authority was in her voice too, Mrs. Barney heard it there—"Go along, Eddie, let the lady fix your knee."

The child submitted, let himself be lifted up on the strange lap. (Good heavens! He weighed nothing. Why, his very bones should be heavier than that!) When the warm water began to trickle over the wound, he clenched his little hands to fists, but he did not cry.

"I'll say 'ouch!' for you, if it hurts *too* much," said the old lady. "It's pretty hard to expect a person to feel it hurt and have to remember to say the ouches, too." But he did not smile. So she turned seriously to the older sister, "See, this is the way you do it—and what is *your* name?"

"Tulane."

"Oh— Well, you see, what you always want to do with a cut is to wash it out without getting any *more* dirt in it. So you let the water flow over it like this. And then you take a swab of cotton and get it good and wet, and do this—and when it's all clean—"

The little girl listened and watched to the end of the operation. When the bandage was in place, startlingly white

164

against the roughened, dark skin, she said painfully, "Mom tries to keep us clean. But she has to bring the water in a pail from the river. There ain't always such a whole lot left. And the kids hate to wash."

Not having put her criticism into audible words, Mrs. Barney now took it back in the same way, silently, with an inward apology. Aloud she said, putting the little boy down, "Well, how'd you and Eddie like to wash up a little now, and have some cookies."

A desperate greediness flashed into Tulane's face. She looked up, speechless. But Eddie only shuffled his feet and drooped his head till she could see only a frowzy tangle of sun-bleached hair. "*I've* got something that'll make Eddie like to wash his hands," said Mrs. Barney, with confidence. She led them into her bathroom—her second bathroom—ran the basin full of warm water and put the soap frog into Eddie's hands. Tulane knew the old lady wanted them to think this funny. So she laughed, and said, "See, Eddie—it's a frog—ain't it comic?" But he did not smile, not even when wet and slippery it leaped in great hops back into the water every time he tried to hold it. His face cleared a little, he washed himself industriously, he did not object but shut his eyes tight in silent endurance when Mrs. Barney took a few layers from his face with a washcloth, but he did not smile.

"He's awful scared of strangers," Tulane said again. She looked around her, a little afraid herself of all these shining wonders. "What's that?" she whispered.

"What?"

She pointed to the bathtub.

Mrs. Barney looked at her in silence for an instant, steadying her voice against a tendency to tremble. Then she explained, "That's where *I* get clean." She thought, "And I have two!" and heard herself go on, "How'd you like to come and take a soap-swim in it some day?"

The little girl asked instantly, "Could Eddie?"

Mrs. Barney swallowed. "Yes, Eddie too. Now let's get some cookies."

She poured them each some milk and made them sit down. She gave Eddie his in the silver cup. Tulane anxiously tried to hold it for him to make sure he did not drop it. "Oh, it won't do any harm if he does. My first baby learned to drink out of that cup. And when he'd finished, he used to throw it right across the kitchen!" Their gravity but deepened. So she went on to serious talk, she and Tulane, of family matters. There were nine of them, she learned, the eldest eleven years old. Amyann her name was, she took care of Martha 'n' Henry who were just eggsactly the same age— no, not twins—"and I look out for Eddie, sort of." That left only the four littlest ones for the mother. "But there's another baby coming before long, Mom says."

Mrs. Barney looked blank, tried to think, changed the subject. Now that Eddie was partially clean, he was visibly very blond, with a fair skin, tow-white hair and blue eyes— at least she thought they must be blue, he had not once looked up. But Tulane's straggling elf-locks were nearly black. "Your little brother doesn't look much like you. Is it your mother or your father who is blond?"

A conscious, uneasy look came into the little girl's eyes. She said nothing, crumbling her cookie nervously instead of eating it. Mrs. Barney backed away hastily, thinking of promiscuity, illegitimacy, unknown fathers and other things that slip quickly into the minds of clean and safe people when thinking of those who live in shacks. She went into the pantry to get them some more milk, and turning around, was a little startled to see that Tulane followed. The child beckoned her to stoop and when she had her lips close to the other's ear, whispered, "Eddie ain't no kin to us at all. Him and Martha and the baby belong to a woman that moved next door to us before we had to leave South Lynnfield and she died and their father run away and Mom took the kids. But she don't want for them to know they don't belong to us."

Mrs. Barney straightened herself, shifted the milk bottle into the other hand and blew her nose. "That was very kind of your mother," she said.

"She had to. There wa'n't anybody else to," explained the child.

"I see," said Mrs. Barney.

The small boy was still eating, eating—starting on his sixth, or was it his eighth, cookie. But his pale peaked face, with the dark rings under the down-dropped eyelids, was guarded and closed. "We'll just see, young man, whether you've got a smile in you or not," Mrs. Barney challenged him inwardly. Aloud she asked, "Do you know the song about the frog who would a-wooing go?"

Still gulping down great swallows of milk and cookies, he shook his head. So she sang it to him, all the endless

167

stanzas. At the end Tulane said eagerly, "Oh, I *wish't* I could sing that one! I betcha Martha 'n' Henry would like it."

"Well, I could teach it to you some day," said Mrs. Barney. Eddie had eaten his fill now, and sat, his head turned away, secretively picking his nose. Tulane flew at him and snatched his hand down. "He ain't but four and a half," she apologized for him. He slipped from his chair and scuttled to lean against her again, his face in her skirt.

Mrs. Barney's spirit was up—"I never saw the child yet I couldn't get a laugh out of!"—she tied a knot in a corner of her handkerchief, slipped her forefinger into the knot and draped the rest of the white stuff about her hand. "Did you ever see the Hanky-Magician, Vizier?" she asked, laying her forearm on the table, her draped hand up-reared, the knot like a turban on the forefinger's nodding head. She began to chant rhythmically, swaying her hand so that the draperies rose and fell with a toy dignity, "His full name is the Grand Vizier of the Sultan's Golden Court, and he has shoed on his overputs, sade himself some mandwiches, thrilled a fermos cottle with bot hoffee and cugar and scream, and come all the way from the land of Xylophone Cakes and Bay-Rum Trees across the sea of Molasses and Ink, straight to our own dear You-*neye*-bed-Statia-Melicum—and *what* has he come for? To march right up to Eddie—" she began to walk the little figure, ludicrously stately in its trailing draperies, across the table—"to ask him—[in a deep voice]—'*Are*—you—a—good—boy?' " She paused, cocking the little turbaned head to one side and the other in listening poses, and then, leaping it into the air, "Oh, goody! Goody! *Goody!* He *is* a good boy. And so I've simply got to—give—him—a —*hug.*" With a whistling canary-bird twitter of excitement she darted the Vizier up towards the child's face, fluttering its skirts in the air.

The little boy broke into a startled giggle. He raised enchanted blue eyes to hers. His mouth was wide open in a laugh. *"Do* it again!" he begged her. Two of his front teeth were missing.

And he was alive.

SECTION THREE

The Cage

THE TWO little sisters had carried the canaries in their cage out on the balcony. "It's such a lovely day," said the younger. "They'll love the sun and the fresh air."

"But won't it make them feel worse about having to live in a cage?" wondered the older child, anxiously bending over the two chirping yellow birds, flirting their tiny wings and tails and hopping from perch to perch, excited by the breeze which came eddying over the roofs of the city.

"Why, they *love* their cage," said the younger. "Just see how nice it is. They have verything in it! Their darling little bathtub, and their nice clean grains any time they are hungry, and low perches and high perches, and us to take care of them, and even that sweet little swing that Father brought for them. What more could they want?"

The older child did not answer. While her little sister brought fresh water for the birds, and gave the cage its daily cleaning, she leaned against the iron railing of the balcony, looking through the curves of its ironwork, far off, away over the roofs. Her eyes were wide and soft. The spring air lifted the curls from her forehead and blew across her cheek. She was looking so far away that (until the other child murmured, "Oh, look!") she did not see a little brown bird, who

173

had flown over the roofs to them and was now perching on the railing at the other end of the balcony.

"Sh-h-h!" said the younger child. The two little girls stood motionless, their eyes fixed on the visitor. He kept his eyes fixed on them too, but he was not silent nor motionless. He chirped volubly, tilted his tail in a quick, irregular rhythm, and skipped on his slim, twig-like legs forward and back on the railing.

"He *likes* us! He's trying to talk to us," said the younger child.

The older one murmured, "He's asking us ugly giants please to go away."

"Oh, you always think something like that," said the younger. But she followed her sister into their room, where they shut the window and, hiding themselves behind the curtain, peeped out to see what the new bird would do.

As they moved, he had flown away with a nervous flutter of wings, but the moment the window closed he came back to the railing, his eyes shining, his tail jerking, his tiny ardent body panting and quivering. He was looking at the birds in the cage.

"He's so sorry for them!" said the older child.

"He wishes he had as much to eat as they," said the younger.

The bird now flew to the floor of the balcony and hopped around and around the cage, cocking his head to one side, ruffling his feathers, incessantly chattering. The birds in the cage paid no attention to him, continuing sagely their usual occupations, hopping up on one perch and down on another, swinging in their little mechanical swing, occasionally cracking a grain in their beaks and eating the kernel with relish.

The children's old nurse stepped into the room now, and the little girls beckoned her to come. She looked, nodded her head wisely, and said, "He wants to get in the cage and live with them."

The older child flung up her head passionately. "Oh, no, *no!* How *can* you say such a thing!"

She spoke so loudly that the little bird was frightened, spread his wings in a panic and flew away over the roofs.

"There!" said the younger child reproachfully. "You've scared him away. You never think what you're doing."

"He'll come back," said the old woman.

"No, he won't!" said the older child. "No, he won't! Never!"

"We'll see," said the nurse, who did not care in the least whether he did or not.

He came back the next day, and the next and the next, flying free-winged over the roofs, through the wide sky, through the spring sunshine, and folded his wings to hop, chirping and voluble, around and around the cage in which the two tame birds cracked their grains, sipped their water out of their little crockery dish, and swung complacently in their little swing.

The children's father, who was a scientist, hearing talk of what was happening, came one day to peep out of the window to see for himself. For he had not believed in the least what the children and the old woman told him. He never

believed what children and women said. He had told them,
"Oh, no, you must be mistaken. The two tame birds are
both males. The only thing that could attract a wild bird
would be a female." But as he looked out from behind the
curtains, he saw just what they had described, and for an
instant he was at a loss.

His older daughter looked up intently, anxiously into his
face. "Mélanie thinks he wants to get into the cage and live
with them. He couldn't want to do that, could he, Father?
Not a *bird!*"

The father considered the matter. "Perhaps he's a tame
bird, who has flown away from his own cage and can't find
his way back."

The older child was even more distressed. "Oh, no, no!
That would be worse yet! If he'd been in a cage, and knew
what a cage was like, he couldn't want to get into another,
once he was free!"

"Yes, he could too," said the younger. "He'd remember
how comfortable he'd been."

"Father!" appealed the older child.

"Father!" cried the younger.

Their father said, scientifically, "Good gracious, children,
don't go trying to settle fact by an appeal to authority. I
don't know any more about it than you. The only way to
get at facts is by experimenting."

The little girls looked blank.

"It's easy. Leave the door of the cage open and see whether
he goes in or stays out."

"Yes, yes," cried the younger, clapping her hands.

176

The face of the older brightened. She was sure that if the door were opened, the two imprisoned birds would fly away and be free.

They waited till the next day. Mélanie arranged a string to the cage door from inside their room, and as the little visitor went skipping and fluttering about on the floor of the balcony she chose a moment when he was close to the door and, pulling on the string, quickly and noiselessly lifted up the little gate.

The pulses of the older child beat so violently that she pressed her two hands on her heart. A mist came before her eyes. When it cleared away, she saw that the little free bird had hopped inside the cage and was bobbing his pretty head up and down over the grain dish. As she looked, he said, "*Queet! queet!*" in his sweet, shrill voice, and springing happily up on a perch, began to preen his feathers.

The father laughed. "That settles it." The nurse gently let down the door of the cage. The lunch bell rang and they all went off to the dining-room.

That night, long after the little girls had gone to bed, the nurse thought she heard one of them cough, and taking a candle in her hand, stepped into their bedroom. The younger child lay asleep, her rosy face calm, her long eyelashes sweeping her rounded cheek. The older child, surprised by the light, flung up one arm to hide her face; but not before the nurse had seen her cheeks flushed and glazed with tears.

"Why, dearie!" she cried, running to the child's bed. "Darling lamb! Are you sick? Where does it hurt you?"

She put her loving arms about the child and laid the hot wet cheek on her soft old breast, trying to understand what it was that the little girl was saying so desperately. She could only catch a few disconnected words . . . "the bird . . . the cage. . . ."

"But, dear heart," she said reasonably, "the little birdie wanted to go into the cage. And he's perfectly happy there. You should have seen how nicely he went to sleep, sitting on his smooth round perch, beside the others, so trusting. Tucking his little head under his wing without a fear. He *wanted* to live in the cage."

The child stopped sobbing and pulled away from the loving arms. She said sternly, "It's . . . it's his *wanting* to . . ."

She looked at her nurse's face, shook her head, and laying herself down again on her little bed, she turned her face to the wall in silence.

The Murder on Jefferson Street

WITH its low, bungalow-style, stucco cottages, and its few high, old-fashioned, clapboarded houses, Jefferson Street looked like any side street in the less expensive part of any American large-town, small-city. And it was like any one of them. Like all collections of human habitations everywhere, its roofs sheltered complex and unstable beings, perilously feeling their way, step by step, along the knife-edge narrow path of equilibrium that winds across the morasses and clings to the precipitous cliffs of life.

Mrs. Benson, the slender, middle-aged, well-bred widow who had moved to Jefferson Street because it was cheap, was the only one of them—as yet—whose foot had slipped too far from that path for recovery. With her every breath since her husband's death, she had slid down towards that gray limbo of indifference in which all things look alike. She was lost and she knew it; but as she fell, she grasped at anything that could hold her for a little longer; till her daughter grew up. At fourteen, Helen, plain, virtuous, intelligent, charmless, needed all the help she could get, if she were to have even a small share of the world's satisfactions.

Although Mrs. Benson went through the normal maneuvers of life, speaking, smiling, asking and answering questions, her secret aloofness from what other people prized was, of course, obscurely felt by the people around her. It was both felt and feared by the Warders, who were her next-door neighbors. It was one of the many things that made them feel insecure in Jefferson Street life. They felt everything, feared everything, started back at the snapping of a twig, all their senses strained like those of nervous explorers cautiously advancing, hand on cocked trigger, into an unknown jungle. For they were undertaking a hazardous feat compared to which hunting big game or living among hostile savages is sport for children. They were moving from one social class to the one above it.

Their family (as far as Jefferson Street knew it) was made up of Bert Warder, his wife, their daughter Imogene and a brother Don, employed in a bank in Huntsville. But this presentable floe, visible above the white-collar surface was the smallest part of the tribe. Below it was a great substructure, sunk deep in the ocean of manual work—overalled uncles who were factory-hands, drab, stringy-necked aunts who "worked out," brothers who were garage mechanics, sisters who sold over the counters of ten-cent stores. Only Bert and his bank-clerk brother Don sat at desks with pens in their hands. Bert, like most of the men who lived on Jefferson Street, was an employee of the great Stott McDevitt Electric Company. His desk there felt to him like a pedestal. His bungalow-home was another. To the occasional Packard car which, trying to locate a dressmaker or a trained nurse, sometimes purred into it and rolled noiselessly out, Jefferson Street looked plebeian and small-employee-ish enough. For Bert Warder and his wife, brought up in tenement houses in

180

a black brutally industrial city, Jefferson Street was patrician
with its small lawns, its shade trees, its occasional flowerbeds,
above all, its leisure-class tennis courts on the two vacant lots
at the end. They could hardly believe that Bert's night-
school-educated brains had lifted them to such a height. The
watchful tips of their antennae soon told them that in the
class into which they were transferring themselves it was
considered no notable feat to live in a home with a yard, so
they took care to speak of the street as other people did, with
amused condescension for its humbleness; but in reality they
all three worshiped it, admired, feared and tried to imitate its
inhabitants, lived in dread that something from their past
might cast them out from it, and did what we all do, passionately collected their neighbors' weak points as potential
ammunition with which to resist attacks on their own. They
would have fought to the death against a threat to their social
standing on the street—as indeed they did, quite literally,
when they felt themselves so threatened.

Tautly on the lookout as they were, they naturally felt
that Mrs. Benson's pre-occupied good manners might be intended as a reflection on their own, and suspected that the
Tuttles (neighbors on the other side) looked down on them
and on Jefferson Street. There was nothing definite in Francis
and Mary Tuttle around which this suspicion could crystal-
lize. It was everything. In their every contact with the
Tuttles, the Warders uneasily felt the need to make an effort
towards more ease, pleasantness, reticence and quietness than
was natural to them. It was fatiguing. And they were never
sure they had quite caught the new tune.

Yet, as a matter of fact, the Tuttles did not look down on Jefferson Street but were as glad to live there as the Warders. And, exactly like the Warders, had escaped to it from a life they shuddered to look back on. It was true, as Bert Warder's quiveringly suspicious nose for class differences told him, that both Francis and Mary his wife had been brought up in a house grander than any Bert had ever set foot in, and that Francis' youth (which he mentioned as little as Bert mentioned his) had been spent not with hired girls and factory hands but with Senators and Bank Presidents. But his past had something else in it—misery and failure, and a period of total black eclipse such as the vigorous Bert had never dreamed of. Francis thought of his past as seldom as possible. Till Mary had dragged him up out of the morass of self-contempt in which he lay, already half drowned, and set his feet beside hers on the knife-edge narrow path of equilibrium, he had taken for granted that his failure in life was inevitable, was because he was an all-around misfit. Living with her, he had begun to hope that perhaps it was only his family he did not fit. He said—he thought—"family." What he meant was "brother." Away from Roger there might be a place for him in the world, after all, he began to hope.

When Mary thought of that past, as wretched for her as for Francis, it was to Francis' mother not his brother, she cried, "Shame on you! Shame!" His mother had long been dead but no tombstone could hide her from Mary's wrath. In the old bad days when both sons were little boys, and the mother's favoritism was at its maddest worst, people used to say, if they noticed Francis at all, "It's hard on an ordi-

nary boy, and rather a weakling at that, to have such a successful older brother. Doesn't give him a chance, really."
But Mary knew that Roger was not the one to blame for the
tragedy of their relation. She had thought him stub-fingered
and tiresome, the sort of successful person who bores sensitive
and intelligent ones; but living as she did—mouselike invisible poor relative—close to both of them, she had always
known that Roger felt wistful and clumsy beside Francis'
accurate rightness of taste, and that he had even a dim divination of Francis' exquisite undeveloped gift. No, part of Roger's exasperating rightness was that he had never accepted his
mother's over-valuation. The older brother had steadily tried
to be friendly; but Francis' mother had early conditioned the
younger to see in any friendliness from anyone only a contemptuous pity for his own ineptitude. "You, *you!*" cried
Mary ragingly to the woman in her grave. "Before your little
poet-son could walk alone, you had shut him into the black
vault with your stupid admiration of Roger's commonplace
successes, your stupid notion that Francis' fineness was weakness. And every year you added another padlock to the door.
What strange hateful mania possessed you, you wicked
woman, with your mean perverted bullying . . ." Whenever
another bitter adjective came into her mind she said all this
and more to Francis' dead mother, ending triumphantly, "But
I know what he is and I've always known—a poet, a spirit
so fine and true that just to breathe the air with him lifts an
ordinary human being to nobility! I, the little poor young
cousin-drudge you never noticed, I married a broken man,
and he's a whole man now—or will be soon. I've given him

children who adore him, *who depend on him!* And I depend on him. He earns their living and mine. He's escaped from the role of defeated weakling you bullied him into. He creates happiness and knows it! He's coming to life. And every day I bury *you* a little deeper, thank God!"

Never a word of this did she say to Francis. He did not recognize personal resentment as one of the permissible elements in life. Not in his life. It belonged in a lower, meaner world than his. Mary had climbed through the keyhole of his vault, had triumphantly thrown open the door and led him out to happiness, without letting him hear a single reproach to his mother or brother at which his magnanimity could take fright. She knew magnanimity to be the air he must breathe or die. It was part of what she adored in him, part of what she loved in the world he shared with her. But she did not practice it in her own thoughts. Francis, she knew, would have cut his hand off before he would have admitted even to himself that the smallest part of his passionate delight in the twins came from the knowledge that Roger's brilliant marriage was childless, and that he had—at last—something that Roger envied. She felt no such scruples. Hugging her babies to her, she often reveled, unabashed, in happy savagery, "You dumb conspicuous go-getter, you haven't anything like *this* in your expensive empty house!" Sometimes in reaction from the loftiness of Francis' ideals she thought, "Why can't he *be* unfair like anybody, and hate Roger, even if Roger's not to blame? It's nature. Who but Francis could feel guilty—not over *being* unfair, but over the mere temptation to be not angelically just? It'd do him good to let himself go."

But she did not believe this. "He couldn't let himself go into unfairness like just anybody," she thought, "for he's not just anybody. He's a poet with a poet's fineness of fiber. And about the only civilized being on the globe."

So there was Jefferson Street: its low bungalows, its awkward high older houses with their jigsaw ornamentation, filled with people who day by day set one foot before the other along the knife-edge narrow path that ran—for the Warders across a treacherous black bog, for the Tuttles along the face of a cliff with crashing breakers below, for the others here and there, high and low, as Fate decreed. Nothing happened. Mrs. Benson was the only one who had lost the path. And she sank but slowly towards her final fall. Three years went by. Her daughter was a Senior, getting high marks; unnoticed by the boys. Bert Warder had held his job, not yet realizing that he would never do more than hold it, would never get any higher; only beginning to feel aggrieved because other men were stepped up over his head. He had also, with what sweating pains and secret study nobody would know, learned to play tennis without betraying that he had never before held a racket in his hand. Imogene Warder had passed her examinations—well, nearly all—and was, with some conditions, a Senior in the high school, intensively noticed by a certain kind of boy. Francis Tuttle had not only held his job and had had two raises in salary, but had learned to grow roses. His June garden now made him catch his breath. And he had written a little shy and beautiful poetry. Poetry not verse. "Give me three years more," cried Mary his wife to Fate. "Give me only *two* more, and he'll be safe." The exquisite happiness Francis gave her and gave their children even softened her heart towards his mother. Once she thought—just once!—"Why, perhaps she was a victim too. Someone may have hurt her in childhood as she hurt Francis, hurt her desperately, so that her will to live was all warped into the impulse to hurt back."

Yes, just once, Mary had a moment of divination and guessed that the will to hurt comes by subterranean ways from pain and fear not from malignancy.

It was but a flash. A partial guess, so weak and new-born a beginning of understanding that it had no more than an instant's universal life before Mary, frightened by a glimpse at the vicious circle of the human generations, seized it and made it personal, "Oh, yes—horrors!—of course, if Francis were still sick with that self-hating Roger-obsession, he couldn't help making the children wretched with it, one way or another. And when they grew up, they would pass it on to their children. . . ."

She looked across the room at Francis and the twins, wrestling together on the couch, wildly, happily, breathlessly laughing, and thought contentedly, "Well, there's *one* misery that won't be handed on. His hurt is all but healed."

Leaning on her sword she stood, negligently smiling, at the gate of the garden where Francis grew poetry and roses, from which she had walled his demon out.

186

II

And then, one day four years after the Warders had moved to Jefferson Street, Fate, unheeding Mary's appeal for only a little longer respite, rode in on the bicycle of the evening newspaper boy, flinging up on each front porch the usual hard-twisted roll of trivial and ugly news. But this time, among the ugly items was a headlined statement about the arrest of one Donald Warder in Huntsville. He had been stealing from the bank he worked for, it seemed; had been playing the races; spending money on fancy women; he would probably get a long term in the penitentiary.

When Bert Warder walked across his front porch on his way home from the office that April afternoon, he was wondering resentfully why dumb-bells like Frankie Tuttle got one raise after another, while he with three times Frankie's pep just barely held his own, with frequent callings-down. "But I can beat hell out of him at tennis, anyhow." He applied his tried-and-true old remedy to his soreness and felt the pain abating. The evening paper was still lying in front of the screen door. He stopped, picked it up, glanced at the headlines.

Although the news took him so by surprise as to leave him stunned, his body acted as bodies do when left to themselves, in obedience to the nature of the soul dwelling in them. He rushed into the house, shut the front door, locked it and jerked down the shades of the front windows. His wife and daughter stared at him, surprised. "Look here! Look here!" he said in a strangled voice, and beckoned them to read the headlines.

They read the news together, dropped the paper, looked at each other in despair. The same thought was in them all— if only they need never open that door, if only they could leave town that night, never again be seen by anybody on Jefferson Street. For they knew that as they stood there, all their neighbors up and down the street were opening screen doors, taking in the paper. And, knowing what their own exclamations would have been, had those headlines referred to someone's else brother, they cowered before the gloating, zestful comments they could almost literally hear, "Say, that must be Bert Warder's brother, Don. What-do-you-know-about-that? Well, *well*—maybe we'll have a little less kidding from Bert about our Harvey's being suspended from high school." "Why, look here, I see in the paper where Bert Warder's brother is jailed for stealing. What kind of low-down folks are they anyhow? And Bert so high and mighty about your mother's being divorced."

Imogene drowned out the twanging of these poisoned arrows by a sudden outcry, "I can't *ever* go back to school. Those mean kids'll just razz me to death. Helen Benson's so jealous of me about the boys, she'll be tickled pink to have something terrible like this on me. Oh, I think Uncle Don ought to be *shot!*"

Her father and mother too had been thinking that Don deserved to be shot for wrecking their lives. For of course they could not run away from this disgrace. Of course they must, and the very next morning, appear before their neighbors with a break in their armor far worse than anybody's. Harvey Starr's suspension from high school, Joe Crosby's not getting his raise, Mary Seabury's divorced mother, Frankie Tuttle's weak tennis, Helen Benson's unattractiveness to boys —they had been held up by the Warders as shields against possible criticism of slips in their manners. But against the positive disgrace of a brother in the penitentiary! And of course, now everybody would find out about their folks— the aunt who was somebody's hired girl, the old grandmother who couldn't write her name. All that would be in the newspapers, now. "If I had Don Warder here, I'd . . ." thought his sister-in-law vindictively. But Don of course was in jail. "Safe in jail!" thought his brother bitterly. *"He* won't have to walk into an office tomorrow morning, and all the mornings, and face a bunch of guys that'll . . ." Like his wife, his mind was full of foreseen descriptions by newspaper reporters of his illiterate tenement-house relatives. He held the newspaper up to go on reading it. It rattled in his shaking hands. Imogene flung herself on her mother's shoulder, sobbing, "Mamma, you *got* to send me to boarding school. Every kid in school will be picking on me."

Behind the newspaper her father gave a choked roar of rage. Lowering the sheet, he showed a congested face. His jaws were set. "Boarding school! More likely you'll have to get out of high school and go to work." They looked at him, too stunned to ask what he meant. Still speaking between clenched teeth he told them, "Our savings were in Don's bank and I see in the paper here where it says the bank's on the rocks because of the money he stole."

With a wringing motion of his hands as if they had a neck between them, he crushed the paper, flung it to the floor, and turned on his weeping wife and daughter as if he would like to wring their necks too. "What's the good of standing there hollering?" he shouted at them. "Haven't you got any guts? Don't take it lying down like that! Stand up to them! Get back at them before they begin!"

He tramped into the next room and they heard him locking doors and windows.

It was true, just as the Warders thought, that the neighbors began to talk about them as soon as the headlines were read. Helen Benson had taken her mother over to the Tuttles' garden to look at the newly opened tulips. Mrs. Tuttle, newspaper in hand, came out of their shabby tall old house, read out the news to them and they all said how hard it was on the Warders. "Oh, I bet there's some mistake," said Francis Tuttle. "The paper just says he's accused of it. There's no proof he's done it, you notice. I remember Don Warder very well, the time he came to visit Bert last summer. He's not that kind at all. I bet when they get to the bottom of it that they'll find somebody's double-crossed him. Maybe one of the other men in the bank. I'm going to tell Bert Warder I bet that's what happened, the first time I see him." Thinking intently of the accused man's probable innocence, he was absent-mindedly fingering his sandy hair which, he had noticed for the first time that morning, had begun to thin a little.

Mrs. Benson said, "It'll be a terrible blow to the Warders.

We must be sure to show our sympathy for them. Helen, it'd be nice if you could think of something specially nice to do for Imogene." She had by now slipped so far from the narrow path trod by those who still cared what happened, that this like all news was no more than a murmur in her ears. But, that Helen might learn what is correct, she brought out the right formula in the right voice.

"Yes, indeed," said Mary Tuttle, in her warm eager way. "People's friends ought to stand close around them when trouble comes."

Mrs. Murray across the street, seeing the four of them standing close together, not looking at the flowers, knew what they were talking about and came over to say compassionately, "I could cry when I think of poor Emma Warder! She'll take this hard."

Helen Benson was awed by her first contact with drama. "My! Imogene must be feeling simply terrible," she said. "I wonder if she wouldn't like to be Vice President of our class. I'd just as soon resign. Mother, how would it be if I went right up now to the Warders and told Imogene . . ."

But Helen's mother said, her sorrow salt in her heart, "No, when people have had a blow it's better to leave them to themselves a little at first. Don't you think so, Mrs. Tuttle?"

Mary, annoyed to see Francis once more passed over as if he were not present, said resolutely in a formula she often used, "Yes, that is what my husband always advises in such cases, and I have great confidence in his judgment."

But Francis had turned away. How like Mary it was to try even in little things to make it up to him for being a nonentity! But sometimes he thought she but pointed out the fact that he was. A little nettled, as any man might be (no, considerably more than a man who had had in his past no nightmare nervous collapse), he walked along in the twilight towards the house. On the other side of Mary's wall his exiled demon kept pace with him, trying hard to reach him with old dark associations of ideas, thinking longingly how easy it would be to tear open that nearly healed wound if only these passing relapses could be prolonged. He succeeded in starting a familiar train of thought in Francis' mind, like a brackish taste in his mouth. "And now to grow bald!" he meditated moodily. "What Bert Warder calls my 'motheaten' look will be complete." His fingers strayed up to his head again to explore the thinning hair. Deep under the healthy scar-tissue forming over his inner wound, an old pulse of pain began to throb. Roger was getting bald too, he remembered, but of course baldness gave Roger dignity and authority, would actually add to his prestige. Francis, bald, would drop to a lower insignificance. "To him that hath, and from him that hath not—the motto of my life," thought Francis. His demon's eyes glittered redly in hope.

But Mary had built her wall high and strong. And inside its safe protection Francis' roses had struck down deep roots. The gardener came to himself with a smile at his absurdity that sent his demon scurrying away into outer darkness.

"Good gosh, only a thin place in my hair, and seeing myself bald a'ready!" he thought, amused. It had been through that mental habit as through a secret back door, he reflected, that many a dose of poison had been smuggled into his life.

He stooped to straighten a drooping tulip. As he stood up, the evening star shone brightly pale in the eastern sky. The inner eye of his intelligence focused itself to a finer accuracy: the world stood before him in its true, reassuring proportions. "Suppose I do get bald—bald as an egg—what of it!" he thought; and, loose, at ease, forgot himself to admire a young pear tree, its myriad swelling buds proclaiming with pride that, mere humble living cellulose that it was, its roots had found the universal source of growth. "And all amid them stood The Tree of Life," thought Francis, his eyes deeply on the miracle.

"Da-d-d-dy," came cautiously from the sleeping porch. The bars of the railing there were high and set close together because of the dangerous three-story drop to the cement-floored basement entrance below, but Francis could make out the twins in their pajamas like little bears in a cage. "How about a sto-o-ory?" they called down.

"With you in a sec," called Francis, running into the house.

The twins rushed out on the landing to meet him, hopping, twittering, and as he snatched them up, planting loud kisses on his cheeks, his ears, his nose. "Praise be to God who gave me life!" sang Francis' heart as he had never dreamed it could. On the swelling tide of this joy, this thankfulness, he rode up with a surge to the highest point—but one—of his long struggle with himself. Quite effortlessly, quite naturally, he thought, "Too bad that Roger's wife can never give him children," and went warm with delight that he had wished his brother well.

III

Francis had meant to tell Bert Warder when he next saw him that he was sure Don had never stolen a cent, that somebody had double-crossed him. But the next time he saw Warder, he did not tell him that or anything else.

The morning after the newspapers had announced the arrest of Bert's brother, Francis stepped out to the border along his front-yard path to get some tulips for Mary to take to Emma Warder, Bert's wife. But there was something so beautiful on the first one he cut that he stood still to look at it, marveling, forgetting the errand his sympathy had sent him on. Dew-drops clung to the flower, every tiny globe a magic mirror reflecting all the visible universe. Francis smiled dreamily down on the extravagance of this beauty. At first he remembered with amusement that he was the man who only last night had thought life hard to bear because his hair was getting thin. Then he forgot himself in contemplation of the divine playfulness that shrinks the great far blueness of the sky, the nearby intricacy of trees, immeasurable space itself, to ornament the white perfection of a flower. The doors of his heart swung softly open, as they do when a poem knocks and asks to be written.

Another door opened, the door of the next house. Through it—because he must—Bert Warder came resolutely out from the safety of his home to face the arena full of enemies waiting to spring upon him. The odds were against him now. He knew that. But he was no coward. He was no man to

194

take things lying down. He was worn with sleeplessness, and half sick with dread of this first impact with a world echoing to his disgrace. But he did not lose his head. He remembered the plan for defense he had worked out in the long dark; he tried to keep clearly in mind the old rule of warfare that the way to head off attack is to attack first. But would he be able to carry out this plan? Cornered by Fate as he was, how could he reach anyone with a first thrust? He had no hope that he could, no hope at all; but he bared his teeth savagely with the desperation of the trapped, and would not give up. The instinct of self-preservation, feeling him appeal as if for his very life, responded with a wild rush of its inordinate stimulants to action. His eyes fell on Frankie Tuttle in the garden next door. He was mooning over a flower he held in one hand, while the other hand in a mechanical gesture drew up the sandy hair over a spot at the top of his head. When a man's hand does that without his realizing it, he fears baldness. The instinct of self-preservation as it can when driven hard by fear, rose to genius, and showed the endangered man how to strike, in all safety, a first blow to ward off the attack he could not parry. He took off his hat, put his hand up to his head and walked rapidly along the sidewalk towards the Avenue, keeping his eyes on Frankie.

When Francis, his heart still unguardedly opened to its very depths by ecstasy, looked up from his tulip, he saw Bert Warder passing by on his way to the trolley, holding his hat in one hand. With the other he was ostentatiously patting and ruffling his abundant dark hair in uncouth caricature of Francis' unconscious fumble. As their eyes met,

Bert let fly his arrow with all his might. His words were but trivial and a little common, but his panic tipped them well with the poison of the wish to hurt, and he put his back into the bending of his bow, his broad beefy back. Long before the meaning of the vapid pleasantry had penetrated to Francis' mind, the malignity of its intention was quivering deep in his opened, softened heart. "That's the way to do it, Frankie!" called Bert in a loud coarse tone, his fingers leaping about grotesquely in his hair. "You've *got* a clearing up there. Scratch 'em up into it where you can get at 'em. Scratch 'em up into the clearing."

For a nightmare second, Francis, like a man who dreams he sees a friend run on him sword in hand, felt not pain so much as a wild incredulity. His eyes widened, his dumbfounded face was blank, his up-raised arm and fumbling fingers froze foolishly where they were. From his confusion a gleam of light shone into the other's darkness. The constriction around Bert's heart loosened. It might really work then, the system of attacking first. He'd sure knocked old Frankie cold, his first try. No man who looked like that, could collect his wits for taunts about jailbird brothers. After the hours of helpless dread that lay back of Bert, his relief was exquisite. And the hope it gave! Hope! He might, after all, be able to defend himself. Drinking in greedily Francis' stunned expression and grotesque attitude, he burst into a yelling haw! haw! of triumph and clutching hope to his breast, ran on courageously to where a fellow-worker stood waiting for the trolley.

By that time the meaning of his words reached Francis' mind. He snatched his hand down from his thinning hair with a betraying jerk. Through the quiet morning air Bert's voice came, loudly repeating his joke to Joe Crosby, who remarked, turning back to look at Francis, "Why, I never noticed he has a bald spot." The trolley roared along the tracks and carried the two men away to the office where Francis was at once to follow them.

By the end of that day everybody over in the Stott Mc-Devitt works and out on Jefferson Street knew that the Warders didn't want to have anything said to them about this trouble. "Some folks take trouble that way," said their neighbors with sympathy.

So, since that was the way the Warders took it, nobody did say anything about it to them. And since it was never mentioned nobody knew exactly what was happening. People naturally took for granted that Bert's first thought had been of his brother's innocence, and that like Joe Crosby at the time of his sister's divorce, he was spending his last cent to pay defending lawyers. Since his face grew steadily more haggardly anxious, they supposed that his efforts were all in vain. They sympathized silently, and read without comment day after day the abbreviated accounts of his brother's trial in the local newspapers.

For they were both brief and colorless. Huntsville was far away in another state; one more revelation of the doings of a dishonest bank employee was hardly news; the reporters apparently found Don too obscure a thief to be interesting. No revelations about a grubby working-class family were ever printed. But the Warders saw in every newspaper mention of Don's trial plenty of other material for malicious satisfaction on the part of their neighbors. When finally Don was found guilty and sentenced to fifteen years in prison Bert Warder said wildly to his wife, "Nobody need tell *me* what they're saying to each other. By God! I'd like to knock the words down their dirty throats."

Drunk first with shame and then with anger—for two weeks after Don's conviction, the bank did fail and the Warders did lose their savings—he had a drunken man's glowering readiness to take offense at nothing. He snarled and hit out in response to harmless greetings; he started every conversation with an unprovoked verbal aggression; he protested every decision made against him at the North Side Tennis Club—as Jefferson Street people called the two vacant-lot courts; he took every happening in the office as flagrant and unfair discrimination against him. His neighbors, his fellow-workers knew that his snarls were cries of pain, and for a time—a short time—said to each other tolerantly, "Poor old Bert, no wonder he's got a grouch." But they had tempers of their own, grievances of their own, their tolerance soon wore thin, his unprovoked attacks began to strike sparks. Two could play as well as one, they reminded him forcibly, at being offensively personal. He was not the only one who knew how to give a nasty dig. Nobody of course dreamed of sinking so low as to throw his brother up to him, Don now in stripes behind prison bars. In fact that story soon passed out of their minds. They had seen Don only once or twice. They were full of their own affairs, their own secret troubles and hidden disgraces. They did not mention the convicted thief, or remember him. But the convict's brother had not forgotten. He imagined in the turn of every exasperated retort a reminder that they had something on him, a threat that he would hear a thing or two about jail-birds if he went too far. So he did not go too far—with them. Every rough rejoinder to a brutal sally from him frightened him into choking down his ill-nature. A sort of approximate balance was found. After a week or so, a Jefferson Street maxim ran, "Anybody can get along with Bert Warder—all you got to do is to tell him to go to hell once in so often."

But there was one among them foolishly unable to return evil for evil. Or to defend himself from boorishness by being boorish. And Bert's first handful of mud had told him where he could fling more without having it flung back on him. Mary, annoyed to have Bert's ragging increasingly center on Francis, used to think, "If Francis only had more vanity! He'd get mad then at teasing instead of feeling ashamed that he's bothered by it; and he'd defend himself." But she was wrong. Against the blackguardism of the wish to cause pain, Francis now as in his youth could devise no defense that he was willing to use. The others on Jefferson Street and in the office snatched up whatever weapon came to hand, dirty or not. If a hit below the belt was what reached Bert's sensibilities most sharply, all right—sure—they'd hit below the belt—why not? But to Francis a choice between committing an ignoble act or suffering from one, was no choice at all. For him only one of those two alternatives was conceivable.

When in an idiotic pleasantry that became threadbare that summer, Bert came suddenly behind him, blew hard on the thinning spot in Francis' hair, rattling off with a noisy laugh, "Let-the-air-*blow*-on-the-head-the-hair-will-*grow*-on-the-head," Francis only jerked away in a gesture of nervous annoyance, and then grinned apologetically for feeling sore. He was incapable of hitting back as the others did, with a jibe about Bert's pendulous paunch, any mention of which, it was an open secret, made him wince, or about his big flat feet, or his bulging eyes, or his occasional bad grammar. He could not understand the idea the men around him had that hurting Bert Warder's feelings eased their own. Rather the contrary, it seemed to him. To find a festering wound in Bert's life and to press on it hard with a word well chosen for its power to cause him pain—how could that do anything but make a bad matter worse? A good deal worse. For Bert's uncouth tormentings caused him only discomfort and annoyance. But it would be shame, as at a real disgrace, which he would feel, to spy upon another's unhealed sores and dash his fist into the one that looked as though it would hurt the most. From his shadowed childhood on, Francis Tuttle had never understood why, with all the unavoidable pain in the world, anyone could wish to add to it.

So he could do no more than try to hide under an apologetic grin the annoyance he could not help feeling when week after week Bert rang the changes about his looking moth-eaten, twitted him with his poor tennis, his mistakes in gardening, his inability to carry a tune. He even managed a grin, though a faint and weary one over a new stunt of Bert's which emerged in June, a strenuous imitation of Francis' tennis serve, winding up with grotesquely strenuous contortions to deliver at the end a ball of a lamentable young-ladyish feebleness.

But it was his watchful demon not he who grinned, when Bert in a chance remark, stumbled on one of the two secrets in Francis' life he was ashamed of. This was the lesser secret, the one he had thought he had quite outgrown. One Saturday afternoon in June, at the end of some doubles, as they were pulling on their sweaters, Bert Warder chanced to comment on the election of his daughter Imogene to be Vice President of her class in the high school— ". . . right over the head of Helen Benson, I understand. She's all right, Helen is, but kind o' slow. No S. A. as the boys say." The other men all knew that Helen had resigned to make place for the Warder girl and had insisted on her election. A self-conscious silence fell on the group. Sensitive to silences as a sick man to draughts, Bert went hot and cold with his usual reflex of panic—were they thinking that because Imogene was a convict's niece—he backed into his corner and bared his teeth.

But Joe Crosby thought of something to turn the conversation. "I never heard that sex appeal is what swings elections," he said.

The casual quality of the remark blew away Bert's suspicion. But his nerves had been shaken. They needed an outlet. A safe one. His eyes fell on Francis Tuttle. "Sure, S. A. is what settles elections!" he cried at random, giving Francis a great dig in the ribs. "That's why our own Valentino gets elected to all the fat offices in town."

Francis was astonished to feel a sharp twinge from old bitterness. He had not then, not even yet, left behind the boyish chagrin over all those elections in school, in college, when Roger again and again had been chosen to any office he would accept, and Roger's dead loss of a brother had never been so much as thought of. It was absurd that he still cared anything about that. But an involuntary quiver had passed over his face, just one. It was enough for his tormentor. "Why for fair, Frankie! There's more truth than poetry in what I say. You never do get elected to anything, do you? Were you *ever?*"

This was the time of course, for Francis to tell him to mind his own damn business. But he could never tell anybody that, and now could think of nothing but a sorry shame that he felt even a last throb of that trivial adolescent hurt. He kept his eyes on the racket he was putting into its case; he fumbled with its fastenings; he was silent. He felt diminished and looked it.

As half-asphyxiated lungs strain joyfully to draw in a life-giving gush of fresh air, Bert felt his own painfully diminished self expanding in the other's discomfort. What suffocating man would hold his hand from the one window he can open? "Poor old Frankie!" he cried gloatingly. "Never had no luck with 'lections. Let's 'lect him to something right now. I nominate him to be Honorary Fly-Swatter to the Ladies' Aid Society. Haw! Haw!"

As they walked down the street together, he composed variations on this new theme. Mary, coming out to meet Francis, heard his horse-laugh, heard him as he turned in at his front walk bawl out, "I nominate Mr. Francis Tuttle to be scorekeeper in the One-legged Men's Athletic Meet. Who will second my motion?"

"What's he talking about?" she asked.

Francis answered, "Oh, nothing."

Sitting that evening over her accounts, Mary chanced to glance up at Francis, reading, and was startled to see an old shadow on his face. He wore the shrunken look that had always frightened her. She had not seen it for a long time now. His relapses in the last years had come seldom and were short; but they still made her almost as miserable as he. Adding up a total and transferring it to the next page she thought, "It is like an old tubercular lesion. Doctors tell you that even when they are healed—or almost—they feel strains that are nothing to normal tissue." Looking down fixedly at her column of figures but not seeing it, she fell for the hundredth time into a puzzled wonder at the inexplicable difference between what people feel about bodily and mental sickness. "If it had been a temporary break-down in a normal lung, acquired in childhood by direct infection from the outside, now almost but not quite healed—why, we'd have told everybody about it, sure of their sympathy. We'd have given it as the natural explanation for the things Francis isn't quite well enough to do yet. There'd have been nothing to hide. Everybody would be interested, and sort of proud and encouraged when Francis recovered. But because it's a temporary breakdown of a personality he's recovering from—and yet that was forced on a sensitive mind by a direct infection from the outside as much as any disease germ!—we have to hide it as though it were a disgrace. He and I can't even talk it over together, and plan what's best to do."

More than by anything else, she was worn by the need to appear unconscious of what was the center of her thoughts. Now, for instance, to be forced to cast about in the dark for a possible explanation of the recurrence on Francis' face of that old look of sickness. Not even to be sure she was not imagining it. What strain could have come into their safe Jefferson Street refuge that was just the same now as ever? Nothing had happened there to change anything. She did give one fleeting thought to Bert Warder's joshing. But he had always been a boor. And anyhow, he was only teasing. Teasing. The word brought up recollections of child play. And child play was always unimportant. The thought re-assured her. She began to emerge from her concentration, set her pen down to the paper again, added 23 to 44, and thought in the phrase she had heard her elders let drop so often, "Oh, teasing's nothing." She shot a sidelong look at Francis again. He was reading. His face looked quiet. Yes, she must have been mistaken. It could be no recurrence of his old trouble, vague and dimmed as that was now. Perhaps his tennis had tired him. Presently the idea occurred to her that he might have a real worry, a present one, something at the office perhaps. No matter how bad that was, it would be less dangerous.

IV

She was right. It was a present worry. About a real danger. But not in the office. In his past, close to the foolish weakness uncovered by Bert's random thrust, lay his other secret—the base and bad one. The two were woven together by a thousand connecting nerves. Bert's hammering on one had set the other a-quiver. Suppose—he thought, horrified, that some day, with a reflex reaction like this, some involuntary quiver of his face should betray his feeling about Roger. That he had such a secret to hide was his shame. That Mary might learn it, was his terror. Great-hearted as she was, she would never go on sharing life with him if she knew of his mean jealousy of Roger—fiercely suppressed, always festering in the dark hollow of his heart. He thought, as he had a thousand times in his boyhood, that there could be no depravity so low as this vicious ill-will towards his unconscious, blameless brother. He told himself once again that he was cheating Mary—he knew why she overlooked his personal insignificance, his poverty—it was because she had the illusion that he was true-hearted, above baseness. If she should learn that he was capable of this obscene resentment of the kind and generous Roger's superiority—she would turn away from him forever. Was there any real difference—no, there was not—between such a feeling towards a brother and the up-raised arm of Cain?

But Mary was looking at him! She had lifted her eyes from her account book! He had not seen when. How long had she been watching him? A man with a guilty secret is always terrified to be watched. Had she guessed? Had she read this thought in his face? He froze. And waited.

But Mary smiled. The room shone. The golden light

around him brought Francis with a start out of his nightmare.

"Why, you've been asleep," said Mary.

"Yes, I must have dropped off for a moment." He thought he had been having a bad dream. What a relief to be waked up!

Before he lay down to sleep that night, he stepped over to the twins' little cribs. Through the high railing of the sleeping-porch the barred moonlight shone on their round faces, bland in sleep. How safe they looked. And it was he who made them safe, their father. His heart grew great with love.

But after he was in bed Mary heard him draw the long sighing breath of disheartenment. "What is it, dear?" she murmured. He did not answer. Probably he was already asleep, she thought.

He was awake. His sigh had been of disheartenment. He had perceived that his love for his little boys was tarnished by satisfaction in his brother's childlessness.

The tide that had been sweeping in so strongly had begun to ebb.

The two vacant-lot courts had never been so busy as that summer. Bert Warder made them the center of Jefferson Street life as much as he could. For there he knew success. By concentrating fiercely on his game, he had made himself one of the best players in the group, and looked forward all through his uneasy days to the hour with his racket at the end, which was almost his only respite from misery. His big unused working-man's body grunted with satisfaction in the hard physical effort and the copious sweat: the strain of his fixed idea relaxed in a momentary forgetfulness of Don in jail: and his perpetual doubt of his equality with those about him fell with the ravening zest of starvation on the chance to inflict defeat.

He steered clear cunningly of the two or three men who could beat him; and naturally played a good deal with Frankie Tuttle. They did not work in the same department of Stott McDevitt, but he scarcely let a day go by without hunting up Francis, inviting him to play, and saying facetiously that he did hope *this* time he might get by Francis' cannon-ball serve and maybe score a few points against him: promising if he did, to campaign for Frankie's election to be town dog-catcher, or chief reader-aloud at the Sewing Society. Day by day he scored more points.

Mary went up to watch the play once and afterwards said, "See here, Francis, why don't you give up tennis for the rest of the summer? You're wearing yourself out." But the turn of her phrase, the quality of her voice, showed Francis how pitiful he looked on the courts, going to pieces under Bert's ragging, trotting about, broken-kneed, like a futile old woman, unstrung, unable to command even his usual modestly competent strokes. If he stopped playing now after such exhibitions of feebleness there would be no limit to the joshing he would get at Bert's hands.

And by this time Bert's joshing did not so much annoy as frighten him. He was terrified at the thought that another chance lunge in the dark might lay open to Bert's rough handling the secret shame he was trying to leave behind. Bert had, so far, never twitted him with Roger, but at any

207

moment he might try that line; certainly would if he guessed that to be a sore point. Francis' nerves tautened in vigilance if he even caught sight of Bert from afar. He seemed to feel Roger in the air, whenever Bert was present.

He was right in feeling that Roger's name was often in Bert's mind. The contrast between Francis' brother, distinguished, wealthy, well-known, and his disgraced convict brother was one of the sorest of Bert's stripes, the worst of all his envies. Glaring across the net at Francis, going forlornly and hopelessly through the complicated wind-up for his serve, he often thought (as he called out in his witty way, "Play ball, bald head"), "There's one sure thing, 'bo . . . you'll never know from *me* I ever heard of that big stiff!"

Mary was rather troubled by the way Francis seemed to feel the heat that summer. But the hot weather would soon be gone. And wasn't he growing thinner? She'd have to start the evening hot chocolate and crackers again. He didn't seem to have the interest in his garden of other summers. Perhaps only that he hadn't much time left over from tennis. He hadn't written a line of poetry for weeks. But of course the wind of poetry blew fitfully. Was he enjoying the twins as much as he did? Or was that only a fancy of hers?

It was no fancy of hers. Coming in to his children after his daily defeat in tennis, worn out with standing guard over his threatened secret, it was soon borne in on him that he had been in a fool's paradise. Now, while his little sons were babies, yes, of course, they were his, as other men's children were theirs. But they grew so fast. Over and over he lived helplessly through in imagination as if it had already happened, how they would turn from him. They would soon naturally be asked to visit their Uncle Roger. They could not but be struck by the difference between the two homes. They would begin to compare their father with his brother. And then they would see how their father always took a back seat, never was consulted, never elected to any office, had no influence. As they grew, they would note people's surprise that a Senator—Roger would probably be a Senator by that time—had such a queer singed-cat of a brother. . . . "And now—" Francis often thought, his fingers fumbling with his thinning hair—"now a mangy singed-cat."

Twenty times a day it seemed to him, he was startled to find that without his knowing it, he was nervously drawing his hair up over the crown of his head.

He was even more startled to discover that he was not the only one to notice this involuntary reflex. "Have you hurt the top of your head lately, Mr. Tuttle?" Mrs. Benson once asked him. He was shocked, and turned on her such a darkening face that she hurriedly excused herself, "I just noticed that you often put your hand up to it."

He snatched down his hand—to his amazement it was once more lifted to his head—and told her shortly, "No. I'm all right." As he moved away a strange thought came to him, one that soon became familiar by repetition. "It would be better if all the hair on my head would come out. And have it over with!" Sometimes he imagined for an instant between sleep and waking that this had happened. And it was a relief. He was sickened to find that he could not control himself even in such a little matter as fumbling with that thin place. How could he hope to hide his secret vice? Every time he found his fingers in his hair he thought anew, disheartened at his own weakness, that he would never be quick enough to hide what would come leaping up to his eyes at a mention of Roger.

V

But until now he had had Mary. As long as Mary was there . . .

Then early in August a tragic telegram took Mary away for a time. Her delicate sister, now a young wife, was lying at the point of death, her baby prematurely born. "Come at once. Florence calling for you," the telegram read. She telephoned the news to Francis who looked up the hour of the next train for her and hurried to draw the money from the savings bank to cover her expenses. Mary, wild with sorrow and alarm, began to pack, interrupted herself to run over to ask Mrs. Benson to keep a neighborly eye on Francis while she was away, tried to think what clothes the twins would need, stopped to telephone the cleaning-woman about getting Francis' meals, stood still in the middle of the floor and wrung her hands. When Francis came with the money, he was startled to see her so distraught. "If it were only time for my vacation, so I could go along to take care of the twins," he said.

"Oh, if you only could be there to take care of *me!*" cried poor Mary, weeping on his shoulder. "I'm scared to death to go by myself. I don't know how to face anything without you now!"

The memory of this cry of Mary's, the thought of her need for him, Mary's real and actual need for *him* hung like incense around Francis as he stood on the station platform that evening looking after the train from which the twins' handkerchiefs still fluttered. It was a sweetness in the night air as he let himself into the empty house. He was breathing it in as he fell asleep, his arm on the pillow sacred to Mary's dear head. Mary had not yet wholly gone.

The next day, the first day since his marriage that he had wakened alone, he arrived early at the office. To his surprise Bert Warder was at a desk farther down the same room, among the apprentices. Francis wondered if this meant that Bert had been definitely put out of the drafting room. There had been some gossip about his mistakes there. Bert's eyes were roving about unhappily. He saw the surprise in Francis' glance. "You, damn you, with your rich brother and your pull! Of course you get on!" he thought, savage over the injustice of the world. To say something he called out foolishly, "Hey there, Francis, I got special orders to report here to keep the air blowing through your clearing." As Francis took out the papers from his drawer he heard Bert's loud unmodulated voice explaining the joke about "the clearing." "Have I got to go all through that again?" thought Francis, shrugging his shoulders wearily. But the men near Bert thought the joke a flat one, found Bert's noise about it tiresome, and took no pains to conceal their impression. Smarting, humiliated, apprehensive, resentful, Bert drew glumly back into himself, waiting bodefully for a chance to pay Francis out for his rebuff.

At lunch he went out of his way in the cafeteria to sit at the same table with Francis, ostentatiously familiar with him and after work he let trolley after trolley go by the corner where he waited till Francis arrived. Knowing that he had been punished for being too fresh, he was impelled by the fatality that hangs over people who have struck a false note, to strike it yet more loudly. Francis had never found him harder to endure. As they walked up Jefferson Street together, he said peremptorily, "Run on in and get your tennis things on, Frankie. We'll have a set before supper. Maybe if I try *hard* I can score a point or two on you."

"It's gosh-awful hot for tennis," protested Francis.

Bert's heavy eyebrows lifted ironically over his bulging eyes, he began a certain menacing one-sided smile which was the introduction to his worst joshing. It was uglier than usual, ominous and threatening. There was but one threat that Francis feared. It came instantly into his mind. He lost his head, "This is the time he is going to bring Roger up—and I have not yet thought what to say or how to look!" and said in a hurried panic, "All right, all right. Yes, let's play. It may do us good."

A couple of hours later he came in. He had lost one love set after another to Bert. Too tired to bathe and change, he sank down in a chair. The cold supper that was to be left for him every evening by Mary's cleaning-woman, faced him on the table. After a time he ate a little of it, and went stiffly to bed. But for a long time not to sleep. Out of the darkness white balls hurtled towards him. Every time he began to doze, he saw one like a bullet, driving straight towards his eyes, and starting to one side to avoid it woke up to find himself sweating, his heart beating fast, all his muscles taut.

The cleaning-woman, come in early by Mary's instructions to get Mr. Tuttle's breakfast, told him, "You don't look so good, Mr. Tuttle."

"It was hot last night," he told her, pushing his uneaten breakfast away.

It was hot all that day too. But in spite of it he lingered in the furnace-like office till the 5:20 trolley. To no avail. As soon as he stepped off the trolley Bert and a couple of others shouted at him to come and make a fourth at doubles. They played set after set, shifting partners in all the possible combinations. But defeat always came to the side that Francis was on. He could have told them that beforehand, he thought, playing more and more feebly.

When he went home he found two letters waiting for him in the hot shut-up living room. One from Mary. One from Roger. What could Roger be writing for? Looking at that letter with apprehension he opened Mary's. The twins were well, she wrote, her sister had recognized her but was not expected to live. The rest was love. ". . . take care of yourself, darling, *darling!* I miss you so! I need you, dearest. I love you. I love you." A murmur as from Mary's voice rose faintly from the paper, but died away in the silence coldly breathed out from the letter he had not read. He sat a long time looking at it, forgetting his dinner. But it had to be read. He tore it open.

Roger wrote to give Francis the news everybody was to see in the newspaper the next day, that through a new busi-

ness combine, he was now one of the Vice Presidents of the
Stott McDevitt Company, as well as of his own. "We'll see
to it that this means some well-deserved advancement for you
too, Francis, old man," wrote Roger pleasantly. His letters
were always kind. "It'll be fine to see more of you and Mary.
We may even decide to become neighbors of yours. Nothing
holds us here. And I certainly would enjoy getting acquainted with my splendid little nephews."

The darkness fell slowly around Francis holding the letter
in a clutch he could not relax. He had not eaten since noon.
His old inner wound opened slowly, gaping here and there,
and began to bleed. No, no, he told himself, shamed to the
heart, it was nothing so clean and wholesome as bleeding;
it was the drip of pus from a foul old ulcer. Well, a man was
a leper, who could feel nothing but mortal sickness over his
own brother's success.

The blackness deepened. Out of it, one after another, there
hurtled towards him bullet-like revelations of his own pitiful
abjectness. He had always known he was a dub at business,
a dub at tennis, a dub at life—everybody's inferior in everything! But till now he had hoped he might at least grow into
a harmless dub. But he was not even that. He was incurably
vicious, with the mean vice of feebleness. The beast in his
heart would not die, starve it though he might. It snarled
and gnashed its teeth over every new triumph of Roger's
and sprang up from its lair, rattling its chain in sordid hope
every time a faint shadow came over Roger's life. He would
rather die, oh, infinitely rather die, than have Mary learn that

her husband could not kill that hope, tighten his hold as he might around its filthy throat.

Through the darkness a voice in a loud snarl came to Francis' ears, "He'll never have any children. And I have two sons." Francis leaped to his feet. Who was there in the dark with him? He had thought he was alone. He snapped on a light and looked wildly around the empty room. He was alone.

Had *he* said that? Or had he only thought it so fiercely that it rang in his ears like a cry? His knees shook. Suppose Mary had been there? Suppose Bert Warder had heard him? Why, he was likely to betray himself wholly at any moment, even without the dreaded mention of Roger's name. How it would be mentioned tomorrow at the office, after everyone had seen the announcement in the morning paper! And he who could control his voice no more than his fingers—he found them again fumbling involuntarily at the crown of his head!

He turned off the light, undressed and sat down on the edge of his bed to think, to plan, to prepare himself for tomorrow's ordeal. Everyone would speak of Roger to him, not Bert only, everybody. And he had only this one night in which to find the right look, the right intonations, the right answers.

Yet when it happened he was somehow equal to it. Tense and careful as a man handling a bomb, he thought he had come through safely. Everybody had said the proper thing about what good luck it was to have his brother one of the Company's Vice Presidents, and he had made the proper answers. At least they had sounded all right when he said them. Why did he still have this terrified uneasiness? Then he realized that his apprehension came from the fact that Bert Warder alone had not said a word to him. He, alone of all the men, had only nodded with a sardonic smile, and sat down silently to work. Francis' heart gave a frightened leap. Bert knew something. Somehow he had found out. Perhaps spying on him from a distance as he had doggedly answered the congratulations of the other men Bert had seen through the mask he had tried to keep closely clamped over his face.

All that morning Bert stuck closely to his desk. But Francis knew that he was not thinking of his work. As the hot morning went on, and Bert said nothing, did not so much as look at him, Francis was surer and surer that somehow he knew. But how could he have found out?

A few moments before lunch time Bert took his hat and without a word went out by himself. He was not at the cafeteria at all. In the alarm over this inexplicable variation from routine Francis suddenly knew how Bert had found out. He had been standing outside the open windows last night listening in the dark, and had heard that cry of evil joy in Roger's childlessness. Yes, of course, that was what had happened.

All that afternoon Francis covertly watched Bert. It was strange how easy it was to watch him without seeming to. Even when his back was squarely turned, he could see Bert continually leaving his desk to go from one man to another, whispering in their ears. And then not knowing that Francis could see them even though his back was turned, the listener would stare at him, nodding, nodding his head with pursed-up lips, as Bert went on whispering, whispering, telling about the shameful secret he had heard as he stood listening in the dark.

Through the breach in Mary's wall the demon had stepped softly in, bringing blackness with him.

V I

Bert said nothing about tennis that day and went home early. Francis got off the trolley at Jefferson Street alone. Forgetting to look in the mailbox, he let himself into the unaired empty house. He did not go about to open windows. He sat down heavily, alarmed to feel his legs shaking under him. He could not afford to be agitated. He must collect himself. His only hope lay in not losing his head. The situation was grave. Bert might even now be coming up the walk to . . . He looked out to reassure himself, and saw not Bert, but a shining limousine drawing up in front of the house.

Before he knew that he had recognized it as Roger's, his trembling legs had carried him in a wild rush of panic to the back of the house. The locked kitchen door halted him. If he went out there he would be seen. Where could he hide? Glaring around, he saw the closet where the mops and cleaning-cloths were kept. He flung himself into it. He was just in time. He had no more than drawn the door shut when the front doorbell rang, and it came to him sickeningly that he could not remember whether he had locked the front door when he came in. He had not breathed till now, when, his lungs almost collapsing, he gasped deeply and drew in to his last capillary the stench from the dirt on the damp mops, decomposing in the heat. The bell rang again. The noise found out his hiding place so accurately that for an instant he felt he was discovered, and gave up hope. He tightened his clutch on the doorknob. Even if they found him out he would hold the door shut, no matter how they pulled on it. He braced himself. A long silence. Had they stepped into the house? He tried to listen. The drumming of his pulse was the only sound. He stood rigid, clutching the doorknob to him, breathing the fetid air deeply in and out of his lungs. Presently from the street the sound of a starting motor came dimly through the closed door.

He waited a long time before he ventured to come out. This might be a trap to make him think they had gone. If he opened the door he might see someone's cold contemptuous eyes fixed on the door, waiting for him. But when he finally did cautiously turn the knob and look out, the kitchen was empty. He tiptoed to the front door, found he had locked it, that he had been safe all the time.

And then, coming to himself for a moment's respite, he turned so faint in a revulsion of feeling that he could not stand. What in God's name had he been doing? But was it possible! It was so remote from anything he wished that he thought for an instant he must have dreamed it. He, Francis, had had no intention of hiding from Roger! Why should he? There was no reason. Suppose Mary had been there? What possible reason could he have given her?

The respite was over . . . *suppose someone had seen him!*

218

A cold sweat drenched him. Someone had seen him, of course. Everyone! They all must have known what he had done. Everyone on the street must have seen him leave the trolley and go into the house. They all knew Roger by sight. They must all have been looking from their windows, saying to each other, "But he's there. I saw him go in just now." Perhaps they had gone out to the street to tell Roger that. Tomorrow they would say to him, suspicious eyes boring into his, "Why in the world didn't you let your brother in yesterday?" What could he say?

He wrung his hands. "What can I say? What can I say?" Then he thought of a way out. It was simple. He could say he had gone at once to sleep, that he had not heard the bell. He would hurry up to the sleeping porch now and lie down so that if anyone came in he would be found there, his eyes closed. He raced up the stairs and flung himself down on the bed, clenching his eyelids shut. It was essential that he should seem to be asleep. Then he remembered that nobody could come in because the doors were locked. He opened his eyes. He tried to get up.

But he was by now exhausted. He fell back, his wide-open eyes facing a new danger. He imagined Bert Warder asking him the next morning, "What were you up to yesterday that you didn't want your brother to catch you at?" He must think of an answer to that question. Perhaps if he went over it all now in anticipation, question and answer, he might be able to . . . Suppose Bert said suddenly, "What did you get into the mop-closet for yesterday, when your brother . . ."

Oh, horror! He had forgotten to keep his eyes shut to

prove to people who came in to spy on him that he really had been asleep when Roger rang the bell. He shut them hard. Then slowly remembered, no, no, that was not necessary. The front door was locked. No one could come in. He opened them again and stared out through the high railing of the sleeping porch.

He had been trying to think what he could answer Bert Warder tomorrow. But how could he hope to control his face to hide his secret when he had no control over his fingers—he snatched his fumbling hand down from his head—over his body—he felt himself cowering again in front of the foul-smelling mop. His desperate thoughts of how to ward off tomorrow's danger were cut short by a sudden cold divination of the present peril. Danger was stealthily closing in on him now, this instant. He felt it creeping up on him from behind. He had known what that danger was. He tried wildly to remember. Oh, yes. He was to keep his eyes closed so that people would think him asleep. He had forgotten that. He shut them tightly, and weak with relief, felt that he had been just in time.

He opened them in the morning, rose and under the cleaning-woman's eyes went through the motions of eating breakfast. He and Bert happened to walk into the office together. He was incapable of speech, all his vitality concentrated on being on his guard. Bert looked pale and out of sorts and said he hadn't been feeling very well yesterday. But he was all right today, he said, goggling his eyes, "And how about some tennis?" Francis saw through this trick instantly. He knew Bert was lying, and why he was lying

. . . to throw Francis off his guard. His plan was to wait till Francis was exhausted at the end of the tennis that afternoon and then suddenly to shoot his question like one of his cannon-ball serves . . . *"Why didn't you let your brother in yesterday?"* Yes, it would come to him like one of those fiercely driven balls he could not return.

All day he tried to invent a way out of the trap laid for him. But it was not till he was on the trolley with Bert that his inspiration came to him. The ride home was triumphal. He told Bert with a happy smile that he was going to change his clothes for tennis, and ran into the empty house. He stepped lightly, exultantly, into the kitchen and putting all his weight against it, tipped the heavy refrigerator to one side. As it toppled he stooped, still smiling, and held his right hand under it.

VII

But of course the bandaged hand that could not hold a racket could not hold a pen or run a typewriter either. When he went to the office, he was sent home on sick leave. This pleased him. It meant he could lie on the bed all day, his eyes tightly shut to prevent the discovery that threatened him, that threatened Mary through him. The moment he opened them—as he must if he went downstairs to eat— Mary was in danger again, might at any moment be dragged in the filth of knowing what kind of man her husband was. But he had grown very clever in thinking of ways to protect Mary from that discovery. "I seem to be very sleepy," he said cunningly to the cleaning-woman. "The doctor who took care of my hand told me the accident might have that effect and wanted me to sleep as much as I could. Just keep some food on a tray for me, will you, outside the door. When I wake up I will eat it."

After this he need not open his eyes. He could lie, hour after hour, reveling in the pain of his mangled hand, glorious anguish with which he was buying security for Mary. He could, waiting till black night, grope his way into the bathroom, find scissors and razor blades by feel, and use them without looking. Without opening those tightly shut eyelids he could find the food left for him on the tray, and empty it out in the corner of his closet so that the cleaning-woman would think he ate it. Mostly he lay rigidly still, as still as if he were in his coffin. Now that there was no longer any reason to raise his hand to his head, his arms lay quiet at his side. What a heavenly rest! He was resting almost as well as if he were dead. And Mary was as safe as if he were dead. He was very tired, but infinitely proud of knowing how to protect Mary.

Sometimes his tense eyelids relaxed and he really slept. That was the best. Oh, that was the best . . .

VIII

Since he no longer knew whether it were night or day he could not judge of time. How long had he lain there keeping Mary safe? A day . . . a week . . . a year? The silence of the empty house seemed to be broken by voices. The cleaning-woman's. And—could it be—it sounded like Mary's!

It couldn't be Mary's, could it, come back into danger when he was so sure he had made her safe? Not *Mary!* This must be a ruse of his enemies to frighten him into opening his eyes.

He sat up in bed, staring into the red blackness of his closed lids. Horrified, he strained his ears and recognized the children's voices. And that was Mary's step in the hall downstairs. His heart beat in time with it as with no other. Mary had come back, walking straight into mortal peril.

Once more he had failed. He had not saved her after all. For a moment he was undone with defeat, and trembling from head to foot sat dumb with stupid panic.

He heard the dear remembered step start up the stairs. With an effort greater than any in all his life, he summoned his soul to rise on the wings of love and be strong. And saw how even now it was not too late. Even now, though Mary's dear step was mounting the stairs, unsuspecting . . . Now, now was the time to play the man, once for all.

He flung himself on his love for Mary, and with one beat of its mighty wings it bore him beyond Destiny that thought to have him vanquished. Weak he might be—his love, immortal and divine, made him, at the last, mightier than Fate.

IX

Only after the excitement of the clearing of Don's name was all over, when the Warders were on the train going home from their exhausting week in Huntsville did they begin to understand all that the proving of Don's innocence meant to them. Their days in Huntsville after the melodramatic dis-

223

covery of the real thief, were so crammed with raw emotion they had been bewildered. They had passed without a pause from their first incredulous excitement to incredulous joy and then indignant sympathy for their brother with all those months of undeserved wretchedness back of him. What a nightmare they had all lived through, they said over and over to each other. They had wept together, and the tears had washed the poison out of their wounds so that now, in the train on their way home, they were faint in the sweet weakness of convalescence. Bert's heart that had been crushed shut by shame and fear, softened, opened and let him out from the bitter desolation of self-pity. His imagination that had been smothered under the consciousness of disgrace drew breath again. He forgot what he had suffered; his thoughts were for his brother. "Poor Don!" he said over and over. "Poor *Don!*" After what he had lived through, it was like dying and going to heaven, to feel love and compassion. He was proud with a noble and new pride that the loss of all his savings weighed as nothing with him compared to his brother's vindication.

The news had been in the newspapers. With headlines. Everybody must have read it. The Warders almost expected a congratulating delegation of neighbors to meet them at the station. But when they climbed heavily down from the dusty train and saw that the platform was empty, they thought at once that it was only uneducated working-class people who made a fuss in public, and laid the lesson humbly to heart.

There was no one to be seen on Jefferson Street when they

stepped from the trolley at the home corner. They set their suitcases down with a long breath, to look. There was their street! It was theirs, with its genteel lawns, its ornamental useless flower-gardens, its dignified parklike shade trees. There it stood brooding dreamily in the blue summer twilight, and welcomed them back.

"I'll carry the bags, both of them," said Bert to his wife, chivalrously. They trudged along towards their home, their own home, redeemed, shining, safe. They belonged here, they thought, with deep content. They were accepted by these refined people who took lawns and trees and flowers for granted. Their purged hearts swelled with thankfulness, with friendliness, with good resolutions. They must be worthy of their good fortune.

As they approached the Benson house they saw that Helen was standing on the front porch, looking at the newspaper. What a nice girl Helen was, they thought fondly. Imogene called, "*Ooh*-hoo, Nellie!" and skipped up the front walk. Stricken by Helen's face she fell back, shocked. "Oh . . . why . . . what's the *matter?*"

Two or three short sentences were all Helen had to say. Her news whining ominously like a loaded shell, flew over her listeners' blanched faces, not exploding till long after it had passed.

They stood like stocks, stupidly listening to the sound of the words they could not understand. Then Bert said in a flat voice, "Not Frankie Tuttle! You didn't say it was *Frankie Tuttle!*" He took the newspaper from Helen's hand. Through the brooding summer twilight the headlines shrieked.

225

Fables for Parents

The paper fell from his hand.

"This very morning," said Helen.

"That deep cement-covered entrance to the basement,"
began Mrs. Benson. "Right over the high railing around the
sleeping porch. Mary had come home—you knew she'd been
away with a sick sister—and she just started up the stairs."

The Warders, stunned, sank down on their suitcases. Bert's
mouth hung slackly open.

Joe Crosby came over from across the street. His lips
twitched. His eyes were red. He shook Bert's hand without
a word. The Warders had been but bludgeoned into stupe-
faction by the headlines. They had not believed them. But
this silence told them what had happened. Mrs. Warder and
Imogene began to cry. A film came over Bert's bulging eyes.
He got out his handkerchief, blew his nose, and took his hat
off, holding it on his knee and looking fixedly down at it.

After a time when they could, they asked the usual questions. And had the usual answers. No imaginable explanation. His accounts in perfect order. His health all right—
he'd hurt his hand of course, but that was not serious; the
doctor said it was healing without any sign of infection. And
everything going extra well with him, seems though—his
brother just made Vice President of the company, the luckiest
kind of a break, his brother thinking the world and all of him
—came right over the minute he heard of this and took Mary
and the children back. To make their home with him. Al-

226

ways. Said he'd always wanted children in his home. No, everything in the business end of his life was fine, couldn't be better. His brother kept saying there wasn't *anything* he wouldn't have done for him. And no trouble at home, Lord, *no!* He and Mary were the happiest couple on the street. Suspicious of their good faith, Bert said it seemed as if there *must* have been some warning. "No, there wasn't. He was just exactly the same as ever, the last time anybody saw him. He'd hurt his hand, you know—was that before you went to Huntsville? No, I guess it was afterwards—and that kept him away from the office for a while. It must have been while he was at home with that, that he . . ."

Bert Warder was shocked at a glimpsed possibility of unneighborly neglect. "For the Lord's sake, hadn't anybody gone in to see that he was all right?" he asked sternly.

Mrs. Benson defended herself hastily, "Oh, yes, yes. Before she left Mary had asked me to look after him, and I went over there every day. Sometimes twice. But the cleaning-woman always said he was asleep. She told me the doctor had given him something to deaden the pain in his hand and make him drowsy."

Joe Crosby confirmed this. "Yes, every time I went in too, he was asleep. I went clear up to his room several times. The shades were pulled down and it was dark. But I could see he was asleep all right." He answered the stubborn question in the other's face. "Yes, I know, Bert, I felt just the way you do, as if we might have done *some*thing, if we'd been any good. But you know there isn't anything *any*body can do when it's a case of . . ." he drew in a long breath

227

before he could pronounce the word, "it was just plain insanity, Bert."

"Frankie wasn't insane!" rapped out Bert, indignant. "He was a *swell* fellow!"

Joe lowered his voice and with a dark shamed intonation and yet with a certain relish of the enormity he was reporting, said, "Bert, when they picked up his body they found he'd shaved his head. All over. Every spear of hair shaved off. Down to the skin. The way you shave your face."

This did stagger the questioner. He said feebly, "You don't *say* . . . ! Good gosh, his *head!* Why, what in the . . . what ever would make anybody do *that?*" and fell back into his stockish uncomprehending blankness.

Mrs. Benson murmured an explanation, "The doctors told his brother that's one of the signs of religious mania—the tonsure, you know. They told his brother that sometimes insane . . ."

"Oh, they make me tired!" cried Joe Crosby in angry sorrow. "They don't know anything about it. Why don't they keep still!"

Bert Warder agreed sadly, "I guess nobody knows anything about what causes insanity."

It came over him that this was no waking nightmare, was fact. But he could not admit it as fact. "It just don't seem *possible* to me!" he told them, his voice breaking grotesquely in his pain. "Why, Frankie and me . . . why, I never *had* a better pal than Frankie Tuttle!"

Poor Miss Maggie

WHEN Marcia Stone emerged from Normal School with her diploma, she was lucky enough to get a position in her roommate's home town. She and Ann had exchanged visits several times. It was very different indeed, as Marcia's mother said, from going off to a strange place where you didn't know a soul. This was what she said: what she thought was that the Clarkes being a lively family—lively but nice—Marcia might in their society get over some of her funny notions. For all that Marcia was bright, and quite pretty—or would be if she ever took care of her looks—and very sweet, Mrs. Stone didn't know how she was ever going to get a husband if she went on being more interested in every mangy dog and sick cat and deaf musty old great-grandmother than in personable young men.

Never having said a single word of this to Marcia, Mrs. Stone supposed that her daughter had no idea how she felt. But of course Marcia, ever since she could remember, had stooped her shoulders to the burden of her mother's disapproval, and was by this time thoroughly tired of dragging around the ball and chain of someone else's standards of conduct. The independence of her life in Melville was what she looked forward to with eagerness. She would be free there from her mother's perpetual barrage of wordless, but very audible objections to her interest in lame ducks.

She even knew what she meant to do first in this new freedom—to go to the rescue of Ann Clarke's Aunt Margaret. On her very first visit her heart had gone out to Miss Maggie limping around the Clarke house like a little ghost, her sensitive face with its beautiful but alas! too visible bones and its deep-set haunting eyes telling the story of the shadow life had been to her. Marcia had longed to move her out of her cheerless north room into a south-looking life with all its windows open to the sun.

It did not seem strange to Marcia that she rather than the Clarkes thought of this as a possibility. She had seen too much of the unimaginative callousness of healthy, red-blooded life-enjoying people to be surprised that Miss Maggie's family brushed past her shrinking figure without ever trying to light up with a smile the patient endurance of her face. Laughing and bustling about as they were, how could they hear a low timid voice asking for her share of what makes life worth living? And of course Miss Maggie never thought of asking for even the smallest part of her share. Marcia had occasionally helped her mother take care of their small flock of poultry and with no idea that her metaphor was not an original one, she often thought that people are like hens, their instinct is to peck at anybody who is under par in vitality, rather than to take thought how that vitality might be brought up to normal. But that was not *her* instinct, and in this first independent life of her own she would be free at last to act on her instinct.

230

She took a room in a boarding house near the Clarkes and began quietly to study Miss Maggie's needs. She had planned to take the older woman out after school hours or on Saturdays, for walks in the open air, to the tune of cheerful chat. But of course the lame knee made that impossible. Miss Maggie could do no more than to get around the house, she told her young friend. "If I try to do more the pain gets worse."

"*Worse!*" cried Marcia. "Is it painful all the time?"

"Oh, I'm pretty well used to it now, my dear, after thirty years," said Miss Maggie with a reassuring smile.

"Can't anything be done for it, Miss Maggie?"

"Oh, I suppose if I were a millionairess or married to somebody who . . ." she began, laughed at her fancifulness, and broke off to say, "No, there's nothing but rubbing it that does any good. And of course, that . . . but see here, dear, what are you worrying about my small troubles for? Young people ought to have their heads full of their good times."

"No, no, I'm not that kind. I *wish* you'd let me rub your knee at night. You might sleep better."

"Oh, *would* you?" said Miss Maggie, catching her breath. Tears stood in her beautiful sunken blue eyes. But, "No, *no!*" she hurried on. "What an idea! A lovely young girl like you!"

"I'd love to!" said Marcia, warm with her first success.

It occurred to her that it might be awkward to manage this without applying a reproach to Miss Maggie's own flesh and blood. But the Clarkes seemed to pay little attention to any-

231

thing that concerned their aunt. Go ahead if you want to, they seemed tacitly to say. She was thankful they put no obstacles in her way.

Talk is a natural accompaniment to massage: Marcia found that the other spoke more freely in these quiet tête-à-têtes than in general conversation. Miss Maggie told her things she would never dream of mentioning to her family, touching things, sad things, that Marcia burned to redress. She was living under all sorts of handicaps, moral and material, from which a little good will could easily clear her path. For instance, she had an ulcerated tooth, often causing her extreme pain, and always pouring poison into her system day and night. Of course her health suffered from this. "But don't you dare, Marcia, to say anything to Henry or Maria about it. They have plenty of demands on them from their own family without wasting money on a useless old aunt! Dear little Caroline really needs a fur coat, and Bob's college life must be unclouded. Promise me you won't say anything to them. I ought not to have told you. But I'll never dare to again, if you let them know."

She was so distressed that Marcia solemnly promised secrecy. But of course that tooth must be treated. "See here, Miss Maggie, you wouldn't have to let anybody know. You could say you were coming to visit my room in school, and then go on to the dentist from there. I'd be *glad* to take care of the cost. It would be a joy to!"

She was astonished by the resistance—very pathetic she found it—which poor Miss Maggie made to this plan. She had apparently gone so long without sympathy or help that she felt she was doing wrong to accept it. "No, oh, no, Marcia! At your age you ought to spend your money on yourself, not on an old woman that's no good to anybody— what difference does it make whether I am in pain or not?"

"It makes a great deal of difference to *me,* dear Miss Maggie!"

It was when Marcia brought their week-long discussion to an end that she first saw fleetingly pass over Miss Maggie's face a singular expression which she did not recognize. With affectionate insistence she had just gone ahead and made an appointment with the dentist on a Saturday, chosen because all the Clarkes would be away. "So you see, nobody'll ever know a thing about it!" Miss Maggie was silent, and out of her eyes for just one instant there looked—what was it? It *looked* like a gleam of—well, what? Marcia was so startled that she stepped back hastily. But Miss Maggie had so immediately exclaimed, "Oh, Marcia, how generous you are!" so sincerely, so fervently that the girl was sure she must have imagined that strange desperate roll of the eye.

So they did go to the dentist, Marcia prepared to spend a month's salary if necessary. But unexpected good luck was with them. The dentist assured them there was no ulceration; the only thing he could find amiss was a small cavity which he filled in half an hour and for which he charged three dollars and a quarter.

"Oh, what a relief!" cried Marcia when they were back in the Clarke house. She gave Miss Maggie a hug of joy. "What a relief!"

"Yes, it *is* a relief," said Miss Maggie. She took off her

233

hat and laid it on the bed. "If that dentist is right," she added.

Marcia had not thought of this possibility, and was alarmed. "Oh, do you think he may not be? Let's go to another one."

"No, no! Leave it as it is!" cried Miss Maggie, sharply. She simply hated, you could see that, to be a bother to anyone.

Nothing was ever said again about her teeth. Marcia often wondered if the filling had relieved the pain, but felt a certain delicacy about making inquiries. And her attention was soon centered on another detail—a small one, but what a tale it told of neglect! She discovered that Miss Maggie had no galoshes! She had no money of her own to buy a pair, and nobody cared enough about her to notice that she needed them. "Now don't you get them for me," she admonished Marcia hurriedly. "You've done *enough*."

She spoke so earnestly that Marcia hesitated to go against her dictum, although she saw now that it was the lack of them as much as her lameness that kept Miss Maggie indoors. Finally making up a whimsical little note about its being a present to celebrate George Washington's birthday, she sent her (thinking it better than taking them to her in person) a pair of the best overshoes to be had, on the 22nd of February.

When she went in that evening to rub the lame knee she found the room darkened and Miss Maggie lying on her bed, a wet towel over her eyes. She had one of her blinding headaches, it seemed. When one of them struck her, there was nothing to do but give up to it. In the dim light, her thin, nobly modeled face was deeply etched with lines of suffering. Marcia's heart was wrung. "Could it be your eyes?" she asked.

"Perhaps," murmured the other.

"Don't you *know?* Haven't you ever had them examined?"

Miss Maggie's mouth silently expressed what her patient words never did, a bitter wonder that the girl could suppose that she had been given the care people thought necessary for others.

"Well, we must see to that!" said Marcia energetically. Miss Maggie said nothing.

"Wouldn't you like me to change your bandage for you?"

"Oh, *would* you?" said Miss Maggie with astonished gratitude. So Marcia spent the rest of the evening wringing out towels and laying them on the aching eyeballs. By half past eleven the pain was a little better. Marcia let herself out of the darkened house, resolved to look up an oculist the very next day. As she dropped wearily into bed, a pile of uncorrected arithmetic papers weighing rather heavily on her mind, she remembered that nothing had been said about the galoshes. Well, of course not!

If it had been hard to persuade Miss Maggie to accept the help a dentist could give her, it seemed impossible for Marcia to get anything done about her eyes. Miss Maggie was horrified at what she had already cost the girl, and would accept nothing else, no matter how earnestly Marcia told her that to help her was what she wanted to do more than anything else in the world. "No, my dear child, I will *not* hang like a

235

millstone around anybody's neck, certainly not somebody who doesn't owe me any duty. I simply will not allow more good money to be wasted on an old woman who's no use to anybody."

Marcia thought of saying encouragingly, "But don't you see, if your eyes and your teeth were all right and your health good, you *would* be able to be of some use." This was the obviously forward-looking and comforting hope to hold up. As soon as she could think of the right tactful phrase to express it, she must be sure to make this suggestion to Miss Maggie who spoke so often and so pitifully about being excluded from usefulness by her infirmities. Judging others from herself as we all do, Marcia thought, "Of course, what everybody needs more than anything else is to feel useful. Why else am I trying to help poor Miss Maggie? Yet do I try to secure any of that satisfaction for her? No, I spend all my time on these mere surface material details."

All the same, eyestrain was serious and must be eliminated before anything else could be tried. And how could it be managed when Miss Maggie refused to let her young friend spend another cent for her, and—oh, above all—refused to allow any appeal to be made to the Clarkes? From the skies dropped the perfect solution. An uncle of Marcia's who had been settled in Denver, had trouble with his heart and moved back to a lower altitude—to Melville as it happened. And he was an oculist. Of course he was glad to do anything for a friend of his niece's. "It won't cost anybody a penny!" cried Marcia joyfully to Miss Maggie. Miss Maggie was silent and over her face came again—for an instant—that inexplicable, almost wild, expression as of someone at bay. But a moment after the tears of gratitude were in her eyes. "How good you are, Marcia!"

It did not occur to Marcia that this too must be kept from the family, since it was to cost nothing, so when on their way out to the appointment, they met Mrs. Clarke on the front walk, Marcia blithely told her their errand.

"Why, don't your glasses fit you any more, Maggie?" asked Mrs. Clarke.

On this, the two before her fell so portentously silent that she hastily answered herself, "Well, of course, one's eyes do change all the time. Your uncle's very kind, Marcia."

Marcia moved on stiffly as in a trance. So Miss Maggie *had* had glasses. Her eyes had been examined. The girl was in a passion of bewilderment. Why ever in the world would she want Marcia to think she hadn't! The house door closed behind Mrs. Clarke. Miss Maggie said quietly, "They gave me an old pair that were found among our mother's things when she died."

Marcia's heart leaped up in relief. But she ached all over in self-reproach. How beastly she was to suspect a friend, like that, before she made a single inquiry.

So the glasses were secured. Miss Maggie did not often wear them. They hurt the bridge of her nose, she explained. Marcia consulted her uncle about this, and got a pair of another construction that did not rest on the bridge at all. For some reason which she could not in the least understand, she felt diffident about offering these to Miss Maggie, and put it off day after day. Was she afraid of that strange roll of the eye? But when she finally took in the new glasses, Miss Maggie was only very, very grateful. "You sweet girl! Is there anybody in this world who'd be so good to a useless old woman?"

The turn of her phrase reminded Marcia that she had intended to try to go deeper than trifling surface troubles. It takes *constructive* thought, she realized, to help another human being. She began to think as constructively as a girl of her age could. Often enough in school hours when she should have been absorbed in geography or spelling, she was wondering what Miss Maggie could do that would give her a place in the ranks of the useful?

An idea came to her. The domestic science department of the school where she taught was lamentably understaffed. The classes were crowded. Many of those who needed it most had little chance to learn. Miss Maggie might be interested in having a group of little girls from poorer families come to her for instruction in plain sewing. Why, yes, indeed! Miss Maggie cried out that she would simply love that! It would be, she said, a sort of justification, the first she had ever had, for living on charity. "Yes, it *is* charity, Marcia. I know what it is. I don't deceive myself." They spent a happy hour planning all the details of the little class. Miss Maggie's room would hold seven at a time easily. The light was good. Marcia would bring the children in after four o'clock, three times a week.

Marcia went home walking on air. She was learning and growing, she thought. When you went down to the fundamentals and called upon the deeper instincts, what powerful forces you released! She could feel herself emerging from childishness, from the schoolgirl's view of life. Full of happy plans she sat down and began to make a list of the fortunate little girls who were to have this opportunity.

Presently her landlady knocked and handed in a note. It was from Miss Maggie, saying she had been struck all in a heap by the certainty that Mrs. Clarke, her sister-in-law, would object very much to having slum children in the house—colds—dirt—sore throats—light-fingered—kidnaping gangs—head lice—noise . . . Marcia's eyes leaped along over the objections Mrs. Clarke would be sure to make, to the end of the page. "Of course if you *asked* her to allow it, she'd be ashamed to refuse you. But she would be furious with *me,* when you were not here. My position would be unbearable. After all what right have I, a helpless burden on my brother's family, to insist on taking people into their home they would object to?"

Marcia sadly scrunched into a ball her half-made list. Yes, she could see that that plan was impossible. The idea was all right. Fine. She must just think of another way to put it into execution. She did think of others, which she presented one by one for Miss Maggie's consideration. But she seemed to have lost all her common sense. Impossible crack-brained plans were the only ones that occurred to her. She had not realized she was such a visionary. Yet who but a visionary would have thought of Miss Maggie's reading stories aloud in the children's room at the public library, when her throat was so delicate that she lost her voice if she even talked long at a time; of her going to the Red Cross room to help mend

239

donated garments when there was such a draught in that place that the first time she tried it she got a cold which nearly ended in pneumonia; of her writing cheer-up letters to bedridden shut-ins, when that brought back to her with anguished vividness the long years she had spent caring for her mother's bedridden old age, so that she was simply sick with crying every time she put pen to paper.

Indeed, poor Miss Maggie's health began to fail so much at this time, that she was all but a bedridden shut-in herself.

She looked frightfully ill, a hunted, anxious expression in her haggard eyes that was, Marcia thought with indignant pity, like that of a harmless little animal almost run down by the hounds on its track. Were the Clarkes horrid to her? Miss Maggie seemed to feel so much more than her usual depressed remorse about being a burden to them, that Marcia suspected them of active unkindness. Miss Maggie looked exactly like a delicate defenseless person who is being unkindly treated, she really did. She was in a panic about her very evidently declining health. "I mustn't get sick!" she kept saying to Marcia. "I must *not* get sick. The demands on my poor brother's pocketbook are so great. It would be the last straw if he had to pay out money for doctor's bills for *me*."

But she did get sick. Her strength ebbed away visibly. She had dreadful vomiting spells. Her heart had hours of throbbing at such terrific speed that she was exhausted and could only lie for hours afterwards on her bed, utterly spent.

Marcia did what she could for her. But that was less and less. She was too weak now to have her knee rubbed. Above all she was too weak to talk or to hear talk. When Marcia tried to bring in a little cheerful conversation, poor Miss Maggie's beautiful sunken eyes grew wild with nervous strain. "Don't! Don't!" she implored her. "Something in my head right there . . ." she put her hand up, "begins to ache like a nail being driven in."

She did not even seem to like to have Marcia send her flowers, or nice things to eat. After a time Marcia had a strange idea that Miss Maggie did not like her to come at all; when she turned her head on the pillow to see who had come in to her darkened room, it seemed to Marcia that more and more often—or did she imagine it?—she caught on the waxen wasted face of the sick woman a gleam of that strange expression which almost looked like—but of course it couldn't be—resentment. But resentment of what? It must be a flicker of anguish from her suffering. The girl was at a standstill.

What *should* she do?

She very soon knew what to do. There happened to her what everybody had thought would happen, because it usually does but what she had never once dreamed might be possible—a young man fell in love with her and she with him. Oh, tremendously in love. You never saw anything like it— except that you have seen it many times. You know from experience just how it looked from the outside because it looked like any love affair. And there's no use trying to tell you what it felt like from the inside (unless you know that from experience too) because there are no words that could begin to describe it. The only fact to record is that they met in

241

April and were engaged by the middle of May. He was a Denver connection of her aunt-by-marriage, so they knew all about each other to begin with; and both families approved so heartily that it would have taken the edge off their engagement if they had not been so simply crazy about each other. He had a good position in Chicago. There was no reason for a long wait. And there was no long wait. Like many another girl educated at public expense to be a schoolteacher, Marcia taught school for just a year before she was married.

Although most girls would have been so absorbed and excited by all this as entirely to forget a poor sick old woman, Marcia was not that kind of girl. Although she felt that she was deserting her old friend just when she was most needed, she told Miss Maggie about her engagement before another soul knew it. The moment she had dreaded turned out a bright one. Miss Maggie's great heart rose with a bound to this test of its magnanimity. She could hardly have been more pleased if she herself had become engaged.

"To Chicago?" she asked, and lay back on her pillows, a smile of selfless sweetness on her pale face, as she told her dear girl how she rejoiced with her. Marcia told her Harold that she felt a perfect criminal to be so frantically happy as he made her while such a dear old person had never had anything for herself, and yet felt only this generous gladness in another's joy. She took Harold to see Miss Maggie who from her bed of pain gave them her feeble blessing. Afterwards Marcia wept her handkerchief to a sop as she thought about the invalid's absence of envy. "She never had a single thing go right for her," she told Harold's shoulder, talking into it brokenly while she held her handkerchief to her nose. "Not one smallest piece of happiness has ever come her way! It's too . . ."

Tightening his arms around her Harold told her sympathetically (although it could not be said that his interest in Miss Maggie was really deep) that she needn't think he knew nothing about it, for they had had somebody like that in their family, a cousin of his mother's. ". . . a poor dreary old creature who . . ."

"But Miss Maggie's not *dreary!*" protested Marcia. "She's wonderful. She's so brave. She *never* complains."

Maybe so, agreed Harold. Maybe she didn't. But his old cousin had. "You couldn't do a thing for her. Momma used to try to, some, but it was no go. As long as she had something to complain about she was O.K. But try to fix her up any better—and good *night!* Gramma used to say to Momma, 'Let her alone, Bessie!' Gramma was Momma's mother. 'You wouldn't pull the crutch away from a one-legged man, would you? Folks that can't stand up to life have got to have an alibi,' she used to tell Momma. 'Of course it makes her mad when you try to get it away from her.'"

What did she mean, Marcia wondered. "Get *what* away?" Harold didn't know what his grandmother meant, and didn't care. And in a minute or two he had succeeded in ending Marcia's caring just then. They were to be married in a fortnight, and were very much wrapped up in each other.

Their wedding was in June as soon as Marcia's school was over, they had an exhilarating time in Atlantic City on their honeymoon, settled in Chicago in a cute little apartment out on the West Side, and began adding to the population of the world. They had a little boy first, a wonderfully fine child, and then a little girl. But she, poor scrap, had eczema terribly all through her first year. Both she and her mother were all but worn out with work and worry and discouragement from that. And then the little boy fell from his kiddie-car and somehow broke his ankle bones and the doctor didn't set them right, and they had to be broken all over again and re-set; and Harold's company went into bankruptcy—he was for nearly a year without a position; they had to sell their car and move to a cheap noisy little flat; and of course that was the time when a new baby was on the way, who was born when things looked blackest.

Something went wrong with that third confinement, per-haps the worries and anxieties that had gone before, and Marcia was still far from well when after six expensive weeks in the hospital, she and the new baby were sent back to the hot smelly flat where her out-of-work husband was struggling single-handedly with the cooking and housework and care of the five-year-old boy and the delicate three-year-old girl. Al-though she had been allowed to come home, the doctors had told her to get off her feet and lie down the minute her back began to ache, and not to walk more than a block. If she was careful, they said, she'd be all right.

So Marcia was careful. She lay down the minute her back began to ache. For fear of exceeding the permitted block, she never walked at all. Her appetite was not good; she could not sleep well; her strength did not return. Rather it seemed

244

to her that she was getting weaker. Her back was worse instead of better. Harold had to do more and more of the work and to rub her back nights and mornings, into the bargain. Yet she slept wretchedly. The ache soon extended up to her shoulders and arms which were so lame she could hardly dress herself. She had her hair cut short because she could not raise her arms to put it up. She spent most of the time on her bed.

If things had been as they were, with a good maid, a nice, airy, convenient apartment, and a safe little court for the children's outings, she would have had a chance to recover, she thought. But all piled on top of each other as they were, in the heat and noise and city dirt, their small savings melting day by day, and no hope of anything better—of course she couldn't get her strength back. Nor did she. "No, children, it's just *all* I can do with my back aching as it is, to . . . I'm sorry, Harold, but I had a bad night and . . ."

On the morning of one of the hottest days, Harold had gone out to do their small marketing, taking the children along to give his wife an hour of quiet. The postman brought a letter from an acquaintance, the wife of a former business associate of Harold's. She said she and her husband were to go back East for their vacation, and offered Marcia and Harold the use of their cottage by the lake for four weeks.

Lying back on her pillows Marcia read this letter with resentment. What could a short stay in the country do for them! Nothing! Compared to what they needed, what was it? Nothing! And here was Mrs. Cantwell ostentatiously lifting a single grain of sand out of the path of exhausted people toiling up a mountain, and admiring herself for being so kind. If they accepted this trifling help they'd be no better off, but the Cantwells would think they had *done* something, would expect a lot of thanks, would want everybody to pretend that because of them, things were better than they really were. Marcia began turning over in her mind various ways to evade this offer which now seemed almost an insult. They could say—Marcia began to think what they might say . . .

But at that instant she had a vision. A real vision, like the ones people have in books. The only time in her life. It startled her so much that she sprang off the bed with a loud exclamation. "Good gracious!" cried Marcia, and even more emphatically, "My . . . goodness . . . gracious . . . *me!*" She flung off her wrapper, pulled a percale housedress on over her head and moved rapidly towards a pile of unwashed dishes in the kitchen sink.

Of course it was not easy to climb back up. She was astonished to find how hard it was. Yet she had not had time to slip very far. And the pressing, immediate, imperative need for her of her husband and children and baby all tugged for dear life against the insidious slipperiness of the downward slope. But what a struggle it was! Climbing with all her might but often falling, she came to have a humble fellow-feeling for those solitary ones not roped to others by the mighty ties of human needs, who lost their footing, and unseen, unaided, slid slowly down and down till they were beyond help.

The four weeks of fresh air, room for the children to run

246

around, and daily swims in the lake did wonders for them all. That stay in the country came at just the right time. When the Cantwells came back, Marcia told them gratefully that it had been exactly what she needed; it had simply made her over. She felt her strength definitely on the return. And it was cooler in the city now; if she stopped to rest on the landings, the stairs did not tire her too much; she could do her own marketing. When the three children—and the weary Harold too, of all things!—came down with whooping cough together, Marcia did not collapse and give up. She just took care of them.

No, it was by no means all smooth sailing on blue seas, those first years of Marcia's married life. But they came through the storm, as families usually do. Harold unexpectedly got a splendid position as Comptroller of Accounts in a college in Minnesota. They moved there, into a nice little home. It was a pleasant college town. The public schools were excellent. The little girl's eczema had long ago vanished, the boy's broken leg was a thing of the past, the new baby was a joy, Marcia's back was as good as ever. They drew breath and looked up. Six years had passed.

They were no longer the boy and girl who had been so crazy about each other. Crazy? thought Marcia on their seventh wedding anniversary, her heart full of sober thankfulness as she walked down through the garden to meet Harold coming back from his office, we didn't know a single thing about love. About anything! "What an idiot I was as a girl!" she exclaimed. Her husband took her into his arms. "I guess we were two of a kind," he said, kissing her fondly.

247

The first summer after they went to live in the college town, they drove back East to see their folks and show the children to their old friends. Letters had kept them in touch with the main events back there, and they were not surprised by gaps in the ranks of the older generation. What did repeatedly take their breath away was to find their contemporaries no longer blooming young people, but grave, often careworn, sometimes positively battered. Nobody had said a word about that change. Well, it was natural, some of them had been through deep waters. Ann Clarke, married soon after Marcia, had had three babies and lost every one of them in infancy. How do people *live* through such blows? Marcia and Harold asked each other, shaken with gratitude for their own noisy, vigorous three.

Of course they drove to Melville to see what was left of the Clarkes. Marcia thought that Mrs. Clarke, a widow now, seemed shockingly broken and aged; evidently Mrs. Clarke found her much changed, for after one look she cried out compassionately, "Oh, my *dear* Marcia!" The surprise was when Miss Maggie came limping in, deprecating and shadowed. She was exactly the same: it might have been yesterday that the young Normal College student had first seen her. But that inexperienced clumsy child had grown up. When Marcia kissed her old friend she made no comments on her appearance, she only said, "Well, Miss Maggie, how glad I am to see you. How are you?"

Miss Maggie said she had been having a great deal of trouble with her spine. Some disease of the spinal cord, a kind of degeneration of its tissue. Long shudders passed along it at times which shook her so that she could not sit up after them. Marcia expressed sympathy for that and for the sleepless nights caused by the passage of heavy trucks before her window. And for the arthritis which often made it impossible for Miss Maggie to hold her brush and comb. Mrs. Clarke, who had been sitting through this talk in a rather absentminded silence, now thought of something she ought to do in the kitchen. But even left alone with Miss Maggie, Marcia did not offer to take her to a doctor for an examination of her spine, nor to try to have her room changed to the quiet back of the house, nor to find some one who would go in to brush her hair. Just before Mrs. Clarke came back, Miss Maggie said, not complainingly at all, a mere plain matter-of-fact statement, that she had not been away from the house for three months, not even down to the end of the block. "My knee keeps me from walking, and of course there's no reason for anyone with a car to think of taking out a useless old woman," she said, with her touching little smile.

Marcia found it touching now as she never had before. Never! But she did not say, "Why, I have my car right in front of the house now. Go put your things on and I'll take you clear out to the river and back." No, Marcia was no longer a shallow, ignorant, self-willed and tyrannical girl. She was a deep-hearted woman who knew tragedy when she saw it. She took the other's strengthless, skill-less, useless old hand into hers and held it close. The tears were in her eyes; and in her heart the first sympathy she had ever felt for poor Miss Maggie.

As I Looked Out of the Window

UNDER the old elms Mrs. S. Herrington Dodd was walking towards the center of town. Before leaving her well-appointed house she had put on as she always did, exactly the right costume. She had plenty of money, plenty of time, and back of her a lifetime of taking thought as to the right costume for each occasion. True, this occasion was but a shopping expedition to buy nothing-at-all in the best shop in town. Not that the best shop in our town was good enough to interest Mrs. Dodd. The fact was she had started out to look at something-or-other to wear in a shop, because after a half-century of thinking about clothes, she didn't know what else to do in an unoccupied hour. However, unimportant as the expedition was, it had not been slighted as to costume. Mrs. Dodd wore a toilet of which every costly simple detail complied with what, by the latest news from world centers, the most highly paid specialists on clothes considered right. Hence it was, quite literally, just as toilets should be, the complete and perfect expression of the personality of the wearer.

Towards her on the same side of the street came Ivy Peters. Ivy's costume was the perfect expression of what Ivy was, too. She had expended more energy, and made greater sacrifices to express herself in this manner than Mrs. Dodd.

But she had not given more thought to it. That would have been impossible.

This is what Ivy wore:—a small bright green sailor hat, well on the back of her head to show the yellow mass of her much-curled hair. Nude-colored, near-silk stockings with a run down one leg. Spike-heeled, pearl-gray kid slippers; a silver-trimmed, green crepe dress, cut rather skimpy wherever it is possible for a dress to be skimpy. Under the dress there was very little of anything. Ivy was on her way to look for a job as bundle-wrapper in a department store. She had gone without lunches for weeks to buy those clothes, and she loved them. She didn't much care whether she got that job or not. Ivy was eighteen; this was a very fine September morning, she was wearing all her best finery.

She teetered a little with youthful springiness as she walked. She saw Mrs. Dodd's perfect costume in all its sinister perfection approaching her (Mrs. Dodd inside it of course) and her teetering stopped. Her light heart sank. She knew clothes when she saw them. She flung her head up and looked down her nose. But she would have run away if she could.

Mrs. Dodd saw Ivy coming about the time that Ivy saw her. That is, she saw Ivy's clothes. She did not stop thinking of her own affairs (just now she was deliberating on the best shape for hand-bags) because Ivy was too insignificant to distract her mind from important matters. But even with most of her mind where it belonged, her practiced eye took in Ivy's clothes.

251

They were quite close to each other now. And now they had passed, their two women's bodies almost touching.

Mrs. S. Herrington Dodd had looked at Ivy. One gray glitter of a look which had started at the girl's badly cut shoes, already losing their shape because they were too small, had stabbed the run in the stocking-leg, had flickered in an instant's insulting amusement over Ivy's absurd dress, had appraised the cheap poor-quality hat, and with a final snake-like intuition that Ivy had not had a bath that morning nor for several mornings, had slid off from the girl into the distance, thence down to the ground, and thence to a discreet refreshing glance at the tailored perfection of her own skirt.

Not a muscle of Mrs. S. Herrington Dodd's face had moved. Nothing but her eyes. She walked along at the same pace, having quite forgotten that she had just passed an overdressed young working-girl. There are so many of them.

Ivy had understood very well what Mrs. Dodd's look had said to her. It had said, "You are a ridiculous vulgar creature of a different flesh and blood from mine. You have not been well brought up by people who know how to buy only the best things and plenty of them. Everything you have on today is awful, frightful. And everything you will wear all your life will be awful and frightful. No matter how many lunches you go without, you will never have a hundredth part enough money to dress as I do. And if you had the money, you'd never have sense enough to buy the right things."

Ivy had known this look was coming. She had tried with all her might to keep it off, by making her eyes say defiantly to Mrs. Dodd, "You think your clothes are swell because you've blown in all that jack on them. Well, they're not. They're lousy. Nobody could *hire* me to dress like you do, like I spent all my time in the front seat at my grandmother's funeral—not for all the jack in the banks!"

But Ivy could not hold up before her the protecting shield of this idea because she did not believe a word of it. So Mrs. Dodd's glance at her encountered nothing more resistant to its poisoned razor-edge than Ivy's poor little heart. It cut deep into that, and left a long bleeding slash across Ivy's self-respect. She felt sore and ashamed, helplessly unable to think of anything except Mrs. Dodd's look and what it meant. (If she had only known it, there was a look that would have protected her against anything even Mrs. Dodd could think, the look that says, "I am young and you are old." But of course Ivy would not know about this deadly look till she herself was old.) So she went along the street, not teetering springily now, stumping stupidly on her stupid high heels, her bleeding wound raw and quivering. She looked into the face of everyone she met, hoping to find a look that would be healing. But nobody else noticed her especially. There *are* a good many of her.

Mrs. Dodd proceeding in the other direction had no idea what her look had meant to Ivy. As I fear that she would have been pleased if she had known, I think it not inappropriate to feel thankful that this was one of the many things which Mrs. Dodd did not know.

She had advanced a few steps when she saw (dimly as the Mrs. Dodds perceive such small matters) that the delivery-Ford of a grocery store was drawn up before a house she was passing, and that the lower half of the grocer's boy hanging down from the back of the light truck suggested that the upper half was rummaging for the packages he was to deliver. As Mrs. Dodd came opposite, he emerged, all of him, his arms full of bundles and paper bags. He began to whistle a lively jazz tune which everybody is whistling this year, but which Mrs. Dodd had never heard.

As she would have turned her head towards a passing dog to verify the fact that it was a dog, Mrs. Dodd turned her head towards the grocer's boy. Her eyes had intended as a matter of course, to express this: "Oh, yes, the boy who delivers tea and potatoes," as they would have said of a dog, "Oh, yes, Mr. Jenning's half-grown Airedale."

But in the grocer's boy's eyes Mrs. Dodd encountered something so horrifying to her, so shocking, so deadly that her look recoiled and was thrust sharply in towards herself. He was only a lower-class young lout, you understand, too ignorant to appreciate Mrs. Dodd's costume. He did not, as a matter of fact, know enough even to look at her dress and hat. What he glanced at, as he started briskly up the walk to the kitchen door, was, therefore, Mrs. Dodd herself. And what she encountered in his careless eyes was a picture of how she looked to him. They said to her, not what she was accustomed to have people's eyes say to her, "O-o-oh! what a lot of money that costume must have cost!" Instead of this, during the instant when his casual glance swept over her, it said: "A flabby trussed-up old woman, cram-jam full of herself! I'm glad my grandmother doesn't look like that."

This not hotly or indignantly you understand, for Mrs. Dodd was less than nothing to the grocer's boy. What the boy's eyes said was poisoned with something worse to Mrs. Dodd than resentment, with cool slighting sincerity.

Yes, for an instant the grocer's boy's expression was a mirror in which Mrs. Dodd saw how she looked to other people. (Heaven save us all from such mirrors!)

Her whole face altered—

I had never thought before that anything in the world could make me feel sorry for Mrs. S. Herrington Dodd.

This look had not had for the grocer's boy the importance it had had for Mrs. Dodd. It had not, indeed, had any importance at all. It had occupied no more than two of the rapidly whistled notes of his jazz tune. He had many more interesting things to think of.

An old man had been sick for a long time in the house to which the boy was delivering his tea and potatoes. He had had erysipelas which is serious at eighty-one, and the doctors had been sure they could not pull him through. He had pulled himself through.

It had been hard to do, all alone, and had tired him so that during his long convalescence, he often wondered whether it had been worth while. That morning was the first time in many weeks he had been out of his bed. He moved slowly, leaning on his elderly nurse's arm, towards the window. He had, for so long, seen nothing but his sick-room that he had forgotten that there was anything else in the world except the ceiling with its network of cracks his tired eyes had followed so helplessly, and the wall-paper that did not join its strips with accuracy, no, not in one single place, no matter how many million times his gaze crept up and down the wall. The narrow smallness enclosed by the six sides of his sick-room, it was not much bigger than a coffin after all. To have made that long frightful effort to keep hold of this! He was often sorry that he had not let go when the doctors did.

He was at the window now. The nurse took her hand from his arm and pulled up the shade. The old gentleman looked out.

Why, there was the world—still there! Not shrunk to the smallness of his bedroom. The sky was greater than anybody can remember unless he has just looked up into it, the sky whose deep endless blue could not conceivably ever have the tiniest crack in it. The tall calm old elms were there, soaring, deep-rooted, their complicated branches and twigs and trunks fitting together with invisible perfection in every tiniest detail of their intricate pattern. And the distance— the grand spaciousness of the distance! How could he have forgotten what distance is like! And all that air, that golden living air!

The old gentleman knew now why he had kept himself from dying. He looked out and took a long breath. Yes, he knew.

The grocer's boy was coming up the walk towards the kitchen when the nurse raised the window-shade. His eye was caught by that and looking up he saw the old gentleman's face when he took his first deep breath of outdoor air, at the very instant when he perceived that the sky is greater than anyone can remember, at the very moment when he knew why he had not let himself die.

The boy thought the convalescent's face said no more to him than, "Well, old Mr. Elliott's going to get well after all. He looks pretty cheerful about it, I'll tell the world."

But far below this thought, something bright, strong, enduring had slid into his young heart to stay—the beginning of a faith in life that does not depend on being twenty years old and in perfect health.

The nurse helped the old man into his armchair. The grocer's boy delivered his packages and went away. The street was empty.

Presently it became filled again. Filled from end to end, from side to side, roaringly filled as by a blowing wind. Mrs. Dennis' Peggy came racing down the sidewalk skipping rope.

Peggy was still quite a little girl. This was the first season she had known how to jump rope, and this was the very first day she had caught the swing so that she need not think about how to do it, but could give herself wholly to the magnificent violence of the rhythm. Into the light, thin, ever-repeated circles of the whirling rope her little body was flung upward at exactly timed intervals as if the earth were playing ball, with a little girl as the ball.

257

Peggy was new to this wonder, this giddiness of passionate, controlled, recurring motion. She skipped harder and harder, more and more furiously, the crack of her rope as it hit the stone sidewalk a ringing refrain to the long soft swish of the circle through the air. Her face glowed. With every leap into the air, it glowed like a nasturtium in full sunlight. She flung back her head; she was a little Bacchante, a mad, life-drunken little maenad leaping down our street.

She saw a woman coming down the street towards her, and still hurling herself through the perfect circles of her skipping-rope, she drew off to one side of the sidewalk to let her pass. As they came close together, the child looked out from the whirling maze of her rope, full at the woman (whom she had never seen before) and dazzlingly smiled.

She did not really see the other human being—little Peggy had not yet come to an age when she could really see or feel anything in the world except little Peggy. Her smile was a recognition that another living creature was there, someone who, being alive, knew and shared this whirling joyful madness of being alive. For an instant, Peggy's blazing smile of ecstasy flung across the other a high-tension live-wire from the mighty dynamo to which with her skipping-rope she had harnessed her little body.

The woman whom she had passed was Miss Agnes Hardman. She is a very good woman indeed, and although that sounds as though I were making fun of her (isn't it odd—and rather sad—that it should?), I do not mean that at all. She is really and truly the best woman in town. She has never once thought of her own interests, she has always been trying to make things better for other people.

She has been at this so long, all her life in fact, that from the habit of trying to make things better she has acquired another habit, that of seeing very clearly that they are not very good as they are. Well, they aren't. She is right, of course. They never are. But—

People who know Miss Hardman have often thought that "but—" Yet they have never said it either to her or to each other, for of course it is only the beginning of a sentence and nobody has had any idea how to finish it. Miss Hardman is forty-seven years old, and she had never even got as far as the "but—"

That morning she was on her way to the City Council to make a well-merited complaint about the city dumping-ground. The city was using its rubbish to fill in a swampy piece of land in order to produce some salable building-lots. They did not of course dump the contents of garbage-cans there, city health ordinances forbidding that. But all sorts of other trash:—rusty battered wrecks of automobiles, broken barrels, smashed packing-boxes, iron junk, splintered fruit-baskets—nothing that smelled badly or would hurt any-body's health, but a horrible-looking mess, such as no well-to-do people would have allowed to remain in their midst for an instant. Miss Hardman often fiercely asked her friends (especially if they were comfortably well off, and certainly never had), "Did *you* ever live close to a city rubbish heap?"

This was what made Miss Hardman's generous heart especially hot, the fact that this frightful eye-sore was in a poor section of the small city. "If it had been in a middle-class residential section," she often cried out, "the city authorities would have had it filled at once with truck-loads of good clean earth, no matter at what cost, and sowed grass-seed on it to make a park." At the very moment when she passed Peggy she had been saying this very thing to herself. (She said that sort of thing all the time she was awake so this is not as surprising as it might seem.)

She had scarcely noticed that a little girl jumping rope was approaching her. Her eyes were always more on her helpful plans than on what was about her. And although she was sincerely interested in the welfare of children, she did not know any children very well. Also Peggy did not look, even from a distance, as though anybody needed to take thought as to her welfare. But even through her kind, good, and busy thoughts, Miss Hardman had dimly noted the crisp regular beat of the rope, as if another pulse than hers had begun to beat in the air. As they passed, still thinking about how to do away with that dump-heap, she turned her eyes absently on Peggy's face.

Full power, with all its incalculable voltage, there sped through her one great shock from the dynamo to which Peggy had harnessed herself. The child's wild enchanted face —her eyes blazing with life-drunkenness—Miss Hardman reeled back from them, halted and stood stockstill on the sidewalk.

The child whirled past. The beat of her rope that was like a new pulse in the air, now pulsed behind Miss Hardman.

As I Looked Out of the Window

Well—*well!* What could you make of that? Miss Hardman
asked herself. How very queer she felt, her heart beating considerably faster than was its usual quiet habit. What was it
about that child that had so startled her? Why had she felt,
as their eyes met, as though a shower of sparks had burst up
between them?

She tried to get back into her usual feelings. What was it
she had been thinking of? She could not remember. She
looked around her as if to catch her forgotten thought as it
drifted away. And what she saw was that it was a remark-
ably fine morning in September, very golden and spacious
and airy. There was old Mr. Elliott, who had been at the
point of death, up and sitting at the window. So he was going
to get well. This did not surprise her. It seemed for the
moment natural that everybody should get well, should be
well, in such golden air. She waved her kind hand to him,
sharing in his new joy.

What was it she had been about to do? Oh, yes, the dump-
heap. It came back to her now. She remembered how it
looked. But now she saw (she had, as a matter of fact, seen
them often, because she often investigated the dump-heap;
and yet she seemed to see them for the first time), she saw
crowds of Saturday-morning little boys, prowling around over
its untidy surface, uncared-for little boys with no recreation
leader to guide them, shabby little boys with wrinkling and
holey stockings, little boys with dreadful fingernails. The
blinding light which Peggy had sent through Miss Hardman now showed something about them she had never
noticed before. In the refulgence of Peggy's stroke of light-

ning she saw—not their blackened, broken fingernails nor their dusty unkempt heads of hair—but their faces alert and alive, the way they leaped about, and ran and climbed, laughing and calling to each other. She saw that their eyes were shining like Peggy's. She saw their free wild look of being at home, where they belonged in the wild free light of Peggy's flash of lightning.

What were they doing there? Miss Hardman had often seen them. She knew very well. But she had never known before. They made bonfires out of the old barrels and broken boxes, bonfires from which rich black smoke and fierce bright flames swept grandly up to the sky; they constructed crazy-looking shacks out of boards they broke off the crates, crazy-looking but all their own; they clambered in and out of the broken, rusty wrecks of automobiles, wrenching at shattered steering-wheels, shouting, excited and purposeful—was it on imaginary journeys they were going?

Miss Hardman walked along the sidewalk now, but very slowly. If all the dump-heap were covered with good expensive earth, sowed to grass and planted with pretty flower-beds and "keep-off-the-grass" signs, where could little boys like that go to find rich blackness and flaming glories and corners of the world all their own and imaginary escapes from out their poor little lives—

Our poor little lives, all of us, and our escapes from them—

You see, Miss Hardman at forty-seven years of age had come to the "but—" for the first time.

262

It was very troubling and confusing to her. It is to all of us.

You can, as a matter of fact, see enough of human life to addle your brains, just looking out of the window.

Remembrance of Things Past

AUNT EMMA was to drive to town that morning to trade in the eggs. Spring weather had waked up the hens and the eggs had been piling up in the brown crock in the buttery, till they had overflowed into several shiny milk-pans on the same shelf. Mother was too busy cleaning house to think of anything else; and as it was the sacred season of spring plowing, of course nobody so much as mentioned eggs or going to town, to Father.

It settled itself that Aunt Emma was to drive Old Iron-sides (whose asthma was much better now the sunny weather had come) and to take Petey with her. Petey was not a little boy but a little girl, and the reason she wasn't at school was that she had had the mumps, and was just getting over them. Aunt Emma was really Great-aunt Emma, Father's aunt, and she lived in three rooms in the wing of the farmhouse, and kept house by herself.

She had always lived somewhere in that house. She had in fact been born there. Once she had been a little girl like Petey; now she was quite old and had white hair (what there was of it) and wore shoes with elastic in the sides. But she still went berrying in the summer-time, and could hitch up a horse as well as anybody.

The eggs were put into two market-baskets and the

264

baskets set on the floor of the buggy at one side of Aunt
Emma's congress gaiters, just below Petey's dangling feet.
All through the long dreamy jogging trip to town, there
came and went in Petey's mind a scaringly funny notion of
what would happen if she should slip forward off the seat
and land in those egg-baskets.

Aunt Emma pulled up the reins, and held the whip at attention. "Did you say half-inch white elastic? Or quarter-
inch?" she called up to Mother who leaned out of an open
bedroom window, a dustcloth in her hand, her dark hair tied
up in a clean white cloth, her black eyes snapping.

"Half-inch," Mother answered, "it doesn't cut into the
little boys' legs so."

From this Petey knew Mother had got the rompers for
the twins almost done.

"Git-ap," said Aunt Emma to Old Ironsides, who coughed
(but not very hard), leaned forward and moved off over the
grass of the dooryard.

Nobody said anything for a while. Aunt Emma seemed to
be thinking. Petey was feeling—nothing special you could
put your finger on, but plenty of it—she was feeling warmed
by the sunshine so bright and alive that it seemed queer it
was silent and didn't sing aloud as it shone down on a little
girl; and she was feeling pleasantly joggled by Old Ironsides' regular trot-trot; and glad she wasn't at school; and a
little dazzled by the green and gold and blue of outdoors.
She had been kept in the house a long time by the mumps.

By and by they came to a place where, if you felt like it,

265

you could turn off the road and drive through a shallow brook. Aunt Emma did feel like it. When Old Ironsides had his feet in the water, he stopped and shook his head. Aunt Emma let out the reins and he stooped his muzzle to the water to drink, and blow, and drink again.

"My father liked this little ford," said Aunt Emma. "He always used to drive the horses down into it, and let them drink. And then stand a minute. It takes me back to do it."

They stood a minute, too, the quick bright water curling and eddying loudly over its pebbles. Beside the sleepy silence of the growing grass on its banks, it seemed like a just-waked-up person talking—talking and laughing and flashing at you.

It had taken Aunt Emma back. Just so had it flashed and laughed into her father's face with his thick brown beard, when the horses drank, and then stood to breathe. For a moment he seemed sitting there beside her again. People who had had a real father could make a guess what the hymn-books were talking about when they spoke of a "heavenly Father." Aunt Emma's father had lived to be a very old man, quite dependent on her in his last illness, so weak that he was like a baby and could only drink if she held the cup to his lips. But there at the little ford over the brook he was always strong and young and all-powerful and kind —the man who had taught her how to guess at what a heavenly Father might be. It had been twenty-five years since his death, but there he sat again, leaning over to look at the bright ever-young water, and once more his little girl sat beside him, dreaming and secure.

"I see a fish in that pool," exclaimed Petey.

"Yes, farther up the fishing's pretty good," said Aunt Emma. "Git-ap, 'Sidesey!'"

Old Ironsides sighed, and digging his hoofs into the gravelly slope on the other side brought them out once more upon the main road.

Ahead of them where the road made a turn it ran through a cluster of very tall old pines, standing dark against the glowing sky. "Oh, Aunt Emma," said Petey, "isn't this the place where Uncle Zed and somebody else saw the bear? Tell me about it."

"Tell you about it?" protested Aunt Emma. "You've heard it a thousand times!"

"Tell me again," begged Petey, "I love to hear about it."

"There's nothing *to* it, anyhow," said Aunt Emma, beginning to tell the story as it was always told. "Nothing happened. It was 'way back in the early days, just after the war of 1812, when there weren't so many people around here as now, and lots more wild animals. Uncle Zed and Grandfather—it was your own great-great-grandfather, you oughtn't to forget that—had been sent up here to the carding mill to get some wool carded. When we go by sometime I'll show you where you can still see a little piece of the old dam where the carding-mill stood. They were little boys to send so far, all alone, but they didn't baby children then as they do now, Uncle Zed always used to say. Each of them had a basket of wool on his arm, and they were scuffing along in the sand just about here—" (they were almost at the turn of the road now), "only the road was just a narrow trail then, with thick pine woods on both sides. That clump of big old trees are all that are left of the forest. And as the boys came around the corner—" (Old Ironsides swung his nid-nodding head around the turn of the road) "right— *there!*—" she pointed with the whip and made a pause—"right there in the middle of the path stood a great—big—brown—bear." She pulled the old horse to a standstill.

Petey took hold tightly of a fold of Aunt Emma's percale skirt, sat a little closer to her and looked hard along the darkly shaded road to the spot where Aunt Emma was pointing.

Aunt Emma went on. "Uncle Zed always said it looked as big as a bull. It swung its head from one side to the other sort of like a bull, too."

"What did the little boys do?" asked Petey in a small voice, although she knew very well what they had done.

"Oh, they *froze*—stood perfectly still, didn't breathe, didn't stir—for about an hour, Uncle Zed used to say. Then the bear swung its head around with a grunt, and lumbered off up that bank."

Petey looked at the steep bank brown with pine needles. Were there not great footprints on it?

"In a minute, the little boys heard it splashing across the Mill Brook, and after that, stones rattling as it started up the slope of the mountain."

268

Petey listened. It seemed to her that she too could hear a distant splashing and a rattle of rolling stones.

Aunt Emma started the horse up again.

"And then what?" asked Petey.

"Oh, nothing. The little boys stood there, trying to get up their spunk to go on. They felt like legging it for home as fast as they could clip it of course. But they just waited till they'd got their breath back, and went ahead to the carding-mill and left their wool. There wasn't anything to be afraid of once the bear had gone away, and they knew that."

"How old were they?" asked Petey. This was not one of the stock questions she always asked. She did not know the answer. She had never thought before about how old they were.

"Let me see," said Aunt Emma. "I could figure that out from my father's age." She sat figuring it out for a minute or two and said, "Why, Uncle Zed must have been about nine, and Grandfather just past seven."

Petey did not say anything. She was almost seven herself. Almost the age of the little boy who had seen a bear, right here, in this very spot. And still had gone on. Had not run home to his mother.

Old Ironsides clip-clopped slowly along. Petey tipped her head back to look up into the big pines. Those very trees looking down on her had looked down on that little boy. For a moment she saw him—for an instant she was the boy herself, her heart beating fast, her knees shaking, listening to the distant rattle of rolling stones. And he had gone on. It was right here he had decided he wouldn't turn back.

269

He had been Petey's great-great-grandfather. She had often been shown his mossy tombstone in the cemetery. But for Petey he was always alive under the big pines at the turn of the road. There he stood, trembling, but not giving up, clenching his little fists together. These same trees had looked down at him.

"Git-*ap!*" said Aunt Emma crossly to Old Ironsides. "You're pokier than ever this spring."

They were approaching the grassy cross-roads which Aunt Emma liked to pass as fast as she could—the cross-roads where, one starry night, she had said good-by to the only lover she had ever had.

She had loved him terribly, everything about him from the quirk at the corner of his red lips when he pronounced certain consonants, to the way his hands folded together on his lap in church. She had loved his old coat, hung on a fence-post as he plowed, and she had trembled with adoration at the ring of his voice, shouting to his horses, as it came drifting faintly back to her across the wide plowed field, mixed with the clear tinkling of the meadow-lark's song.

He was her father's hired man, one of the Metcalf tribe who never amounted to anything, and he had not a penny to his name. But she had not cared. She was proud to "keep company steadily" with him, to have him drive her to church and singing-school. The touch of his hand as he helped her into the sleigh or buggy made her giddy. Those nights she lay awake, feeling the warm firmness of his young fingers as though he lay there beside her, clasping her hand in his. She never dreamed of anything in her future but marrying him and worshiping him forever.

Then one day, in summer-time, she had seen him looking across the church at Nettie Purdy. That had been enough. He had never looked at her like that. Yet she knew—she knew with every beat of her heart, what such a look meant. But she could not believe it at first. And she was hard and passionate and asked herself, what of it? He was—as such things go—pledged to her. Nettie was very poor, and weak too. Emma was sure she could hold her own against a Nettie.

She watched them together for a month after that, a month of such horrid misery that even now, an old woman, appeased, quiet, near her end, she winced to think of it.

When she knew and could not tell herself she did not— she knew also what she must do—for his sake. One summer night, as they were walking home together from a picnic, there at the cross-roads, she had stopped him and told him that she didn't want to keep company with him any more. She guessed that she didn't care so much about him as she thought she had. And she'd rather walk the rest of the way home alone. She wasn't one to be afraid or lonely.

For form's sake, he had tried to protest. But she who knew every intonation of his voice had not been able to endure the flat falseness of his accent. "Don't talk to me like that!" she had blazed out. "No, don't touch me either!"

Those were the last words she had said to her love, hard hateful words.

271

She had turned and run away down the road. But she had looked back. In the starlight she could see him, starting up the hill road to the left. Nettie's home was the first house up that road.

Well, she had walked the rest of her life alone. But she had been lonely.

He had married Nettie, and she had lived through it. Had lived through the far more awful years when she saw the radiant young man she had loved turn slowly into somebody else, into a shiftless, lean, ignorant, bald-headed farmer, who chewed tobacco and was always behind with his work—into just another Metcalf. For many years she had known the most awful thing of all, that he had never—save in her imagination—been anything else. Even her dreams had been killed for her by life.

He had been dead a long time now, and Aunt Emma's hot terrible madness had died long before he did. But neither was quite altogether dead. Always when she passed the crossroads, there he stood, still, the ghost of a dream. Over him a black sky was always silver-bright with stars; and before him stood a passionate-hearted girl driving the knife steadily into her own side, for the sake of true love—that she might not stand between the man she loved and *his* dream.

They passed the cross-roads, the old horse jogging steadily. Aunt Emma looked down tenderly, piteously at the little girl by her side. How horribly girls could suffer.

"Are you all right, Petey dear?" she asked, tucking the laprobe more closely about the little knees. "Wouldn't you rather curl up on the seat and put your head on my lap for a while?"

"No, I'm all right," said Petey, dreamily. "I like to watch old 'Sidesey's hips hump up and down."

They were not far from town now and ahead of them, off to one side, was the big meadow where, every fall, the county fair was held. Strangers never could see anything in it different from any other sizable field. But people who'd grown up around there looked at it very specially whenever they passed. Its grass was like any other grass now, growing silently, glistening new in the new sunshine. But Aunt Emma and Petey saw it hectic and important, trampled with hundreds of feet, strewn with peanut-shells and paper-bags. And although it lay so vacantly open to the sky now, only a cow or two grazing on it, the two passers-by caught hanging close above it a transparent shimmer of bright tents and flags and fluttering colors; and from the corner where the merry-go-round always stood, there streamed up into the still country air an inaudible echo of the blare of the steam piano.

Aunt Emma smiled to herself. She was an old woman now and had lived through what makes life—love and the death of love and the birth of selflessness. She had known awful hours, great hours, dull hours, happy hours; but never an hour like the one when her mother had set her for her first ride on the merry-go-round. No steam-driven, massive, gilded, be-mirrored edifice in those days. An old horse patiently treading around and around pushed the bar which set the painted horses whirling. A music box tinkled out its steely notes, like so many pins piercing the air.

But Aunt Emma had been six years old. She did not need gilt and mirrors. She was six, and her heart beat like mad in her little breast as her mother lifted her up and strapped her upon the prancing wooden horse.

The music had begun, her horse reared nobly on his front feet—she clutched at his mane—she looked wildly for her mother. But her mother was gone; and the whole world, the great stable world, was floating majestically past her—the tall plumed elm trees gliding along, the blue hills slowly changing their positions.

Oh, there was Mother's face—in the crowd watching— but gone in a twinkling. She did not see it again. She did not look for it again. She was no longer a little girl with a Mother—the music soared up to the sky and she with it— she was gliding rhythmically with a rhythmic moving world. How beautiful it was to have everything moving in time to her music—the hills, the rooted trees—the very earth slid smoothly and sweetly with her, faster and faster through space.

She was filled with the magnificence of her progress—had she ever lived in a tiny body?—been no more than a little girl? She beat her wings and flew up and away from all she had ever known, out of the limitations of time and space—

"There!" said Mother, lifting her off, "that's enough for the first time. You look real pale. I shouldn't wonder if it made you sick to your stomach. Sometimes it does."

274

But it had not. It had only broken a way out from stony barriers for little Emma's imagination, had once for all swung her clear of herself, up and out to bigness, which from that time on was always waiting there for her to explore it again.

Sometimes—Aunt Emma was getting really old—as she lay awake at night, sometimes she thought about death, and what it would mean to die, and at once there came into her mind that old flight into the infinite, that first glimpse of boundlessness, with everything that had been stable float-ing fluently and surely through space with her—and she unafraid, upborne, magnificently free from all that kept her down—music in her ears.

"Did you ever ride on the merry-go-round, Petey?" she asked.

"No," said the little girl. "Mother's always afraid it would make me sick to my stomach."

"I'll take you, come next fair-time," Aunt Emma promised her.

And now they were in front of the store, and old Mr. Eldon, the storekeeper, who had been sitting on the front-steps, smoking his pipe in the sun, came out to the buggy, saying how-de-do to Aunt Emma.

"My sakes, what a nice mess of eggs!" he commented, looking down at the two big basketfuls.

"Yes," said Aunt Emma, putting the whip back in the socket, "there's nothing like Leghorns for laying."

An Unprejudiced Mind

THERE was a young composer who every morning went out to write music in a little shack made of rough boards and roofing paper. The shack had been built one winter, years before, by some lumbermen cutting wood on the mountain, who needed a place where they could sit out of the storm in bad weather and eat their lunches. They had built it carelessly, and it was now half-fallen to pieces, but it was quite good enough for the composer who wanted nothing from the world but to leave him alive till he had written his music.

Almost anything is enough to keep alive someone who wishes nothing for himself but time to write music—he had found that out. He slept at a farmhouse on the edge of the forest, and mornings and evenings ate a hard-fried breakfast and supper there. He paid for this partly by splitting wood and helping with the milking, and partly with a little cash left over from the last time he had stayed out in the world giving music lessons. In the morning when he went off from the farmhouse to the shack, he carried with him a lunch of bread and butter and milk, and whatever new note-sequences had come into his head during the night.

The shack stood in a small clearing several miles from the farmhouse. The path to it was a narrow deeply shaded woodland trail. As his sure, wiry, strong young feet took him swiftly along, each morning and evening, the composer let his creative imagination step out of its usual field and wander about in the motionless battlefield on which the silent, violent struggles of forest life take place. He tried himself out fancifully in one role after another of that— tragedy, comedy, melodrama—he could never decide which it was, always throbbing full-pulsed in the green shadow of the trees. Now he hurried with the mushroom to take advantage of a rainy day before the diabolical sunshine should reappear to shrivel up that exquisite and divine damp- ness which is the real meaning of life, and was as proud of the achievement of a whole day's existence as of a century's cold patience when he threw himself into the long ordeal of the hemlocks, crouching gnome-like and watchful under the arrogant leafiness of the deciduous trees.

Now he lived stolidly under the cool philosophic shell of the snail, letting the feverish world go by with no notice taken of its undignified ups and downs; now he panted excitedly under the quivering striped skin of a chipmunk, flickering from tree to tree, sharing with an artist's abandon the fears, the hopes, the angers, the loves of life's wild drama as lived by creatures with few brains and impressionable nerves.

He had accepted the forest world and was accepted by it. And yet one day when he turned the corner of the shack and saw, on the flat stone before the door, a gracefully coiled snake sunning itself peaceably in the morning light, he started back in an entirely human recoil of his flesh. The

277

snake was as startled as he, and after one terrified spasmodic contraction of alarm, painful to see, writhed away, panic-struck, into the grass of the clearing.

The composer was very much put out by this happening. Not at all by the snake, for his parents, broad-minded enlightened people, had taught him to laugh at superstitions, and had given him well-illustrated readable books on Nature in all of which he had read that there are almost no venomous snakes in a temperate climate, and that most of them are as harmless as chipmunks. No, his composure was not ruffled by the appearance of a snake in his domain, but by the brutally primitive way in which his skin had risen up in goose-flesh at the sight of it. Of course he knew about reflexes as educated people do know nowadays, knew the simple cause of the goose-flesh, and as he settled himself before his work-table, he reminded himself that embedded in his young body were very old muscular and nerve habits, habits dating back probably to the times before the cave-age period, when his ancestors had swung themselves with short-thumbed hands from one tree-branch to another. The appearance of a snake was of course enough to send the whole naked tribe shrieking in terror into the flight which was their only defense.

Then, all during the time his forefathers were coming down out of trees and taking to caves and then to huts and then to houses and cities and subways, those old reflexes that had been useful and now were causeless, had been allowed to go on unchecked, contracting in nervous spasms, because those were times of antiquity, medieval times, Victorian times, when man had not learned to honor above all else the unprejudiced inquiring mind which is to lead us at last, out of the dark tradition-ridden Egypt of slavery to unreason, into the Promised Land of the new humanity. The train of his thoughts having now led him as it always did, to his music, he set to work on the page he had left unfinished the day before.

For the music he was trying to write was to be the voice of the age just dawning, the age in which men, instead of exhausting themselves in the despairing, futile search for affirmations great enough to silence all questionings, should learn to find their joy, their serenity, their fulfillment in the very act of questioning, of searching—as, so he had been taught, modern minds must do or perish. He knew that he had by no means originated this idea. What he hoped to do was to find a new compelling way to express it. Modern science has for a century told men that their highest destiny is to question, yes, but only with the matter-of-fact dryness which states facts as they are, makes no comment on them, and hence reaches but few minds. What was flaming like the Burning Bush in the young composer's generous heart was an exalting passion to proclaim this new Gospel of Questioning in the many-toned voice of emotion, to write music that would lift the heart and not merely the mind to the beauty of seeking. When all is tentative, relative, shifting, it is base, he thought, to use the magic of one's art to prop up the old false cult of stability. His music, if he could only live long enough to learn how to create it, would leave the listener soaring up and out upon the parabola of a melodic curve not to be completed and resolved by scholastic combinations of notes according to the old conventions of harmony, but seeking its release in the flight towards Infinity.

Yes, this was the unearthly and divine antagonist with which the young Jacob wrestled daily in the old shack. This and not making money was the noble goal towards which he pressed with every nerve, gladly spending the ardor of his youth on the mere chance that he might in the end be one of those who cleave the rock and let the army of the faithful through. It was not surprising that he did not care that his shelter was rickety, so long as the roof was tight enough to keep the rain from his battered piano and his work-table. Often he forgot to eat the bread and butter and drink the milk brought from the farmhouse. Sometimes he was recalled to what is usually spoken of as "reality" only when twilight veiled the lines on his music paper, and when opening his door with a hand trembling from long tension, he saw a new moon gleam above the trees, or the evening star. He often stood for a moment there, his chest heaving, as though he had forgotten to breathe since morning. And of course, on the day he saw the snake, he had forgotten the incident by the time he was fairly settled between his piano and his table.

But the next morning, as he approached the shack, although he was already thinking about his work, a faint stirring in the striped muscles of his viscera, reminded him of yesterday's goose-flesh. He disliked this tyranny of the body over the mind, was always annoyed by the conditioning of human moods and emotions by bodily mechanisms. In fact he detested them, because of the obvious idiocy of the body's

processes, its ignoring of reasonableness or logic, the way it
goes stupidly on for centuries wasting your energies with
warnings no longer valid. When, after stopping for a moment
to take thought as to the cause of this slight disagreeable
sensation which felt like dread, he discovered that it came
from the memory of the beautiful little snake he had seen
sharing the clearing with him, he was out of patience with
himself. Walking lightly, not to startle it, he slowly rounded
the corner of the shack. The snake was there. She was rejoic-
ing in the sunlight, her supple body voluptuously lax and
off-guard, basking in the warm rays with a delight very
familiar to the impressionable young artist. Why was there
in his intimate being a recoil, a repulsion, anything but the
brotherly sympathy he would have felt for a dog so obviously
enjoying himself in the sun? Considering this, and forcing
himself to look steadily at the prettily marked serpent, with
the intricate pattern of its harmonious colors, he tried to bring
to mind a larger number of the enlightened principles on
which he had been brought up by his parents, striving as
they did to form in him a personality with no inhibition his
will could not control, a mind without prejudices, moving
freely in the open, beyond tabus, beyond Good and Evil.
But by some random mental association, what came before
his memory was a picture of his grandmother. She had been
an old-fashioned woman with a very prejudiced mind and no
information whatever about the mystic interlocking com-
pensating relationships of the many parts of the great Pattern
of Life, in which a snake is as necessary to the scheme of
things as an old woman. He remembered that his parents

had been fearful lest the example of her life, conducted mostly, as they saw it to be, by rote and unquestioned ritual, should cast a shadow on the glad courageous acceptance of Nature, which they were trying to instill into their little boy. He recalled hearing them trying to make her understand that in the climate where they lived, snakes are almost never poisonous, that they are needed in the economy of Nature, are as harmless and useful as hens. "You don't hate and fear a hen," they told her. "Why should you hate a snake?" They had assured her that if she only made an effort to control herself, she could soon get rid of those reflex contractions of disgust, which made her scream and run away so foolishly from the gentle little garter-snakes in the garden. But the old woman had quite missed the point of their reasoning. She had assured them that she highly valued any feeling that would keep her clear of snakes, and would not for the world lose it. One of her great-great-grandfathers, she told them, had died of a snake-bite, and she felt it behooved his descendants to cultivate goose-flesh when they saw one. His parents had laughed at this story, and afterwards told the little boy this was an example of the tyranny of Tradition, the dead hand of the past.

At this point, although he had been standing very still, the snake became aware of another presence, and gracefully glided away, leaving on the retina of the composer's eye curves which his mind told him were lovely, and from which the core of his being drew back with a shudder.

Before he set himself to work that day, he set himself a mental exercise, the first of a series with which he meant to

282

free himself from this as from any other baseless nervous reaction. He called to mind what he had learned in college about biology and evolution. It was rather hazy now; he was no longer sure of many of the details; but there was plenty enough left in his memory for his purpose. He recalled a professor of zoology who told them that snakes represent one of the many laboratory tests in flesh and bone of the great experiment of finding out how best to construct beings fit to inhabit the globe. Reptiles have certain obvious advantages over our human construction, the teacher had pointed out. The composer remembered how flexible the snake's backbone had looked and felt, that yes, his own was as stiff in comparison as a dead tree. They were also really beautiful to look at, if one could only divest his mind of the idiotic fortuitous human association of ideas which connected evil with that beauty.

Now, of a morning, as the composer walked along the woodland path, he was not whirring and spinning lightly with the Mayflies in slanting rays of light, or striking long unconquerable roots down and down till they reached life-giving food, like the birch-tree whose fate had been to be born on a rock. He was emancipating his mind from prejudice.

Having done a good deal of this in his life, he had invented a very workable technique for it. He varied his devices. One day he adopted one sort of mental gymnastics, the day afterwards turning to something quite different. One day he concentrated on the idea of the great Economy of Nature, the interrelation of one part to another, the interdependence of one on another; he recalled all he had been taught of the way in which ignorance and prejudice, rushing in with conventional ideas of what is good and what is evil, upset the exquisite balance in which the Wheel of Life is poised. He had heard—although he could not now bring it exactly to mind—what useful part is played by snakes in our world—was it perhaps to keep down the numbers of field-mice? At any rate it was something. Something discovered by unprejudiced scientists who, probing into nature's housekeeping with disinterested eyes, naturally see what is actually there, not what they think would be decorous to see.

On another morning he set himself the exercise—rather amusing—of thinking how repulsive he and other humans must look to snakes, queer, graceless monsters, hitching themselves forward by falling from one long bone to another, of an ugly monotonous grayish white as to skin, without one single spot of color or arabesque of line such as flows in gracious designs along the back of the humblest member of the snake family. And of what use could they be—these clumping elephantine destructive creatures? The composer found this a very useful device, easily kept up and elaborated.

Another morning he brought to mind the evident fright of the snake the first time he had trodden so near her, the agonized fear expressed by that spasmodic coiling contraction of all her body. He remembered now having read that snakes, far from being aggressive, are very timid, have poor eyesight and know it, and suffer greatly from apprehension. He began to school his mind to compassion for the poor creature. The clearing around the shack was the only place she had to sun herself. And that poisoned by a noisy clown!

He got on very well in these mental exercises, familiarized himself so thoroughly with the idea he was trying to plant in his mind that he was able, before the summer was over, to watch almost unmoved the pretty timid thing as, on his arrival at the shack, she slid gracefully from his door-step. Yet, walking home one afternoon, thinking fixedly of his music, he saw from the corner of his eye the shadow of a dead branch move writhingly on the path before him. With a cry he started back, breathing fast, his heart beating thickly in his throat. There was still much to do, he saw, before he had wholly driven prejudice, tradition and convention from his life.

But at least he had removed the dim feeling of dread from his mind so successfully that often now as he approached the shack, he had quite forgotten that the snake might be there, his thoughts already leaping forward to his vision of the apotheosis of questioning which hung gloriously in the air over the work-table in the battered little shed, taking shape more firmly every day.

One morning, indeed, absorbed by a phrase which he had been obliged to leave half-finished the day before, he not only forgot that the snake might be there, but as he approached the shack, did not observe that she really was there. He stepped jarringly with his clumsy heavy human tread upon the door-step where the snake lay sunning herself.

The pretty creature was terribly frightened, for the composer had been rightly informed, she was very timid indeed. And it was also true, as he had been taught, that her reactions were not different in any way from those of a harmless barnyard hen. A startled hen in a flurry of nervous self-defense pecks hard at whatever seems to threaten it. Just so the startled snake, in a panic, coiled and struck hard at the nearest object her dim eyes could see. For the nature-study books read in his boyhood by the composer had been accurate in stating that snakes have very poor eyesight.

The nearest object happened to be an artery in the bare ankle of the composer. And it was a snake not a hen who struck, a snake moreover—as it happened—belonging to one of the rarely seen venomous varieties. So the composer died before he could get back to the farmhouse for help. And that was the end of his music.

Silver Poplars and the Father

AS MARTIN WARNER plodded past the Bates bungalow on his way home from the garage he saw young Mrs. Bates sitting very still on the porch, her new baby at her breast. She was looking down on the small round head so steadily she did not see the man till, as he turned the corner, his lunch-pail flashed in the sun, now very low. She looked up then with a start, shifted the baby hastily to the other arm, pulled her clean, rumpled, percale dress over her breast and called after him, "Oh, Mr. Warner, wait a minute. Your wife just telephoned from Troy that the dentist had kept them so long she and the children missed the last train north. She said to tell you that they'd stay with her sister overnight, and come up on the early morning train."

"Oh, did she?" said Martin. He stood still, surprised by a variation in the regularity of his life's pattern. He thought about the news for a moment, till it had had time to sink into his mind. Then, as there seemed nothing special to say about it, he remarked, "Well, all right. Much obliged for telling me."

The young woman recited the rest of the message competently. "Mrs. Warner said to tell you there is some corned-beef hash in a bowl all ready to warm up, and cold boiled potatoes to fry and plenty of ripe tomatoes in the garden to slice, if you feel like them."

"Oh, *that*'ll be all right!" Martin reassured her—any man to any woman—about his capacity to get himself enough to eat as instinctively as, in thinking about his food, she had put herself in his wife's place—any woman to any man.

"That'll be all right," he said again. He felt now that he ought to show some interest in the Bateses, to pay back Mrs. Bates' neighborliness in taking the telephone message, so he asked (although he had never before paid enough attention to the baby even to know whether it was a boy or girl), "How's your baby these hot days?"

The young mother's face glowed. "Oh, he's just *fine!*" she said, in quite another voice from the one that had told him about the hash. She looked down ardently at the little round head, and did not look up again. Martin knew how women look down at nursing babies. He thought she had forgotten he was there, and moved on. But she was thinking about him as much as about the baby, thinking what a nice man Mr. Warner was, even if he was very ordinary looking and only a mechanic in a garage. She didn't believe there was another man on the street who'd remember that hot weather is hard on babies and think to ask how Junior was. He was a good father. That was the way fathers should be. She hoped her Ralph would grow to be like that when he was Mr. Warner's age. Sometimes it seemed to her that Ralph didn't take the baby very seriously.

Martin was clumping over the footpath which crossed the field in front of his house. He was thinking mildly to him-

288

self that most women were like Mrs. Bates, sort of off their heads about babies. What made them?

He opened the gate to his side yard, passed between the two poplars he and Clara had planted the year they were married and came to live out here, and went up the path to his porch. He did not see the poplars at all. He seldom did, being so used to them he had forgotten they were there.

The house seemed rather queer without anybody around, but he was prepared for that, and was not at all a fanciful man to think much about it. The corned-beef hash in the bowl was there all right. Since he was by himself, he did not bother to wash. He got the hash out, heated it, fried his potatoes, made himself a pot of tea and carried his food out to the table on the side porch, where they ate in summer. It was queerer yet, eating all alone, without a sound around him. If he had known, he would have bought him an evening paper, he thought. But he was too tired to walk all the way back into town to the railway station to get one. So he had nothing to do but to listen to himself chewing, and watch the evening settle down over the little stretch of grass which he saw from the porch, and the two poplars on each side of the gate leading into the fields. He noticed them now, how tall and black they stood, motionless in the darkening sultry summer twilight.

He was tired. He sat slumped down in his chair, his food heavy within him. He felt as though he were made of lead. It was hot in there under the porch roof. He lifted his arm to wipe the sweat off his forehead and smelled the rankness of his unwashed body. After a time he felt that it must have grown hotter. It was stifling. Perhaps there was more air under the open sky. He walked across the grass and sat down at the foot of one of the poplars, his back against the trunk. It was now quite dark. He thought to himself that he must have sat there mooning on the porch longer than he had realized. Perhaps he had dozed off for a while. He wondered what time it was, and took out his big nickel watch. But it was too dark to see the hands, he found he had no matches, and he was too tired to get up and go into the house to find one.

How still it was! One of those hot nights when it seemed as though everything were suffocating and couldn't make a sound. When had he been so alone, with nobody expecting anything of him? He couldn't remember when. At the garage there was always plenty of noise, people and cars coming and going, and always something to be done for them. Here at home the children were always hollering and carrying on and laughing and running around, and teasing him for something. And Clara—even in bed, he was never by himself like this, there was always somebody there, moving, breathing, living, saying something, waiting for him to say something.

And now there was nobody—but himself. It made you think about yourself, not to have anybody else there. To think about himself made Martin uneasy. As the stifling moments lagged by, Martin was more and more aware of himself, a heavy, shapeless, sweating mass in the dark, dark and silent as the poplars. Why was he sitting there so long without a word? It was as though he too were waiting for

Martin to say something. But what? Martin certainly had no idea what to say to himself.

He slid down and lay flat on the grass, his head on a root of the tree thinking that really he couldn't remember when he had ever been so quiet and alone. And yet, an odor that rose, pungent and keen from the grass, from the garden, reminded him of another time, very long ago. The dew must be beginning to fall, he thought, to make the earth in the garden have that damp smell. How it took him back to that other solitary moment. Why did he remember it so well? Nothing had happened—it was only the way he had felt early one morning when he was a little boy. He had wakened and run out just at dawn, while his father and mother were still asleep in the house. He was the only person in the world who had waked up. The grass and the earth had smelled exactly like this. How strange that a smell could make him remember so exactly how that dawn had looked and felt to him!

Remember? It wasn't something faint, like remembering. He was overcome with the vividness of it. He did not look back on the child dazzled by the dawn, he was that little boy, and the little boy was the dawn, was the beginning. There he stood, barefoot in the new beginning of the day, of his life —he was again the little boy who felt the whole world waiting for him to begin to run along the white road leading him to life.

Then, like a light winking out into darkness, the dewy early-morning freshness was gone. He was the little boy in the dawn no longer. He was a middle-aged man in overalls, who didn't know what to do with himself on a hot black night, a mechanic in Peter's garage. He had gone along that white road as best he could, and where had it brought him? To tramping home from work and warming over some corned-beef hash. That was all that had been announced by that dreadfully beautiful dawn.

Three noisy children, who had to be fed and clothed and sheltered and taken care of—that was all he had to show for it. And they would turn out just as he had. What else could they do? He would go on working for wages to bring them up till they were big enough to work for wages to bring up their children. And some hot dark night, when they had too much time to think about things, it would all come over them like this.

He shook his shoulders and growled. Why did he lie there and let the blues ride him? He was a man grown with some sense. He could get up and go somewhere else, couldn't he? And slam this door shut which did nobody any good to have open. He walked heavily back to the porch and sat down on the old sofa they left out there, his head in his hands, wondering why in the world, on this particular hot black night, he should have been carried back to that moment in his little-boy life? And why should it hurt him so awfully to remember it, when it was something he'd liked? There were very few things in his boyhood he liked to remember. Usually any sudden recollection made him wince and groan as though he had suddenly bitten down on a sore tooth—like the time Alice Barnes laughed at him that winter night, when he saw all the stars shining in her eyes and tried to tell her so. Her laughter, so scornful of his clumsiness, of his shyness, of his not having any money, of his stammering, of the foolishness which made him want to say such things—it crackled in his ears now, as it had so many times, driving him back all his life long to shamed silence. He shrank together and hung his head again, tonight, before the sharp unkindness of her pretty face as he had when he was seventeen years old. Why must he pick *that* out to remember so vividly that it happened all over again when he thought of it? Poor Alice, dead and gone, years ago. Why should her unkind look and jeering laugh go on living for him, after she had lain down in her grave? Why couldn't he remember other things about her, things he'd loved and that had never hurt him? For Alice had been the one he loved. He had never pretended to himself that he loved Clara. When Alice wouldn't have anything to do with him, he'd drifted around with Clara, and then they got married. He knew now that Clara was a better woman than Alice, a thousand times better. But Alice was the one he had loved. And now she was dead, all her pretty looks and ways—the lift of her eyebrows, the way her hair shone in the sun, the limber way she bent over to tie her shoes. They were dead, and only her unkindness went on living and hurting him. When he thought of Alice, her mocking laugh was all he could remember.

He tore his collar open more widely, rubbed his fingers back and forth through his sticky sweaty hair, and growled again. What was the matter with him tonight to start remembering things? Once you began you couldn't stop. And what had he to remember—who hadn't got anything he wanted out of living? He'd never had anything he wanted—he'd never even seen what he thought he might want. He'd never had but one short look at it—like the way that fiddling man had whipped his bow over the strings. Martin couldn't recall at all the music of that long ago night's entertainment when a man had played the violin. He had not known enough about music to make any sense of the sound of it, so he hadn't remembered that. But he had never forgotten the look of it, the look of something fine getting done just right. He could close his eyes any time in all the years since then, and see again those clean, knowledgeable, strong, strokes of the bow, so sure of themselves, just what they were meant to be. There was something he'd have wanted—to be sure of himself, to know just what he was up to, to be what he was meant to be. But all he'd ever had had been uncertain and smeary and higgledy-piggledy fumbling from one thing to the next, day after day, just as it happened, without any sense to it.

How hot it was! And no air at all. Why didn't he go to bed, instead of sitting there, feeling as if he were in his coffin with the lid closed, under six feet of earth—nothing in his head but remembering that he'd never had anything he wanted.

Something struck him with a soft, weightless violence. He lifted his head with a start. The moon had risen and was thrusting a long bright ray upon him. His eyes followed it back to the open, out to the garden blooming with white light, out to the poplars, every one of their thousands of leaves now shining silver. He groaned. All that silver, all that shiningness for a tree, and not even a little shiningness for a man's life! It shone upon him, the light which turned to silver every crisp leaf of the poplars, as clean in line as that remembered stroke of the bow, the same light shone in on him, on his hands lying across his knees. He looked down at them, grimy, knotted mechanic's fingers, with the involuntary crook of the stubbed fingers, as if they still held the tool which was all their fate. They looked uglier, stiffer than ever in that flood of light. The moonlight made fun of them, as Alice had.

He looked back at the poplars. They were tall pyramids of carved silver. Glittering, motionless in the pride of their beauty. He ached as he looked at them, they were so lovely, so much lovelier than anything in his life. They stood, still, bright, proud—and everything around them, far and near, was still and bright too—everything except Martin, dark, misshapen, with nothing to be proud of. The fields beyond stretched away as if there were miles and miles of them— so far, so still—and in all that shining distance nothing for Martin but to work in a garage.

Martin's heart swelled and hurt him so that he twisted his grimy fingers together hard. It hurt him like something in a dream. Perhaps he was dreaming. He had never felt like this awake. He wished he could wake up and stop staring his eyes out at the silver poplars, clean shining brightness like what he'd have liked to have a little of and never had had. He heard his voice saying over and over, "Oh, what is the use? What is the *use?*" He heard his twisted finger-joints cracking in his own grip.

Something happened to the poplars then. And to Martin. A little wind sprang up, blew softly across Martin's hot sweaty face and started into quick, flowing life the stiff carven splendor of the poplars. Every silver leaf woke up from its frozen pride and stirred, sparkling and shimmering, tossing and turning sweetly back and forth. It was as though they had burst into song. They were as much lovelier than they had been before, as they had been lovelier than Martin's life. Because now they were alive.

Martin was alive, too. Quick life ran all through him, like the flashing and shimmering of the poplars. He put out his stiff rough hands to them with love, not with envy. Their beauty was part of him now, not a grievance and a reproach. He had left his bitterness and sorrow buried safely under six feet of earth, had risen into this silver light without them. He did not even remember what his own life had been, what he had wanted and had not had. It did not seem of the least importance.

His eyes fixed on the silver poplars were bright with their brightness. His ears now divined a faint singing from the stir in their leaves, lovelier than—lovelier than anything the ears can really hear. How could he have tormented himself, because he had not got what he wanted! What he had, then, at that moment, his eyes full of glory, his heart at peace, was so much more than he had ever known how to want! Yes, it must be a dream. But now he did not wish to wake up. Only in a dream could a man's life lie lost in wide quietness, mile on mile, like moonlit fields.

If he could only think of some way to say this—to say this

all out, he would be safe for always. But how could he say anything beautiful—he who had never been taught to do anything fine just right, who could not draw a bow cleanly over strings, who could not even tell a woman she was lovely without being laughed at?

What he wanted to say, if not in words, by a cry, a gesture, an act—it was what was being said to him by the living silver poplars—that it was no matter if you didn't get what you wanted, that was no matter at all, in the bigness of a silvery peace like this. There was something so much better than getting what you wanted—so much sweeter and surer, that—that it made a grown man cry for happiness only to guess at it.

If only he could somehow put this into life, so that it would last! Martin was crying now, crying like a little boy, because he was so glad to know that everything was all right, and because he could not think of any way to say this so that it would last. The tears ran out of his closed eyes down into the pillow on the old sofa where he was lying. For Martin was asleep now, quite asleep.

He was wakened by little Lottie who said, "Oh, Poppa, Momma says she hates to wake you up, but it's half-past six and she's got breakfast ready."

He sat up with a start. How'd he happen to be out on the porch and not in his bed? Oh, yes, he remembered, it had been so hot last night, he'd lain down there and must have dropped off.

"Hello there, kid," he said, rubbing his face up and down with his rough palms. "Did the dentist hurt much?"

"He hurt awful," said the little girl. "But I didn't cry. I didn't want to make Momma feel bad."

"That's fine," said her father. What a good little kid she was. She was going to grow up like her mother. He put his hand on her head, every tousled hair of which was shining like gold in the morning's new light. The hairs on the back of his ugly knotted hand turned to gold, too, in the same kind daylight brightness. He sat looking at them dreamily. "Momma says breakfast is ready," Lottie repeated.

They went into the house together. Through the vapor and hiss of cooking, his wife looked at him with gentle, faded eyes. "Hello there, honey," she said. "Did you get a good sleep? We came up the walk on tip-toe, so's not to wake you up. Was it too hot to sleep in the bedroom? If I'd ha' thought, I'd ha' made a bed up out there on the porch for you."

"Yes, wasn't it hot," he said. "I couldn't get to sleep for ever so long. And I must have dreamed like everything too. I feel kind o' numb, the way you do, after you've had a whole lot of dreams." He drew out a chair from the table but his wife said, "Don't you want to wash? I've got the water hot."

So he washed, all over—his hair too. It felt fine to get the smell of old sweat off. That had been a good idea of Clara's. When he stepped back into the bedroom he found a clean shirt on the bed. She was a good wife.

He put on the clean shirt, combed his wet hair, went back

into the kitchen and sat down to eat his breakfast. He felt fine. His wife poured him a cup of steaming coffee. It had a grand smell. There was nothing that did you more good than coffee.

Little Paul came into the room now, looking pale and hollow-eyed with the heat and the fatigue of traveling. But he never did look very strong, the poor kid.

"How's yourself, 'bo?" his father asked him.

"All right, I guess," said Paul listlessly.

Then, inside his own mind where there had been nothing at all the minute before, Martin found he had an idea about Paul, clear and sure as though he had thought about it a long time. "Say, Paul, how'd you like to start in to take music lessons?" he asked. Now what on earth had made him say that? None of his folks ever had had music lessons. They'd always been too poor. Nor Clara's either. Nor any of the children they went to school with. What a queer idea to come to him. Like that. Without his ever having thought of it before.

Paul stared for a minute, too surprised to take in what his father had said. Then his pale serious little face brightened and shone. What did it remind his father of, that brightening into life?

"Why, Poppa," he cried. "Do you mean it? Honest?"

"That's a splendid idea," said Clara. "How'd you ever think of it?"

"Oh, I don't know," said Martin, pouring molasses over his pancakes. "One of the things I dreamed about last night —come to think of it, that's the only thing I can remember about those dreams—was a man I saw fiddling once years ago. Maybe that put the idea in my head."

"Maybe," said Clara.

"I'd *love* it," said Paul, his face shining.

"Well, we'll see," said his father, as if he needed to think it over. But he did not. He was quite decided.

"Here's your dinner-pail," said Clara, when he stood up after breakfast. "I put iced-tea in the thermos-bottle, instead of coffee. It's going to be hot again today."

"That's good," he replied absently. He was not thinking of what she said. He was thinking about music-lessons. What would they cost? He hadn't the least idea. Oh, well, a little extra time, nights, at the garage, and he could make enough to pay for them.

He passed between the two poplars, looked up at them and saw their bright greenness glistening in the hot sun. My! How those trees had grown since he and Clara had stuck in two little saplings! They were regular beauties now.

He walked along the footpath, his heavy shoes jarring on the hard-baked earth, he turned into the dusty road at the corner of the Bates house.

"Oh, Mr. Warner," called Mrs. Bates from her porch, "did your folks get home this morning?"

"Sure, they got home all right," he answered, stopping a moment to look at her and the baby in her arms.

"How's the boy?" he asked.

"He's fine!" she said, hugging him closer.

"That's good," said Martin.

He walked on, beginning to whistle, along the dusty road.

Yes, it would be nice for Paul to learn to play the fiddle. He was that kind of a kid.

He followed the dusty road till it ran across the concrete highway. Then he turned right and walked along the concrete road till he came to Peter's garage. He was still whistling, softly and absent-mindedly, "Turkey in the Straw" when he stepped inside, hung his hat on the usual nail, set his lunch-pail on the window-sill where he always put it, took up a wrench and went to work.

Memorial Day

ANYONE watching from the cemetery could have seen in the distance the little cloud of dust which announced the approach of the first Ford. But there was no one watching from the cemetery. The dead lay quiet in their graves; the grass and trees and all the growing things thrust their roots deeper into the earth and lifted their heads towards the sun. There was no one who cared in the least that the first Ford was approaching.

Presently it appeared and ground slowly up the sandy road, a small American flag waving from its radiator cap. Similar flags, new and paper-crisp, fluttered from the wreaths of flowers held by the little country boys who filled the car to the brim, perching three deep on the back seat. When it stopped at the gate of the cemetery, they spilled themselves out without waiting to open the doors. Like the grass and trees and other growing things, they were quivering and glistening with vitality. They wore their best clothes, everyone had a neck-tie, their hair was brushed back from their well-soaped faces. Over their arms hung the wreaths for the soldiers' graves.

"Now, don't go and put them on the Masons' graves, the way they did last year," cautioned the driver of their car, as he slammed the Ford into reverse to turn it around. "The kids last year didn't pay any attention to what they were doing, and got everything all mixed up. Look for the graves that have the G.A.R. standard and a flag. Take out the old flag, put in your this-year's one and lay your wreath down near the head of the grave. No, better lean it up against the tombstone. It sheds the rain better."

The boys listened seriously, nodded to show they understood these directions, and walked through the gate into the cemetery. It made them feel important to be walking. They were small boys, who usually skipped or ran.

More cars were arriving now, from which more clean-faced boys with wreaths were clambering out. In one of the cars sat the minister who came to "say a few words and pronounce the benediction." At the gate, a golden cloud of dust hung in the air.

Inside the cemetery there was no dust. It was not considered decorous for cars to roll in over the weedy gravel of these driveways. The boys, ten or twelve of them now, walked forward, the smaller ones once in a while giving a skipping hop to keep up with the bigger ones. When they reached the older part of the cemetery where the grayer tombstones stood, they separated and began to hunt out the graves where a faded last-year's flag drooped from the metal standard.

JOHN HEMINWAY ANDREWS

Died in Camp Fairfax, Virginia

In the Twenty-second Year

Of his Life

The round-cheeked little boy did not read this, but he saw the drab grizzled flag. He stepped around the grave and set his wreath up against the tombstone. As he did this, he leaned his hand for an instant upon the stone. Instantly a silent scream burst up from the grave. The first of the soldiers had awakened.

All the year around they lay quietly and rested in their graves. They had been country-men. They were at home under the open sky. Neither the furious rages of winter nor the heat of the summer suns disturbed their sleep. Year by year the shroud of their oblivion was thicker and softer. If only little boys could be kept away from their grassy beds— little boys with honest eyes and well-washed faces and small harmless hands. At the touch of those hands, the dead men who had been small and harmless little boys themselves, awoke in the old agony to what they were trying to forget. John Andrews, who had died in Camp Fairfax in 1863, had died screaming his heart out while the surgeons were amputating his leg without anesthetics. When his sleep was broken, once a year on that day in May, it was in the midst of that shriek that he awoke. But now it was at the little boy he screamed, to warn him, to tell him, to let him know— He could never think of words for his warning he was so horrified by the child's rosy calmness, by the candor of his eyes, by his awful unawareness—he could only shriek silently from his grave, till the trees above him quivered to it, till the clouds echoed it back. But none of the little boys ever heard him. Nor did this one.

304

He looked carefully at the standard to make sure it was the right one. The metal was so rusted that the letters were almost illegible but he thought he could see G.A.R. Were those the letters he had been told to look for? He tried to remember. He had no idea what they meant. Older people always take for granted that children know. But little children are always new. They are not born with any knowledge of what older people have lived with.

The little boy took out the dingy flag and carefully set in the bright new one. It was the first time he had been old enough to do this on Decoration Day. He was a good obedient child who tried to do just as he had been told.

Well, he thought, there was *one* wreath disposed of! Where was another grave?

On a near-by grave an older boy was already placing his second wreath. This was his second year in the cemetery on Decoration Day, and he knew what to do. He took the old flag briskly from the standard, set in the new one, and laid his wreath of lilacs up against the tombstone. His mother had told him not to take longer than he need, because they were all to go fishing that afternoon.

Under the matted grass of the grave he had just decorated lay a dead man who had been very poor and who had gone away to war because he had been offered five hundred dollars to take a rich man's place. With the money, he and his young wife had planned to buy a farm of their own, and have a home in which to bring up their children. Very dear to him were his three little sons so like this little boy who

305

now bent his round child-face above the old grave. The dead man had never been very bright, and knew that never in any other way could he earn so much money as five hundred dollars. It had seemed an easy way to provide a home for his children and his young wife where he could take care of them all as they grew up.

Like the little boy, he had been obedient, and had done as he had been told. He had killed and maimed men whom he had never seen before, who had never done anything to him; and after a time one of them, doing as he had been told, maimed and killed him. He had died in battle, an expression of astonishment on his face (he had never been very bright and had not at all understood what was happening to him). The last thing he had seen was the unknown face of the unknown man who was killing him. Death had sealed the stranger's face upon his eyes, so that when, with a start, once a year, he awoke from his sleep, he saw two faces —the set, strange features of the man who was driving a bayonet into his side, and a little boy's face, fresh and harmless, like his own little boy's face. He had died without a sound; but now, as the child leaned upon his breast to set the wreath in place he broke into a moan of "Misery! Misery!"

But no one heard him. The little boy brushed his hands together lightly to dust them off, and was about to turn away when he saw a fly buzzing in terror in a spider's web. He stooped, broke the threads and freed the small flying thing, which spun up into the air with a whir of gauzy wings.

At this the soldier in his grave strained terribly to be heard, groaning and sobbing "Misery! Misery! Misery!" till the blades of grass growing over him shook with his violence.

The child, having placed all his wreaths, skipped down the weedy path to join his mother.

A thin little boy who ought never to have been born was standing beside another grave. The little boy's mother was "not all there," so her country neighbors said, and his father was dying of tuberculosis. There were six children already, all of them thin and white and sober-faced. This was the oldest one at home. He was eight years old. An older sister, who was nine, was already in a sanitarium, her bones rotting away in her father's disease. The little boy with the wreaths knew very well why she had been sent away from home, and he was keeping carefully hidden a sore on his knee that did not heal. He told no one about it, and if anyone noticed that he limped, he always said he had stubbed his toe.

He was happy now beyond any dream. Although his mother was not bright, and his father was shiftless and sick, he had been chosen just like any other boy to decorate the graves. In his smileless face his eyes shone. It was the first time in his life that he had held a position of trust. He had had a ride in an automobile, with other boys, well and strong and well-dressed, whose fathers worked regularly and whose mothers were clean and knew how to read and write. And now, just like anyone, he was laying wreaths on the graves—trusted—nobody watching him to see that he did it right—

responsible. He walked carefully, trying not to limp, and glanced down at his knee once in a while to be sure that the oozing matter from his sore had not soaked through the thin material of his trousers.

He laid a wreath on a grave—a very fine grave with a great marble tombstone, marked with the name of Captain Elijah Hatwell on it. He was not going to take a mean poor grave when he could just as well have a fine one.

Under the great marble monument lay a happy man—a man who like the little boy ought never to have been born, who had come to know this and to wish for death; a man whose sick-minded fathers had passed on to him a sick brain, and who had seen the fate waiting for him. It had taken his wounds a long time to kill him, months of torture in one hospital after another, and all of it had been sweet to him, because he was dying, because he was escaping the fate of his fathers. Soundly he slept. When clean-faced little boys laid their small hands upon the old graves he did not waken as did his comrades who had not wished to die.

But today he stirred and felt his stilled heart begin to suffer once more. "Come—come—come—" he murmured pityingly to the limping child. "Come—come—come—" he called so compassionately that a thrush about to sing on the tree above his grave stopped to listen.

But the little boy did not hear. People were gathering at the other end of the cemetery, near the entrance, for the "exercises," and he hurried towards them. This was his day of glory. He must not miss any of it.

A sturdy, broad-chested playmate of his called after him, "I'll be there in a minute. I've got to find me a grave for one more wreath."

He looked about for a last-year's flag. There was one. He ran towards it, headlong and heedless, as he ran in his games, tripped and fell sprawling across it, his wreath flying out of his hands.

The soldier beneath him had been sturdy and broad-chested, too. He too had loved games, had loved everything in his free, outdoor country life. But when his country's unity was threatened, when the call came to help free fellow-men held as slaves, he had shouldered a rifle and gone away to war. He had been proud to die for his country's unity, for human freedom. Year after year, when his dead comrades lost their courage, wept and cried out, he kept a stern righteous silence. He had winced as much as they at the touch of little boys' hands, but he had folded his lips to rigid stillness. It was an ordeal. Year after year he hoped that his grave might be overlooked. But he had never broken his silence.

It was so late on that morning in May before steps came near him, that he had thought he was safe. He was already sinking back into blessed blackness, when the impact of the child's falling body startled him out of oblivion. He had no time to prepare himself, to stiffen, to resist. When his eyes opened, he was gazing full into the little boy's eyes, clear, clear—and ignorant. Their utter, empty ignorance of what the soldier knew, drove to his vitals like the bullet that had killed him. As he had screamed then, he screamed now—the thing the little boy did not know and that he knew. "Blood!

Blood! Blood!" he shrieked noiselessly.

It was the word he slept to forget. All eternity would be too short a sleep to forget that word. Awake now, with a clear-eyed living little boy lying on his breast, his screams of "Blood! Blood! Blood!" rose from his grave like a scarlet spray and fell back in red drops upon the child's beautiful body.

The child sprang hastily to his feet and looked about him, fearing to be scolded for his awkwardness. But no one had noticed. Near the entrance of the cemetery the exercises were going on. The light breeze brought some of the phrases to his ears— "—over our fair land—the last meed of true devotion—with unflinching heroism—"

Turning their backs on the graves where they had left their wreaths, the little boys straggled back towards the entrance. In front of them a group of people stood about the minister who was finishing his remarks. "—unfailing grateful remembrance of our fallen heroes," he said, with a solemn professional intonation.

Back of the little boys, the dead soldiers had all taken up the cry of the last awakened, the strongest, the best, the one who had always till now been silent, the one who had never till now admitted that he had been wrong. Now they knew what it was that must be said and heard. "Blood! Blood! Blood!" they screamed after the harmless little boys, trotting through the flickering tree-shadows.

The minister slid into the benediction;—"and now—" he raised his hand and lifted his face. The little boys stood still and looked down at their shoes, "—the peace of God which passeth all understanding—"

"Blood! Blood! Blood!" screamed the soldiers soundlessly.

The exercises were over. The little boys swarmed up over the sides of the automobiles and perched three deep on the seats. Some of them took off their neck-ties and put them in their pockets. The little sick boy's face shone. Someone had given him a flag to keep (they were bought by the dozen anyhow, and one more or less—). He had never had a flag of his own before. He looked at it with love and waved it with all his might as the Ford turned and started back down the hill. It had been the happiest day of his life. For once he had been an accepted part of things. He thought with pride of the great stone monument where he had laid a wreath. None of the other boys had had so fine a one. It came to him that he too would like to be a soldier when he grew up, and have, perhaps, a fine marble monument put up to him when he died. A throb of pain from his knee made him look down with apprehension. No, it had not soaked through his trouser, yet.

The dust cloud dying away in the distance marked the departure of the last Ford. The dead soldiers fumbled with their dead hands to draw up over them once more the blessed black of oblivion. Nothing else in all the year could reach them to tear away that sheltering pall—if only no little boys came near them, little boys with clear eyes and honest faces and kind, small, harmless hands. Raw and shaken, the dead

311

soldiers huddled down among the shreds of their torn forget-fulness.

The thrush rolled his liquid note into silence. The trees and grass and all the rooted living things quivered and glistened with vitality. In the hot sun the flowers of the wreaths, their life oozing from their amputated stems, began to hang their heads and die. The little new paper-crisp American flags, bought at wholesale, stood stiffly at attention. The last cloud of dust died away in the distance. The cemetery lay quiet.

The soldiers, having been remembered, were now once more forgotten.